Copyright © November 2020 by Brenda Trim
Editor: Chris Cain
Cover Art by Fiona Jayde

* * *

This book is a work of fiction. The names, characters, places, and incidents are products of the writers' imagination or have been used fictitiously and are not to be construed as real. Any resemblance to persons, living or dead, actual events, locales or organizations is entirely coincidental.

WARNING: The unauthorized reproduction of this work is illegal. Criminal copyright infringement is investigated by the FBI and is punishable by up to 5 years in federal prison and a fine of $250,000.

All rights reserved. With the exception of quotes used in reviews, this book may not be reproduced or used in whole or in part by any means existing without written permission from the authors.

✽ Created with Vellum

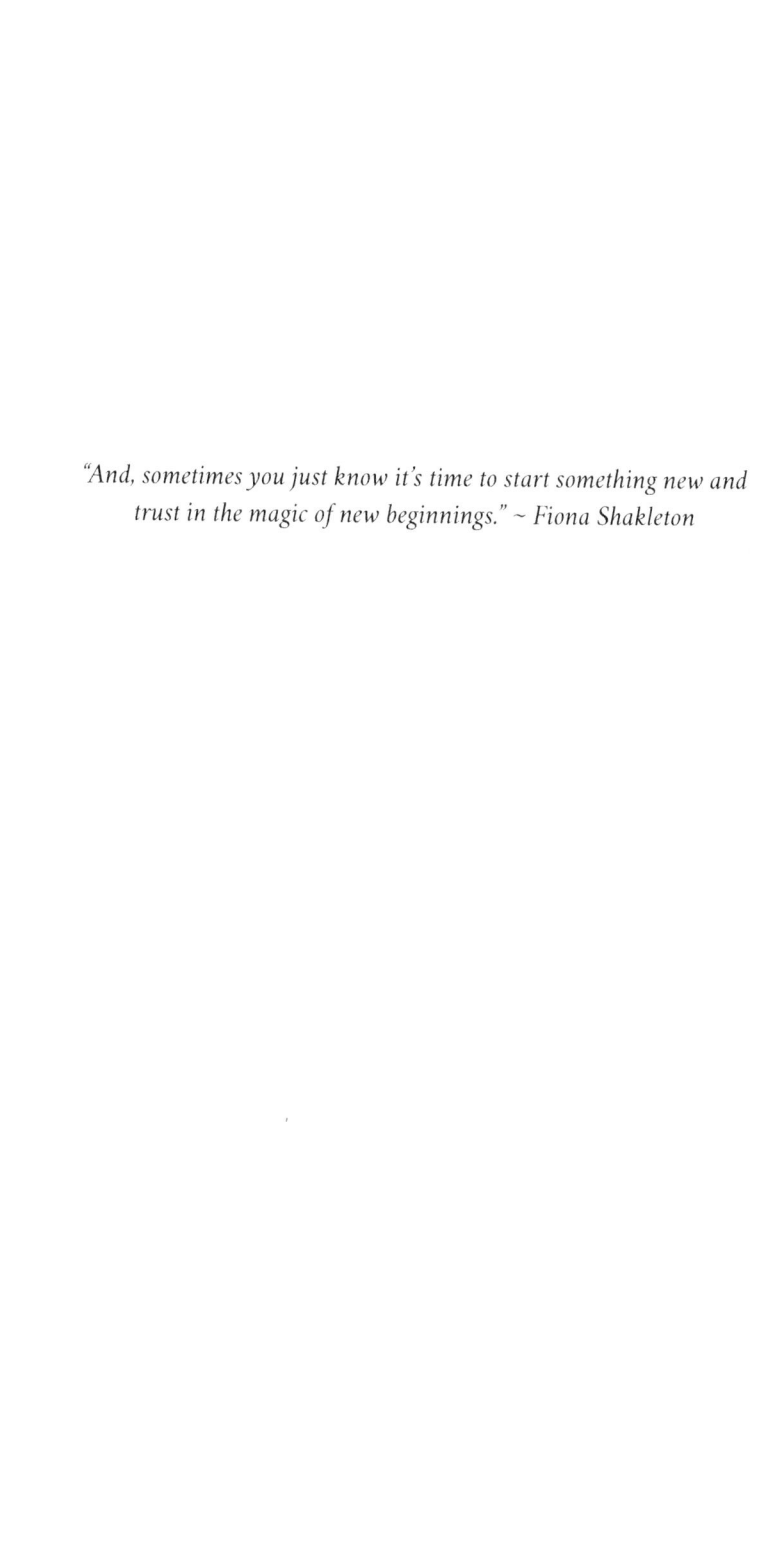

"And, sometimes you just know it's time to start something new and trust in the magic of new beginnings." ~ *Fiona Shakleton*

CHAPTER 1

*E*mmie released me and wiped a tear from her eye as she looked around the grounds. "I can see why you don't want to leave here. This place is amazing, mom. Well, aside from the eerie cemetery and mausoleum. I always hated that when we came here as kids, and it isn't any better. Anyway, knowing how much you love it will make being so far from you completely worth it."

I squeezed my oldest daughter's hand and nodded my head in agreement. I never imagined I would feel this way when I came to England to say goodbye to my grandmother. "For the first time since your father died, I feel like I'm home here at Pymm's Pondside. The only downside is not being able to hop in a car and visit you and your brother and sister."

"We don't mind coming to you, mom. You've done more than enough for us. It's about time you have something just for you," Skylar, my youngest daughter told me as she jumped into the conversation. She was leaning against the white picket fence that surrounded the massive garden my grandmother kept in pristine condition. That was one thing I wasn't looking forward to maintaining. The knee that gave me more problems than my son ached at the mere idea of so much bending.

Greyson turned from the pond at the front of the property I'd just inherited and rolled his eyes at his twin. Skylar was my sensitive one, where Emmie was the responsible one of my three kids, and Greyson was hotheaded. "Stop sucking up. Mom isn't going to fly you out to England every time you're homesick."

My head started throbbing with the familiar argument. Emmie had been away at the university for two years, but the twins just started. And being my sensitive one, Skylar came home nearly every weekend. The three-hour drive didn't faze her at all, where Greyson almost always remained on campus. By staying in England, I will be making it impossible for them to come home for a weekend visit.

I was a horrible mother because leaving my kids without their home base close by didn't make me change my mind. Every cell in my body screamed that I was supposed to be at Pymm's Pondside. No. It was where I *needed* to be. I've lived the past twenty-two years for someone else. Now was my time.

I wrapped one arm around Greyson and the other around Skylar. "What have I always told you, Grey? It's your job to take care of your sisters. They do enough for you. I expect you to make time for her as we all adjust to this new setup."

Greyson's head dipped, and he took a deep breath. "Sorry, mom. You're right. I won't get lost in myself."

"I won't let you," Emmie added. "I never thought I'd be happy to move back in with you nutjobs, but I'm excited."

Dust billowed into the air as the car I arranged to take them to the airport turned down my dirt drive. Emotion clogged my throat, and my eyes burned with tears. I'd lost so much in my life, and it felt like I was losing them now, too. "I'm going to miss you guys."

Skylar squeezed me tighter. "We will miss you, too, but this isn't forever. You never know. We might decide to move here after college."

I released the twins and embraced Emmie next. "Now, remember you guys are closing on your house before the term begins. The agent will be contacting you, Emmie, to set up the date and time, but all three of you need to be there."

The second I stepped foot onto the property, I called a real estate agent in Salisbury and arranged to sell my house. I swear the gods were on my side because it sold before the week was out. Emmie was all too happy to find a place for her to move into with the twins. In no time, the three found the home they wanted. Thanks to the money from my house's sale, I put in an offer for the kids on the two-story they selected.

"I've got it handled, mom. Don't worry about us. We will be back next summer."

"If you need anything, call me." I hugged them each once more then sent them on their way.

Turning around, I took in my new home. Pymm's Pondside was the name for the white cottage. When I visited as a kid, I thought it was neat that they named their houses here. But to call it a 'cottage' was misleading. The thing was nearly as big as my house in Salisbury, but it had charm coming out of the eaves.

The brown roof reminded me of a thatch design. Every angle was rounded, creating a soft, inviting look to the five-bedroom home. The brown shutters on the windows matched the roof, and the ivy growing up one side was straight out of a fairytale. I'd always thought that, and now it was mine.

I even owned a cemetery. I never thought I'd say that in

my life. And the craziest part was that it made me feel closer to the family I'd never known. I turned my head to the left and glanced at the headstones. Towards the back of the place were a couple of mausoleums. Yeah, it's super creepy but also pretty neat. I mean, there was a graveyard a hundred feet from where I slept. Good thing I have always loved them, or I wouldn't have been able to stay in the house.

Turning away from the cemetery, I glanced at the garden I had spent days wondering if I should remove. Not only did I cringe at the thought of so much bending, but I didn't have a green thumb. I wasn't as bad as Violet, my best friend, but plants didn't flourish under my care. And I'm starting a new life now. I admit that I have no desire to weed the damn thing. I was reluctant to pull the plants up. They're a part of the place's charm.

I headed to the pond and smiled as I looked at the large watering hole. I've seen deer, rabbits, and miniature bears drinking late at night or in the early morning. At least I thought they were tiny bears. They looked odd and had large floppy ears, and I swear they understood when I cooed at them. I was excited to have animals so close. And with woods surrounding the entire property, I hoped to see more. The area was lush, thanks to the rainy weather in Northern England.

Opening the small gate in the fence around the garden, I searched for some basil to add to my tomato sandwich for lunch. There were so many herbs and plants, and I knew what maybe a third of them were. Rosemary and mint were the most obvious. The rest I would learn in time if I didn't lose it all to weeds.

I found what I was looking for in the far corner closest to the cemetery. My gaze shifted to the fresh grave. My vision blurred when I read my grandmother's name. A pinging started up in my head. That was the only way I could describe it.

Something was hitting the walls of my skull, almost like a bee trapped under a cloche. I've never experienced it before in my life. The stress of the past month must be getting to me.

I took a deep breath and thought about my grandma. Isidora Shakleton was unforgettable and an integral part of the town. Most of the residents of Cottlehill Wilds showed up for her service.

The pinging was gone by the time I turned away and walked back to the house. The inside was just as cozy as it appeared on the outside. The back door went right into the kitchen, where I dumped the basil before heading through the small living room and up the stairs to my bedroom.

The patchwork quilt my grandmother made was still on her bed. I had my clothes and a few of my favorite keepsakes shipped to me. The rest was going to the kids.

I need a new comforter. And sheets. Badly. I made plans to head into the city to pick up a cozy down quilt and maybe a new mattress. I swear there were more lumps in the thing than there were on my butt and thighs. And that was saying something.

Being my age, it was shocking if you didn't carry an extra fifteen or twenty pounds. I know I certainly had the extra cushion. Along with aches and pains, I thought as I bent to pick up the towels Skylar left on the wood floor.

That was one thing I will not miss. The kids, much like my late husband, never picked up after themselves. And boy, did that get on my last damn nerve. I spent my entire life caring for others—both at work and at home. I swear being a caretaker was woven into my DNA.

After graduating with my bachelor's degree in nursing, I worked full-time in the ICU at a local hospital for twenty years then took care of Tim at the end. Perhaps that was what was so inviting about my grandmother's house. I didn't need to take care of anyone here.

After washing the toothpaste from the sink, I turned and yelped. "What the fuck?" My mouth got away from me when I noticed the towels back on the ground. What the hell was going on? I just picked them up and put them in the laundry basket.

I headed into the other bedrooms and stripped the beds before straightening the covers over the mattresses. By the time I returned to the room where Greyson had slept, the sheets were no longer neatly folded. Instead, I tripped over the tangled mess.

Pausing, I thrust my hands on my hips and glanced around. Was someone there messing with me? I didn't find anything else out of the ordinary, so I picked up the pile, added it to the basket, and then carried my load downstairs.

When I entered the tiny room at the back of the kitchen where the washer and dryer were, I stopped short when I noticed the soap tipped over on its side. "Alright, grandma, if you're haunting the place to scare me, there's no need. I'm not going to make too many changes."

It felt almost as if the house sighed around me. Shaking my head at my idiocy, I put a load on then entered the kitchen. The sight of the scuffed wooden stool sitting at the butcherblock island reminded me of all the days I used to sit there as a kid and listen to my grandmother tell me stories about Fae and witches.

I envied her creativity. I could never come up with the elaborate ones she did. She wove tales about portals, fairies, dragons, and gnomes. When I became a mom and my kids started asking for stories, I used my favorites from the ones she told me.

Skylar's favorite was one about a pixie that sought asylum

with a witch. A vicious beast had been hunting her. She was on the edge of her seat when it came to the part about the pixie barely evading the creature when she came up against a barrier. She pounded her tiny hands on the barrier, begging for help. The witch helped and provided the pixie with some woods to live in, and the fairy gave the witch fresh flowers in return.

Emmie's favorite was about a gnome family escaping from some barghests. While Greyson preferred stories about dragon shifters that needed to get away from the vile King that created them to ravage and kill.

I was making a sandwich while my mind traveled down memory lane when movement outside the window caught my eye. I sucked in a breath and immediately started choking on my food. Smashing the food in my hand, I raced for the back door and burst through.

I was still coughing when I dashed down the steps. After a couple more hacks, I managed to clear my throat. "Can I help you?" It still felt like food was stuck down the wrong pipe.

The woman paused with her hand on an herb in the garden and looked up at me. She looked like she was in her late twenties, maybe early thirties, and had stunning red hair. My hands smoothed down my pink t-shirt when I took in her crop top and flat stomach.

She lifted one hand and smiled. "Oh, hi. You must be Fiona, Isidora's granddaughter. I'm Aislinn. I thought you'd be on a plane home by now. I saw the car leave hours ago."

I crossed my arms over my chest, smearing mayonnaise over my left boob. I was a hot freakin' mess, but I didn't care at the moment. I had no idea how my grandmother did things, but I didn't want people wandering on my property whenever they wanted.

"This is my property, and I have decided to stay. Listen, I'm not sure what arrangement you had with my grandmother, but I would like a heads up before you go prowling around stealing my stuff."

Aislinn's eye bugged out of her head, and her hand dropped to her side. "I apologize. Like I said, I figured you'd be gone. I just needed some thistle for a potion, and Isidora has always allowed me to grab the few ingredients I need in exchange for helping with upkeep in here."

That brought a smile to my lips. My hands dropped, and pieces of tomato fell from between the bread. "In that case, you are more than welcome. Honestly, I was thinking about getting rid of the garden. I swear I have a black thumb. Besides, I have no idea what all this is or what it is for."

Aislinn chuckled and cut a couple of sprigs of the plant she'd been holding. "If you're Isidora's kin, you'll be able to keep things alive, but I am happy to help. Gardening has become my therapy since my husband left me a year ago. Is your husband not staying with you?"

I shook my head from side to side as a lump formed in my throat. Anytime I talked about Tim, I was close to losing my shit. Enough time had passed that I should be beyond this by now. But I knew better than anyone that there was no such thing as closure. Grief was a roller coaster that would catch you off guard when you least expected it. The loss of someone you love never stopped hurting, no matter how much time passed.

"My husband passed away a few years ago. Cancer." I preempted the inevitable questions about what killed him. "My kids went back home to school. They will visit, but they won't be living with me."

"I'm so sorry about your husband. You're starting over. That's good. It'll help to create a life that is separate from him. That way, the grief won't suck you under every time you turn around."

My jaw dropped open at the young woman's insight. I

would never have expected her to be so wise. "Honestly, I never thought about that. I had the hardest time letting him go. Despite how much it hurt to eat at our favorite restaurant and go to our park, I ignored it because it felt like a betrayal to do anything else. It wasn't until I got here and felt this sense of belonging that I started giving more thought to my desire to create a new life for myself."

Aislinn exited through the gate and stopped by my side. She was at least three inches shorter than my five-foot-five frame and skinny as a rail, but she exuded this green aura. I must be thinking that because she enjoys gardening.

"As a Shakleton, you belong here. I need to get home to make this potion, but if you ever need anything, I work at Phoenix Feathers. You should come in some time for a drink. On me."

I extended my clean hand and shook hers. "Thank you. I will be in touch, I'm sure."

I watched her walk away. I missed where she turned off my driveway because standing on the other side of the path was a man. He was muscular and intimidating. I wouldn't say he was gorgeous. He was too scary for that, although his beauty was undeniable.

I lifted my hand and waved at him. "Hi. I'm Fiona. I just moved into my grandmother's house." The guy didn't say a word as he stood with his feet braced apart and his arms crossed over his chest while he narrowed his brown eyes at me.

I waited a few minutes before realizing he was not going to introduce himself. Swallowing hard, I turned back to my house. By the time I got inside the kitchen, he was gone. Maybe I would ask Aislinn who the attractive yet angry man was.

Pymm's Pondside was turning out to be a pain in the butt in so many ways. I wanted to scream when I turned back to the kitchen to see silverware strewn over the island. It felt like the place was haunted. Well, too bad. This was my house, and I wasn't leaving.

I lost my Grams, quit my job, sold my house, and moved to another country. I couldn't exactly pick up where I left off. That life was in the wind now.

CHAPTER 2

"Ungh!" I grabbed my head as that pinging started up again. I wondered for the millionth time if this was a perimenopausal symptom. The hot flashes had been happening more and more, and I found one gray hair yesterday, so it wouldn't surprise me. They say forty is the new thirty, and I agreed. At forty, there wasn't much that slowed me. At forty-five, I'm not so sure. There were moments I felt ancient.

I pushed the irritation aside and forced my feet to carry me to the coffee maker. In the past week, I realized I needed to find something to do with my time. I've always worked full-time and can't stand not having something to do. I have enjoyed not having the stress of the hospital, but I needed something.

I wished Violet had more time. It was nice living in the same town as her now, but she owned a bookstore and didn't have time to hang out with me all day. I thought about asking if I could help at the store but didn't want to overstep. It was one thing to talk on the computer and another to stop by all the time.

It didn't help that the warm welcome I experienced when I first arrived at Pymm's Pondside had subsided. It was more that it seemed as if some force was trying to get me to leave. The house seemed to want me there and be pushing me away at the same time. It was an off-putting game of push-pull.

I was able to take a deep breath as the pinging stopped. That was when the knocking started up. It sounded like the water heater was about to explode, but I was reluctant to call the plumber from the city to come back out here. The last time he stopped by, he told me he saw no reason for the sounds. It didn't help that he never heard it in the hour and a half he was there.

Deciding not to give it a second thought, I poured a cup of java and sipped the caffeinated beverage as I looked out the window at the pond. Mornings here were my absolute favorite. The greenery surrounding me spoke to a part of me that I rarely got to feed living in Salisbury. Not that it was as barren as Texas, but Cottlehill Wilds put both areas to shame in terms of plant life.

The quiet solitude surrounded me. I'd gotten used to living alone, but there was always noise. I lived close to downtown, which meant I heard vehicles all day long. It never occurred to me how much noise pollution there was where I lived.

Opening the back door, I stepped out and crossed to the table set under a large maple. Sitting at the wrought iron table, I drank my coffee while planning my day. I needed to figure out if there was something I could do in town. It was the other thing I loved about living here.

There was a main street filled with quaint businesses. The bakery had the best-clotted cream I've ever tasted, and Violet's bookstore had a great selection. Maybe I'll ask if they need help at the liquor store. They carried a fabulous selection of merlots.

MAGICAL NEW BEGINNINGS

The excitement over this new phase in my life still bubbled just below the surface. Never before have I spent so much time on myself. It felt decadent to spend so much time wondering what I wanted to do with my time now. Up to this point, decisions had always been a no-brainer. Selecting the university that I wanted to attend had been an easy one, and I met Tim during my first year. Things just happened from there.

Not that it was love at first sight, but I knew we were going to get married. When he asked me in our final year, it was more a formality than anything else. Having three kids, a career, and a husband kept me busy enough that I hadn't brought my twins to visit my grandmother very often. Guilt over that took some of my excitement. I should have gone to see her more.

I should have made an effort to come every few years. I knew better. My parents were killed in a car accident during my second year at the university, and I regretted not picking a school closer to home. I missed so much of the last of their lives.

That made me think about the decision to stay here. I wouldn't see my kids much. I had enough money to buy them plane tickets once a year without draining my savings, but so much would happen in their lives between visits.

At least I had Violet here. She and I had been friends for as long as I could remember. I met her during my early visits to my grandmother, and we'd kept in touch throughout the years. She'd been the first one I called when anything happened, and a big reason I visited the few times I had throughout my adult life.

And then there was Aislinn. I hadn't spent a ton of time with her this past week, but she'd come around several times, and I watched her tend the garden while we chatted. I liked how she spoke her mind, even if she was odd, and talked about potions. I was still adjusting to the terms the English used for home remedies.

Then there was the mystery man I'd seen the day my kids left. Violet informed me his name was Sebastian and that he lived close by Pymm's Pondside. I'd seen him lurking about several times, but he never said anything as he stood there watching me.

My eyes scanned the forest surrounding me. The guy had haunted nearly every waking moment. I knew nothing about him, but his grave expression and sexy body wouldn't let me be, so I kept chewing over why. I hated not understanding. When I got a puzzle, I couldn't put it down until I figured it out.

With a sigh, I got up and went to grab a breakfast biscuit. The second I entered the house, the knocking started up, followed by the stairs creaking. The hair on the back of my neck stood on end. That was the first time the stairs made any noise.

My breath caught in my throat as I snatched a knife from the butcher block. Holding it in front of me, I searched for an intruder. Tiptoeing from the kitchen, I poked my head around the corner. There was nothing on the stairs.

A scream left me when one of the doors on the pie cabinet in the sunroom slammed open. *This place is freakin' haunted!* "Grandma, is that you? I'm sorry I didn't come more often over the last ten years." My cheeks heated, and I rolled my eyes at myself.

The place wasn't haunted. But I would love to be able to talk to Grams again. She always had the answers. And at the moment, there was no doubt I was missing something. The problem was that I have no idea what it was I hadn't figured out. Hurrying up the stairs, I checked the rooms on that floor. There was no one in the house.

Back in the living room, I stood next to the worn sofa

with my hands on my hips. "I don't know what's going on, but this is my house now, and I won't tolerate any more BS. That means you can stop making scary noises and opening and closing doors. I'm a Shakleton, and I'm not going anywhere."

I blew out a breath, but before I could turn away and grab my food, electricity flooded my body. It zapped me, sending my heart into SVT. I couldn't lift my arm to check my pulse, but I was sure my heart rate was well over two hundred thirty beats per minute. It was so fast I couldn't catch my breath.

I tried to take a step, and at first, I didn't think I moved an inch. Then my arm smacked into something that sent me reeling backward. I bounced off something behind me next. My eyes were wide open, but I saw nothing in front of me. I swear there was an invisible force field around me, and I could see the dust motes falling around it. *Girl, you need to lay off the Star Wars and stop talking to yourself. It makes you sound crazy.*

The electricity turned to unusual energy that filled every cell in my body. The nuclei went from shriveled raisins to plump grapes in seconds. I never realized I was dehydrated or depleted until It restored me. Only it wasn't fluids that filled me. *Power.* I shivered as the word raced through my mind.

It had to be a delayed reaction to the caffeine. That was the only explanation, unlike the sounds in the house. My analytical mind told me the plumbing was the reason for what I kept hearing. One snag in that theory was that the plumber assured me the pipes in my house were in pristine condition. That's when my grandmother's influence reared its head, and I conjured spirits as the real reason.

Did I piss the ghost off? Talking to myself and declaring the house likely made me insane, but my mind reacted before

I had time to censor what came out. Gritting my teeth against the continued flood of energy, I refused to back down. The house was mine, as was everything in it. I inherited it from my grandmother, and I intended to do right by her.

Lights flashed all around and swept me up into a funnel. It became even harder to breathe. *Am I having a heart attack?* It didn't feel like it. Women's acute MI symptoms were nausea, heartburn, dizziness, cold sweats, and unusual fatigue.

The sweat that dripped down my back was the devil's ass crack hot, and my gag reflex was doing push-ups in my throat. The next thing I knew, black spots danced in my vision as the pressure built in my body. My eyes slipped closed, and the blackness took over.

* * *

"Fiona! Fiona, are you okay? You have to wake up."

"Ughh," I grumbled at the frantic voice. My head was killing me, and I wanted to sleep some more.

"Oh, thank the gods. I thought you were dead." The voice was familiar, but my mind was slow to process other than the fact that someone was in my house.

My eyes flashed open, and I sat up in a rush. My hand went to my head while I scanned the room. "Aislinn? What the hell happened?" My blood felt thick as it rushed through my veins. My mind was sluggish, and I was having a hard time focusing on anything at the moment.

Aislinn sat on the floor next to me and sighed deep and heavy. "I have no idea. I came over to see if you wanted to go to lunch with me. When you didn't answer your door, and I saw the old beater that you bought off George in the drive, so

I checked the lock and came inside when it turned in my hand. I found you unconscious on the floor."

As if in response to her observation, my back started bitching loud and clear. My side ached, and my shoulder hurt like a mother-trucker. There was no doubt I had been on the floor for some time. God, it was no fun getting older. If I sat anywhere for longer than five minutes, I needed a crane to get me up.

"I was electrocuted." I felt my hair, surprised it wasn't a frizzy mess.

Aislinn tilted her head and glanced at the outlet closest to us. We were in the middle of the living room at least five feet from every wall with no appliances or lamps nearby. "Ummm. That makes no sense. What exactly happened?"

My shoulders lifted and fell. "A few minutes ago, I believed the house was haunted, and for a second thought, maybe a ghost attacked me, but that makes no sense."

Aislinn chuckled and got to her feet. "That's not how ghosts work. They aren't capable of producing energy like that, and they aren't conductors either. They barely have enough vitality to manifest most times."

I accepted her hand and grunted as I got to my feet, as well. She made it look so much easier than it was. "What do you mean they don't have enough power? Are there actual ghosts?" I recalled all the stories my grandmother told me, but none of them revolved around spirits.

Aislinn watched me closely for several seconds. The silence, coupled with the way she was looking at me, was highly uncomfortable. "Ghosts exist, and I have thought for weeks now that your grandmother must be hanging around in some form. It's the only thing that makes sense. You haven't shown power until now, and something has to be keeping the protections in place."

A million thoughts and questions scrambled through my

mind at once. What did Aislinn mean Grams was still around? And, what power? I couldn't decide which question to ask first, so I headed into the kitchen and grabbed the tea from the cabinet. After filling the kettle with water, I put it on to boil.

Taking a deep breath, I turned to find Aislinn had followed me and was sitting at the island where I used to as a kid. "Okay. You're going to have to explain this to me slowly. I know something is going on here, but ghosts don't exist. Right? Whatever it is, I want to understand."

Aislinn smiled and nodded her head. "I'm probably not the best one to explain all this, but I'll do my best. Violet is at the bookstore, or I'd call her over to help me. You know magic exists, right? And, you have it."

"No, it doesn't." The scientific part of me spoke up. I wanted to guffaw and dismiss her outright before asking the crazy lady to leave. But I forced myself to consider her words. "Since moving here, I'm not so sure that's right. Stuff keeps happening that I can't explain."

She had to be wrong. I'm nothing more than an ordinary middle-aged widow. Something niggled at my mind from when I was a kid. Unless my memory was playing tricks on me, my grandmother used to light candles with a snap of her fingers. And then there was the time she turned the pond turquoise. For the longest time, I believed she was a witch. Then I started high school and went to university and realized she'd used some kind of dye to change the color.

"Your grandmother was one of the strongest witches in our town. She surpassed anyone else, and we all expect you to as well. Although, I admit some have assumed you're nothing more than a mundane seeing as you haven't displayed any abilities or produced potions to sell at Staves and Stoves."

I grabbed two mugs and placed tea bags in them. "Grams

was nothing more than a normal but eccentric grandmother. What are Staves and Stoves? And what do you mean by potions? I'm not into home remedies. I'm firmly on the side of modern medicine. Although I admit, many plants have healing properties. They're also ingredients in many medications."

Aislinn chuckled and shook her head. "One thing at a time. First, have you ever done something odd or made something happen when you were angry or scared?"

I paused the racing thoughts and considered her question. There was no truth to what she was saying. Or was there? "Does blowing up tires count?" My tone was teasing as I picked an unrealistic phenomenon only to realize that I selected that very particular example because of an incident I couldn't explain from decades ago.

Aislinn lifted one eyebrow as she smirked at me. "Now that you have to explain."

The kettle started whistling, and I poured the hot water into the mugs then handed her one. I added three spoons of sugar and a splash of milk while I tried to recall everything and silence the denial screaming over everything else.

"When I was at the university, there was this girl that lived in my dorms. She believed the world should revolve around her. One day she asked my husband Tim, only he wasn't my husband at the time, to meet her at the restaurant where she worked and take her out dancing after her shift. Neither knew I was listening from my car parked two stalls over from hers. I was so mad I wished her tire would go flat and she'd miss work. To my surprise, a few seconds later, her tire popped, sending her on her ass."

Aislinn was laughing by the end of my explanation. "That's absolutely magic. Tires don't just explode like that. You made that happen. It seems like you did inherit your grandmother's magic after all. I was right. The rest of what happened this morning was because you are the new Guardian. But there's more. Or I wouldn't have felt the flux earlier."

"Guardian? What the hell are you talking about?" I was quickly reaching my limit. I didn't want to get upset with the only other person in the town that spoke to me. However, I wasn't a fool.

I opened my mouth to chew her out for thinking I would be so gullible as to believe the tall tale she just told but snapped my mouth closed. The energy bubbling through my body told me she was right. It fizzed like antacid tablets in water. That was not normal. *And, neither are you.* I flinched at the voice inside my head. It sounded an awful lot like Grams.

"Like I said, I'm not the best to explain all this, but you are the Guardian of the portal. Your family has been in charge of ensuring Dark Fae don't cross to this realm for over a hundred years now. And you have stepped into that role." Aislinn's expression was one hundred percent serious.

My jaw dropped, and my heart skipped a beat. A part of me knew she was right, but my scientific mind refused to believe it. I stood there while my mind battled itself. The part of me that made me an excellent nurse pointed out I likely hit my head and was still unconscious, suffering from a brain bleed. That none of this was real.

A hidden part of me rose to the surface. It was something that only came out when I was at Pymm's Pondside. The part recalled all of the oddities I'd seen from my Grams coupled with the incidents that had occurred since I took over the house.

I pinched my arm to see if I was, in fact, awake. "Ow! Oh my God. That's why the electricity hit me after I informed the house it now belonged to me, and it wasn't going to drive me away. Although, I'm not sure I believe in magic. This is all too freakin' much."

Aislinn grabbed the cookie jar I kept in the middle of the island and lifted the lid. Picking up an oatmeal raisin cookie, she took a bite. "What do you mean too much? Isidora never told you anything? How could she leave you out of the loop when she knew it would fall to you?"

I shook my head. "So, there's magic? And Fae? Are those like tiny Tinkerbells?"

Aislinn's jaw dropped, and she shook her head side to side. "Not all of our kind look like Tinkerbell. I'm a Fae. Well, half anyway. And there are all kinds of creatures in our world. Goblins, pixies, nymphs – both wood and water, barghests, Grimms, and so much more. By the way, it was a fairy that revealed herself to Walt Disney years ago that inspired Tink."

I pursed my mouth and narrowed my eyes. "You're one of these Fae? Are your ears pointy?"

Aislinn finished her cookie and brushed her hands off. Standing up, she crossed to the sink. "Indeed, I am. I am not as powerful as a full-blood, but I have some abilities. And, no, I don't have pointy ears. My human side diluted that trait." She reached out and touched the end of the aloe that had been half dead when I arrived. The thing perked up and turned vibrant green instantly. Gone were the drooping, browned stems.

I slumped against the counter and barely kept myself from falling to the wood floor for the second time that day. "What the hell am I supposed to do with all of this? It's insane. Wait," I gasped as a ton of bricks hit me. "All of my grandmother's stories are true!" There was no question that if what Aislinn was saying was correct, my Grams had been preparing me my entire life without coming out and saying it. "Holy shit."

"Knowing Isidora, they were indeed experiences she'd had. I used to love hearing all the creatures she had encountered. She was infamous for kicking Fae ass and denying them permission to enter our realm."

"Is that what a Guardian does? Is that what I'm supposed to do now?" The idea sounded exciting. I was bored out of my mind and considering taking a position working at the wine shop.

Aislinn nodded and picked up her mug. "You will decide which Fae to allow to cross and which to keep out."

My heart raced at the mere thought of denying some evil asshole the ability to come to earth. "I don't know what is more shocking that there are other planets from ours or that it's up to me to say who can come here. Or that magic exists. I can't wrap my head around it all."

Aislinn chuckled. "I wouldn't want the job, but I know it's important. King Vodor has been trying to get a foothold here for centuries. If he does, he will take over this realm as well."

I finished my tea and rinsed my cup, then glanced back at Aislinn. "I'd ask you how I am supposed to make those decisions, but I've hit a wall. You up for that lunch?" I was ravenous. I'd inadvertently skipped breakfast and needed to do something mundane for a bit before my mind went back to the bucket of unreal that I had just discovered.

CHAPTER 3

"Are you sure you want to walk home? It's at least two miles from here." Aislinn looked up from her handbag with her keys in hand and a skeptical expression.

Yeah, I'd be doubting myself too if I was in my right mind. But I wasn't. And I hated that her question made me feel like I was old. "I'm positive. I need fresh air. And the exercise will be good for me." All of that was true, but it wasn't the real reason.

Once I was home alone, all of the racing thoughts I managed to keep at bay run rampant, and I wasn't entirely sure I wouldn't have a meltdown. My head turned without permission and focused on the dwarf in the café we just exited. Was Bruce, the owner of Mug Shot, a supernatural dwarf? Or another type of Fae? He had some kind of magic to make sandwiches taste so damn good.

"He's a type of Fae we call dwarves. Very different from little people," Aislinn said as if she were reading my mind. Wait. Could she do that?

"Can you read my mind?" That would be awful. I'd have to

stop spending time with her, which would suck because I liked the feisty woman.

Aislinn chuckled. "Not at all. It's pretty obvious where your mind was. I don't blame you. If I hadn't grown up on stories about the hidden world that exists in few places outside Cottlehill Wilds, I would have checked into the nuthouse by now."

A laugh burst from me. "Trust me. I'm close. But my grandmother was always telling me stories about magic and the Fae. I never considered she was telling me the truth. Anyway, thank you for lunch. I'll see you soon."

I forced myself to start walking away. The town was bustling as I took my time down Main street and past the square in the middle. On the surface, the place was like any other small municipality. However, everything looked different to me today.

There was a glow around some shops and not others. The Sapphire Clam restaurant pulsed with energy as I passed. Plants that gave the place, and teatime, a green aura, and vibrant feel. By the time I reached the turn-off to take me closer to the cliffs and my house, I was convinced there was some kind of phenomenon present in these locations. It was almost as if it was an indication the place was owned by a supernatural.

I turned right instead of left and stood on the edge of the cliffs looking out over the sea in the distance. When I was home at Pymm's Pondside, it was impossible to tell the ocean was a mere mile away. Standing there, it felt like another world to me.

My legs were ready to give out after the mile I'd already walked. It wasn't that I was necessarily out of shape. It was more than the aches and pains were enough to make me regret not having Aislinn drive me home.

Shaking my head, I turned around and started down the

road that would take me home. The hustle and bustle of the town receded quickly, leaving me surrounded by trees and shrubs. The houses this far from the center of Cottlehill Wilds were spread out rather than right next door or connected.

I haven't visited anyone out here and had no idea what their property looked like behind the wall of plant life, acting as a sentinel for their homes and providing privacy. Kicking a rock, I watched as it bounced off an invisible barrier to my right. I barely ducked out of the way when it bounced back at me.

I wondered where Sebastian lived. Violet had told me it was close to my house. I had shocked myself when I ventured into stalker territory and asked Aislinn and Violet who the mysterious guy was. It said a lot that the moment I described him with his brooding brown eyes and muscular build, both women knew who it was. It surprised me that they knew him well enough to refer to him by a shortened version of his name. He didn't seem like the type to talk to anyone ever.

The image of his crossed arms and scowl popped into my head. Bas, as Violet and Aislinn referred to him, made sullen sexy. I couldn't imagine him ever-smiling, yet that didn't deter me. I was drawn to him, regardless. I couldn't deny I was curious if his face would soften when he kissed me. *What? Nope, not happening!*

I reached my house in no time and paused to look over the garden. Weeds were starting to pop up, so I headed through the gate and grabbed some gloves from the table set up to the right.

"Crap," I groaned as I lowered to my knees. That might have been a mistake. I might never be able to get up. Not to mention the pain in my joints would keep me awake tonight. As I knelt there, yanking weeds from the ground, Sebastian intruded into my thoughts once again.

Crap. I came out here for a distraction.

Tugging on the stubborn weeds, I pulled one after another while forcing my mind to focus on the task at hand. Unfortunately, it had been too damn long since I'd been kissed or touched in any way. For the years since Tim died, I did not react to men. I certainly had not been so attracted that I wanted to take one to bed.

I was used to living with that part of me dead and gone. Yet seeing Sebastian standing there with a scowl on his face had done something to me. Now my body was awake and wouldn't let me ignore my needs.

Sitting back on my ankles, I closed my eyes and sighed, trying to push the heated ache outside of me. It was something I'd gotten very good at during Tim's illness. The sound of rippling water jolted me, and I jumped to my feet. "Shit," I yelped when my knees started bitching immediately. Getting old sucked.

The sight of flowers blooming on the lily pads stopped any thought about my creaking body. I limped over to the gate and hurried through. *What the heck did I do? And how?* I had made little things happen here and there throughout my life, but nothing on this level.

The pond was at least thirty feet across and twenty-five feet wide and covered by lily pads that now had stunning white flowers on them. My mind refused to believe I was responsible for this development.

They had to be on the verge of blooming before. It was a bright, sunny day. The rays had to have coaxed the buds to open. Only there hadn't been any buds or any hint of them. Standing there gaping in disbelief, I found no other explanation when they hadn't existed moments ago.

Pulling off the gloves, I set them on the table, then went inside and washed my hands. That started a cleaning frenzy. I cleaned the countertops, then moved onto the cabinet doors before beginning on the pantry. That stupid pinging started up in my head again.

It took a lot out of me, and I was losing steam when I finally finished with the kitchen and entered the living room. Before I stopped for the day, I had to rearrange the furniture so it fit me. When my husband died a couple of years ago, I learned there was no need to keep the house a homage to his memory. I loved him, but he was gone. It didn't matter if I changed the arrangement or bought new furniture that he would have hated. I would still love him. Nothing, and no one, could change that fact.

My back protested when I pushed the sofa to the opposite wall, and the pinging was still driving me crazy. My grandmother had arranged everything around the fireplace. There was nothing better than a fire in the winter, but I planned on creating a place I could watch television when mine arrived next week.

There was no cable service in Cottlehill Wilds, but there was internet service. Thank God for streaming. I switched when Emmie started college to have something to access without paying for it.

When I moved the love seat, I stood back and hated the new arrangement. The coffee table didn't fit with the new setup. I opened the door on the side of the house and shoved the short, wooden table outside. Turning back, I groaned at the mess I'd made.

The aches had evolved into agony, and I could barely move. *Time for a bath.* Grabbing a bottle of wine and my e-reader, I practically crawled up the stairs and into my bathroom. I needed a break and had to stop this damn pinging.

Crossing to the old-fashioned claw-footed tub, I turned the faucets on and plugged the drain. My grandmother had several jars filled with liquid on a wood shelf in the bathroom. I had tossed the ones that reminded me of her and kept the rest. Pouring some that smelled like jasmine and apple, I turned to take off my clothes and froze.

I hobbled to the window, and my eyes flew open when I saw Sebastian standing outside near the family cemetery. I was running down the stairs despite my protesting knees a second later.

By the time I made it outside, he was nowhere in sight. I stood there and turned in a circle, then cursed. What the hell was he doing here again? If he wanted to talk to me, why did he take off? On a good note, the pinging finally stopped.

I had no idea how to find Sebastian, so I went back inside. When I heard water upstairs, I remembered the bath was still running. I tripped in my haste to get upstairs. I pushed my creaky body too far today.

I made it to the bathroom just as the hot water started to flow over the side. Turning the handles, I pulled the plug and allowed several inches to drain away. Checking the window to make sure no one was watching me, I tugged the shirt over my head, followed by my shoes and socks, then the rest of my clothes.

God, it felt good to sink into the fragrant water. My aches subsided, and I grabbed my device and pulled up the latest book I was reading. It was no wonder I enjoyed stories involving paranormal and fantasy creatures. It was part of who I am.

I lost myself in the story until the water went cold. With a sigh, I set my glass of wine down and got to my feet. I was pleased to discover my knees and back held me without much complaint. Whatever the oils were, they had to have magical powers. A bath had never felt quite so good before.

I was dried and dressed as the sun started to set. I was hungry again after a long afternoon of walking, weeding, and cleaning. When I made it downstairs, I hit my limit of the impossible for the second time that day.

"How did I make this one happen?" I asked no one as I stood in a perfectly arranged living room. The sofa and love seat were on the opposite side, with the chair finishing off the seating. All I saw above the mantle were empty brackets. The painting of a landscape that used to be there had disappeared. Precisely where I planned to hang the flatscreen TV.

I needed to figure my shit out. Although, I didn't mind making flowers grow and getting the house to clean itself. I turned and went into the kitchen to grab a light dinner. Nothing sounded good, and I had no desire to cook.

For a split second, I stood there wishing for some fish tacos like a fool. Part of me hoped I could do things merely by wishing for it while the rest knew it wasn't possible. Eventually, I was forced to admit defeat and grabbed an apple and some peanut butter along with a pop. I stood there eating when relentless heat broke out over my body.

Sweat poured from every pore, and I became lightheaded. I opened the freezer and stood in front of it, hoping it would cool me down. I thought about walking outside when I noticed the trees swaying in the breeze out the window. The cool air from the fridge felt too good to move.

A second later, the back door blasted open, and the winds blew through the house. Freaked out, I shut the freezer door and headed outside to look for what caused the door to open like that. The sun was just setting, and the sky was a beautiful mix of pinks and oranges.

The crunch of gravel intruded on my quiet moment of peace, and I turned to see Sebastian striding down the lane. "Are you following me, Sebastian?"

His head jerked, and his eyes flared before they narrowed. My hands went to my mouth, and I wanted to crawl into a hole. I'd just proven to him that I was the worst kind of stalker alive.

"I'm not following you. I came to Pymm's Pondside." His

voice was rougher than the gravel beneath his black boots and rubbed me in ways that shouldn't happen.

Clearing my throat, I crossed my arms over my chest. "I can see that. Why do you keep coming here? Do you want something?"

He watched me without saying anything. Aislinn's words about my new job as Guardian popped into my head. The woman hadn't given me any helpful information. Perhaps he wanted to cross into Faery.

"Oh, um, do you want to cross to..." My words faltered as my cheeks heated. I had no idea how this worked. I didn't want this guy to think I was an imbecile.

His head tilted. "To Eidothea? What do you know of the portal to the Fae realm?"

My shoulders lifted and fell. "I don't know anything." It stung to admit that fact. For some reason, I wanted him to see the brilliant woman I was. I picked things up faster than anyone around me and graduated at the top of my class from nursing school. It was why I was the only nurse able to connect patients to ECMO at my previous hospital. "I'm not even sure I believe anything Aislinn said about magic, the Fae, and my supposed job."

"I was worried about that. It's why I've come by."

"Why? Are you here to help me?" Please be here to help me. I was in over my head and needed someone to teach me about everything. There had to be rules that I should be following. The last thing I wanted to do was make a mistake because I didn't know any better.

Oh, God! What if I let some Fae serial killer through the portal?!

Sebastian didn't reply, just stared at me. Lightning bugs flitted by my head. I waved them away while keeping my eyes on Sebastian. The buzzing became persistent until I finally turned to see I was wrong about what was flitting around me. They were tiny people flying around. *Just like Tinkerbell!*

These creatures had iridescent wings and vibrant colored hair and clothes. "What are they? Aislinn never told me what they were."

Sebastian closed some of the distance between us. "They're pixies. And those are brownies."

I followed his finger and noticed small brown creatures crawling under the fence and into the garden. "What do they do? Are they trying to cross?"

"You need to learn your shit before King Vodor sends something horrendous through to establish a foothold in this realm." With those growled words, Sebastian stalked away.

My mouth compressed into a thin line to keep from cursing him as he left. Swallowing the anger and frustration wasn't easy, especially when I considered how this job dropped into my lap, and he was expecting miracles.

With a growl, I stomped my foot on the grass. Electricity shot out of my hands. I screamed and waved them through the air. Suddenly, a bright white stream flew to the left and slammed into a tree.

Flames erupted on the bark, and a tall willowy figure separated from it, shouting. I ran around the pond and reached her in a flash. My heart pounded against my rib cage as burns sprouted along my arms.

Acting on instinct, I ran to the pond and scooped water into my hands. By the time I turned back to her with a handful of water, the fire was out. She stood there staring at me while I poured the liquid over her arm. "I am so sorry. I didn't mean to harm you. I lost my temper."

Her thin pale brown lips stretched up at the corners, and her green eyes sparkled. "It's okay. Bas has that effect on people. I'm Theamise. Your grandmother invited me to live in the maple when it was dying from a fungus."

I nodded my head as if I already knew that. Every time I turned around, there was something new thrown at me. Except I did know that. Grams had told me the story about the tree dying and making a deal with a nymph to save it.

It seemed impossible that these creatures even existed. If not for the stories my grandmother told me, I would be far more shocked. I hoped it got easier to accept this was real because I couldn't continue having the same arguments in my head. Seriously, I made schizophrenics look sane.

I was no longer in my twenties. Being hit with all this was taking a toll on my mind. But like all Shakletons, I refused to allow it to overwhelm me. With a start, I realized my mom ran from all of this. I didn't think she denied it existed. After all, she sent me to her mom every summer. But why didn't she or my father ever tell me about any of this? I couldn't help but wonder what made her move away.

None of that matters right now! Right. I needed to get a handle on the situation before it got out of hand. Something was going on in my new world, and I had to know what before it put me on my ass, literally.

"I'm sorry about your tree. I hope I didn't do any permanent damage, but I need to run and talk to a friend real quick."

"I understand. I will heal, as will the tree. Do not worry about us." Theamise waved me away and went back to the maple.

I raced inside, grabbed my handbag and keys, and jumped into my car. Violet didn't live far, and I needed to ask her if she knew anything about what was going on. Maybe she had a book that would help me. Regardless, I need my bestie to help with a reality check. I parked in front of the Pleasure Bound.

The bell jingled when I opened the door, and Violet looked up from the register. "Hey, Fiona. What's wrong?"

I should have known she would pick up on my distress. I checked down the aisle next to me then the next one before I approached her. "I need your help." I proceeded to explain what happened that day and what Aislinn told me earlier.

Violet sighed and gave me a sympathetic look I'd seen a thousand times before. "She's right. Your grandmother was the last Guardian, and you are her only living heir, so when you claimed the house, you claimed the position."

"How did I never know about all this? Why didn't you ever tell me magic existed?"

Violet bit her lip. "I assumed you were born a Mundie, and that's why your parents moved away with you. It's difficult for a Mundie to grow up among supernaturals. I wasn't going to be the one to tell you about the world that existed around you, especially if there was nothing you could do to protect yourself from it."

I picked up one of the fuzzy tipped pens from a display and rubbed it between my palms, needing a distraction. "I can't believe all of this is real. That all of Grams's stories were true."

"It's a lot to take in. I imagine you feel like the rug was pulled out from under you," Violet said as she watched me fidget.

"Exactly! Sebastian was no help, and Aislinn told me some, but not what I need to know. I want to stick my head in the sand and pretend I never heard any of it."

"But you won't," Violet interjected with a knowing smile. "You face things head-on, even when they seem impossible or are painful to deal with."

"You know me too well. I can't ignore any of this, which is why I'm here. I need to know how I am supposed to guard this portal. I don't even know where it is. Do you have anything that can help me?"

"I might be a witch, but I can't give you those answers.

That's information only your family is privy to," Violet informed me with a wince.

My shoulders sank, and I felt like hitting something. "How the hell am I supposed to do this job when I have no information? Sebastian just told me King Vodor would send something awful through the portal, and I would be responsible for the end of the world. Don't you have a book that can at least give me information on what I'm dealing with?"

Violet waved a hand through the air. "First of all, don't listen to him. He has made brooding an art form. Second, I wish I had something that would help. My best piece of advice is that you look through your house. Your grandmother had to have left something that will help. She knew you'd come back eventually."

"She could have mailed me a letter. Or even left one on the kitchen table. Hell, she could have emailed me. Anything to give me the information I need. The weight of the world is literally on my middle-aged shoulders, and they're about to give out on me."

Violet chuckled and shook her head. "Sounds like you've been running yourself in circles all day. Let's get dinner. After that, I can help you search through your house."

I nodded, emotion suddenly overwhelming me. Something clicked into place inside my chest.

Violet bounced in place with a broad smile lifting her lips. "Hey, did we just form a coven of two?" She must have felt something similar to what I did.

"I think it's more like three. Aislinn would not like being left out," I corrected.

"You're right about that. Let me close up shop, and we can get out of here."

"That would be fantastic. Thank you." I had no desire to do this on my own. It was nice to have someone supporting me.

I might have stepped into the twilight zone, but there were plenty of people around to help me navigate through the darkness. I wasn't alone, and that eased my worry more than anything. One thing I'd learned in life was that you needed to surround yourself with supportive friends and family, or you'll be eaten alive by the twists and turns.

CHAPTER 4

"Is this anything?" I held the book aloft, unsure if the strange markings on the book's cover meant anything.

Violet poked her head into the craft room a second later. Her eyebrows furrowed, and she scanned the brown cover in my hand. "That's not your grandmother's writing or your family, Grimoire. It looks like a book from Faery. That is the Fae language. I don't imagine Isidora would have left you notes in that."

I shook my head and blew out a breath. "Well, I haven't come across anything. This is futile. It seems as if my grandma didn't think to leave me a note or clue me in on this world. Maybe I should return to North Carolina with my kids."

Violet crossed to me and squeezed my hand. "You mentioned something clicking into place. Do you feel differently now?"

Glancing out the window, I watched the pond and the flowering lily pads. "Honestly, I'm overwhelmed, but I still feel like this is where I belong. But I have no idea how I am supposed to be this Guardian. And that pisses me off. I'm not used to not knowing."

Violet chuckled and headed out of the room, tugging me with her. "Now, that sounds like Isidora. She was the go-to in town for most people, whether they asked about potions or recipes or how to help loved ones. What matters is that you feel like you belong."

"That's not all that matters. I can't help anyone with anything. I don't even know what potions are. I would say I have no magic to even learn with, but I know that would be a lie."

"That's something, then. The fact that you are certain you have magic is vastly different than the woman I spoke with a few weeks ago. Are you saying that because of the information you received? Or has something happened?" Violet let go of my hand and went into the kitchen.

I continued past her when she went to the stove. "I made those flowers appear when I was in the garden pulling weeds. I was overwhelmed at the time and sent the feelings out of me. But when I look at my life, I think there has always been something under the surface. When I was in labor with my kids, I caused the fetal monitors to fritz. People who made me mad in some way experienced things like spilled drinks, wardrobe malfunctions, and diarrhea when I sent my anger towards them. I never gave it a second thought, assuming I was reading too much into it. After the last few weeks, I have considered the events differently."

Violet braced herself on the counter as she bent over and laughed. "Diarrhea? That's classic. As far as learning magic, I can help with potions and other spells with the witchcraft part. But you are also part Fae, and I can't help with that half. Nor the role you've accepted as Guardian. That's where your family Grimoire comes in handy."

"You mentioned that before. That's a book, right? Can you

describe it? I haven't found anything with my family history in it."

Violet turned on the stove and set the kettle on to boil. "I've never seen it, but it's far more than your family history. It's an accounting of spells and magic your ancestors created. And, I would bet there's information about the portal and your duties in it, as well."

"Then it sounds like I need to find the damn book." I suddenly felt defeated. I'd searched most of the house but didn't find anything there. "Can you tell me why my family has this role? Why can't I pass the job off to someone like Sebastian? He'd be able to fight off anyone that isn't supposed to cross to earth."

Violet shook her head and grabbed the milk from the fridge. "Having him in charge would be a disaster. He would never allow anyone through. I don't know the entire story, but I do know your family settled in Pymm's Pondside long ago when there were many bridges from Faery to this world. As the magic dried up, the portal on your land remained. I suspect someone in your line created it as a way to visit family here and tied its existence to your bloodline when the Fae realm started losing its power."

I swiveled to face her and nearly dropped the mugs I had just grabbed in my shock. "How can an entire realm lose power? That seems impossible."

Violet sighed and put tea bags in the mugs I set down. "It has to do with the king and when he took the throne. He consumed a significant portion of the magic in the realm and even stole some from his subjects. It was the only way for him to beat the previous king."

That was fascinating. "So, is there like some hidden royal family that can take the throne back and restore Faery to its former glory?" It was a common trope in fantasy novels, my favorite genre.

Violet chuckled at that and removed the kettle when it started whistling. She poured the hot water into the cups. "The stories don't mention that. I'm not Fae, but I can see that whoever wants to rule takes the throne by force from what I have gathered. It's not something someone passes down from heir to heir: the strongest rule Eidothea and its people. There is an upper echelon, and only those top families can fight for the throne. I suspect your family belongs to that higher tier."

I reared back as if she'd slapped me. I wanted nothing to do with beings that would exploit others for personal gain. "Ugh. Thank the gods. I'm not some vile person that would steal from others so I could take the throne."

"Faery needs a ruler that thinks of the greater good. Maybe then the balance between our worlds can be reestablished." Violet poured sugar into her tea then brought the steaming mug to her lips.

I lifted mine and let the aromatic steam calm me. "What would that mean? I can't see humans accepting Fae exist. They'd deploy nuclear bombs to destroy us all if they learned mythic creatures were real." There was no denying the way we reacted to fear. I considered getting a gun after Tim died. In the end, I realized it would pose more of a risk than it would help.

"That's true. It doesn't matter right now anyway. There's no one alive that will challenge King Vodor."

A gasp left me, and I dropped my tea when my hands flew to my head. That awful pinging had started again and was far more potent than it had ever been before. "Are you okay, Fiona? What's wrong?" Violet's voice came to me from far away. I couldn't concentrate on anything except the noise and tugging in my chest.

"My head," I said through clenched teeth. "There's this pinging."

A hand ran up and down my back, rubbing circles. *Find the source of that awful noise!* I took several deep breaths and focused on the sound for several seconds. Violet was asking if she should take me to someone or something named Zreegy. I had no idea who or what Zreegy was.

All I could think about was settling the pinging and tugging. It was getting worse and was now downright painful. After several seconds, I dropped my hands and looked into Violet's wide blue eyes. The concern was the reminder I needed that there were some in town that cared about me.

"Are you okay?" She asked after a couple of seconds.

I nodded my head and licked dry lips. "I'm good now. I've felt this pinging ever since I arrived, and it is getting worse. I thought it was coming from the house, but now I suspect it's coming from outside."

Violet turned and went to the pantry. "You might be sensitive to the power coursing through the leylines, but we will go out and find what's causing it. Not yet, though. Stay where you are. You're barefoot, and there are ceramic pieces all over the floor."

I hadn't even heard it break. I kept focused on the pinging, which was now getting softer and softer. "You know I'd be lost without you and Aislinn. Knowing I can turn to you both erases any doubt about my decision to stay. But what do you mean ley lines, and why would I be sensitive to them?"

"Leylines are pathways of condensed magic. Here in Cottlehill Wilds, several different ones converge. That draws supernatural to our location and is one reason we have a significant population living here. The other is the portal. I suspect the convergence made it possible for the creation of the portal here."

"I reiterate that I wouldn't survive without you. I get the

concept you are describing, but my mind refuses to believe it outright."

Violet dumped the sharp debris into the trash, and I mopped up the liquid with some paper towels. "I've felt a kinship with you for as long as I can remember. I wish you'd known about your magic when Trent left me for his secretary. We could've hexed him with loose bowels like we joked. That would've turned the twenty-something bimbo off."

I barked out a laugh and stuffed my feet into the boots I kept in the mudroom. "Now that's magic I can get behind. Why do men do that when they hit their forties? As if that will turn back the clock? He will have to work twice as hard to keep that young woman. Dumbass. You deserve so much better."

Violet snorted and followed me out of the house. "From your lips to the gods' ears. Now, let's see what we can learn out here. Do you have any idea where it is?"

I thought about that as the cool night air surrounded us. The scent of nightshade and jasmine filtered to me from the garden. I needed to do some research to discover what I had out there. And how to make potions. Perhaps I could find Violet's ex and slip him something to give him cramps.

"I haven't got a clue. It happens intermittently and at odd times. I assumed it had to do with the house because it started right after I informed Pymm's Pondside that I was staying."

Violet lifted a hand and muttered, "*Revelare*." I had no idea what foreign language she was speaking, but energy pulsed through the air, and my skin started tingling in response. A light blue glow seeped from my pores a second later. There was a green glow coming from the garden and various ones coming from the cemetery.

"What did you just do?" I turned in a circle and took in the forest and plant life around me. The maple with the nymph glowed brown and the flowers scattered about glowed brighter, as well.

I focused on the gravestones wondering why each one displayed a different color. And then there was the crypt. Pretty much every color in the rainbow emanated from the stone building.

"I cast a reveal spell. It's all about intent with magic, and I wanted to reveal anything your grandmother may have concealed. There's far more hidden here, so it isn't going to help us." Violet waved her arms to encompass everything.

"What's that?" I was moving through the foliage before Violet responded. There was this black glow that pulled me forward. It was menacing, but there was a darkness that spoke to the grief I'd been carrying for far too long.

Violet's steps were loud behind me as I kept going. "This is all your land. Your grandmother took in strays and allowed them to live on Pymm's Pondside. You'll find many out here."

"How can I find out everyone that lives here with me? It's creepy not knowing who's close by." Trees glowed randomly, as did hollows in the trunks and shrubs. The moon was high in the sky, telling me it was late. I hadn't been out after eight for many years. It was nice to be out at this time of night. It almost made me feel like I was twenty again. Well, if I ignored the aches and pains, hot flashes, and fatigue.

Before Violet could respond, I stopped in my tracks. Sebastian was standing in the middle of the forest with his arms crossed over his chest. "What are you doing out here?"

"You live on my property?"

A growl rumbled from his chest. "No. You left Pymm's Pondside about ten feet back. Go home."

Violet stopped next to me. "Hello to you, too, Bas. Lovely evening isn't it?"

"Why did you cast a reveal spell? I didn't want her

knowing where I live." The look he sent my way was enough to make me cringe and tuck tail then crawl home.

"I don't give a crap where you live. I'm trying to understand my role. We don't have time to argue with you," I informed him and continued walking. In the distance, I caught sight of an iridescent bubble.

"I wasn't arguing with you, Guardian. But you should leave before you're hurt. You're in over your head."

I stopped walking and turned narrowed eyes on the guy. "I wouldn't be in over my head if you'd pull that stick out of your ass and offer me some help."

His jaw dropped open for a second before he snapped it closed. "Why would I do that? If I wanted to be involved in this shit, I would be back in Faery. Not here close to the likes of you."

"What is your problem?" I practically yelled at him. Violet sprang forward and grabbed my arm.

"Let's continue. I'll be by to get my athame later this week, Bas," she called over her shoulder as she dragged me away.

"That guy is an asshole. Does he like anyone? No, you know what? I don't care. What's an athame?" I wanted to know why Sebastian loathed me. Not that I believed he was overly friendly or anything. Brooding was his resting demeanor. Although, he seemed to save his extreme dislike for me.

"An athame is a ceremonial blade. It's the main ritual implement or magical tool among witches. We use them in ceremonial magic rituals. Your grandmother should have left you one, but if you can't find it, Bas is the one you want to buy another from."

"No offense, but I won't be buying anything from that man, no matter how sexy he is."

Violet made a choking sound that ended in a coughing fit.

She looked back over her shoulder then picked up her pace. "Bas is a Fae with exceptional hearing."

The blood drained from my head at the same time my entire body lit up. I refused to see if he was watching me. What I was feeling was nothing more than a hot flash. Or so I told myself. "You could have told me that sooner. Anyway, it doesn't matter how attractive someone is if they're an asshole." I said the last louder, hoping he would hear that.

Violet shook her head and pointed ahead of us. "We've reached the edge of the town border. That offers some protection for us."

I lifted a hand and reached for the iridescent barrier in front of us. A zing traveled through my fingers when I touched it. "Is this like a protection spell or something?"

Violet shook her head. "Not really. It's more of a warning to the town. When a human with no magic or Fae blood passes through, it sends out a signal so those of us that stand out can hide. It also helps hide the existence of the portal in our town. That's why Fae in this world don't overrun us."

I scanned the area around us and dropped my arm. The cliffs were ahead of us, with Cottlehill Wilds behind us. The barrier ended to the left but wasn't visible from the other direction. "I had wondered how you manage to remain hidden. It must alert you to any newcomers. I never saw the pixies or gnomes when my kids and I first arrived. Now they're everywhere."

Violet headed back toward my house but took a path several feet from the one leading to Sebastian's property. "You're right. It tells us when someone that has magic and doesn't live here crosses the border. Now that you've claimed your place here, you won't trigger the spell. Your kids will every time they come to visit."

We walked in silence as I took in everything that had happened that day. The night was clear, and stars filled the sky. Everything looked familiar yet also felt fresh and foreign.

Violet's steps faltered when we came across an area where the foliage had died. All plant life was dried and brown in a three-foot circle. "This doesn't look good."

Fine lines fanned out from the corners of Violet's blue eyes as they lifted to mine. "It's not. I can't say for sure what it is but be on alert. Something might have crossed the portal after your grandmother died and before you arrived. She gave us potions that should have prevented that, but there were a couple of hours between when she passed away and was found."

My heart started pounding against my rib cage, and my breath caught in my throat. "What do we do about it? Do we need to make a potion or something?"

Violet shook her head and walked so fast we were practically running back to my house. "No. When you took the role as new Guardian, it fortified the spell around the land and blocked the portal. You need to find your family Grimoire, or at the very least, the portal so you can physically monitor it. Sebastian was right about one thing. None of Vodor's minions will be able to cross over and take Cottlehill Wilds for their own now that you are here."

"No pressure," I retorted as I huffed and puffed. I wanted to get home, take a hot bath and go to bed. All of this bullshit could wait for morning. I had reached my limit. My crackly body needed the soft bed that had just arrived and several uninterrupted hours of sleep.

CHAPTER 5

We hadn't made it twenty feet from the dead section of the forest when rabid dogs with glowing red eyes sprang out of the shadows. Violet came to a dead stop, and I tripped over my feet and slammed into a tree before I managed to catch myself.

"What the hell is going on?" I was screeching, but I couldn't help it. There were giant black dogs with canines as long as fingers dripping with saliva. Plus, tiny grayish-brown things that were a grotesque cross between chihuahuas and alligators. Only these things had smooth, leather-like skin and long pointed ears.

"Seems like I was right. Dark Fae came through alright." Violet's hands were shaking as she watched the creatures circle us.

Keep your shit together. I was always calm in a storm. It's one thing that made me a good nurse, but this was in a whole other spectrum. "And, what do we do about these things? Can we just keep walking?"

One of the dogs snapped its jaws and jumped toward me

as soon as the question left my lips. "Apparently, not." I tried to concentrate on the self-defense classes I took when I was in my twenties.

It was so long ago, but I never forgot the instructor telling us to hit the nose, groin, and instep. Sensitive places that would injure the attacker. That applied to people. What about dogs and goblins, or whatever those small things were?

I saw angry red eyes heading for me as a dog lunged for me. I threw my hands up on instinct right as Violet shouted something in a foreign language. She was likely casting a spell. It sounded like what she'd spoken a few hours ago.

I needed to use my magic, too. But how? I knew nothing about being a witch. She mentioned magic being about intent.

When teeth sunk into my forearm, I screamed out in pain and kicked the dog latched onto my arm. The thing yelped and snarled at me but didn't let go. My fist punched the beast's nose over and over with no effect.

"Get off me," I demanded and brought every ounce of desire to the front of my mind. I had no idea if I was performing magic and was about to give up when the dog yelped and let me go.

Warm liquid dripped from the wound on my arm, but I didn't have time to think about that when two more headed my way. I couldn't rely on whatever magic I had to fight off these creatures, so I snatched a stick from the ground right before one of the goblins launched himself into the air.

Gripping the tree limb with both hands, I swung and sent the creature sailing away from me. I wanted to fist pump the air, but another was behind that one. "That was absolutely bonkers," Violet called out.

My smile died when sharp teeth cut through my existing wound. The flesh burned and was now sizzling from the injury. My blood thickened, and despite the way my heart raced, it barely pumped through my veins. I became light-headed and dizzy.

The goblin latched onto my arm shook its head, tearing the skin. I barely registered that on top of the pain from the previous attack. "I can see why we don't want your kind here. You're a violent leech." That was the only thought that came to mind as my energy seemed to drain from me.

My hand reflexively closed around the stick, so I didn't drop it as my fingers went numb. I needed to get this thing off me. The fingers of my left hand wrapped around the goblin's large ears and yanked. He opened his mouth reflexively, and I acted as fast as my limp body would allow and removed him from my body.

I tossed him away from me and winced when I saw the mess of half-masticated meat left behind. Growls and snarls warred with the need to close my eyes and go to sleep. If I was a hybrid, wouldn't I have more power than a middle-aged woman with bad knees?

Said knees gave out, and I collapsed with a loud crack followed by pain shooting up my thigh. That was going to hurt worse tomorrow, and that was saying something because I couldn't move at the moment.

My hands flew out to catch myself. Agony shot up my right arm, but a zap of energy followed it. I dug my fingers into the soil and relished the tingling.

I was part Fae and part witch. Thinking back to the stories my grandmother told me, I recalled her saying something about a connection to the four elements, especially the earth.

Opening my mind, I called the power to me. I needed to heal my arm and fight off these creatures. Violet screamed next to me, right as electricity traveled from the ground to my core.

I jumped to my feet as tiny white streaks of lightning traveled up my arms. It hurt my wounded arm while also invigorating it. My head swung in my friend's direction. I flung one of my hands out and caught the hindquarters of a dog that had its claws embedded in her chest. The thing growled and turned to look at me. Violet shoved it off and rolled away.

"There are too many. We need to try and run." She was pulling herself up using a tree. Neither of us was in any shape to run.

I limped over to her and wrapped my good arm around her waist. "Not sure how far we will get, but it's better than standing here while they kill us."

We hadn't made it three feet when a goblin scurried in front of us and slashed out at our legs. I managed to swivel out of the way, but I lost hold of Violet as I did. She collapsed to the ground with her eyes closed.

"Shit, shit, shit." I cursed as my breathing quickened and my heart raced. I scanned the area and noted the two dogs and four goblins were still circling us. The wider they wound around us, the more the trees and plants decayed. They were using life to fuel themselves. I could see the green aura flow from the shrubs to the creatures.

It infuriated me. These dark Fae were destroying my home. I may not own these woods, but it was a matter of time before they took over everything, including Pymm's Pondside.

My entire body heated, and sweat poured from me in buckets. Why the hell did I have to suffer the worst hot flash of my life when I was facing half a dozen creatures that wanted me dead?

If I've learned anything in my life, it was that I had to work despite the bullshit ragging through my head. I could multitask in my sleep. Fanning my face with one hand, I knelt and buried my hand in the dirt. The Fae started circling me, and I focused on the connection to the element.

Anger surged through me once again, and I used that to fuel my determination. I cried out when fire shot out of me in a wide arch. I had no idea how I did that, but I was grateful.

The goblins waved their clawed hands at me. The dogs turned tail and tried to run away. The word burn flashed through my mind and was on repeat as I fed my intent to have the flames eat these creatures into the spell.

I tried to will the flames to extend further and catch every one of the dark Fae. Something light landed on my back, and a scream echoed from my throat. When sharp claws dug into my flesh a second later, I reached up and tried to grab the goblin that had managed to catch me off guard.

My fingers wrapped around one leather ear. I yanked and held the beast up in front of my face. What little energy I had drained from me every second I willed the flames to catch the next dog.

It shouldn't surprise me that I was weakening. Magic, like anything else, took power, and I had no idea what I was doing. No doubt I was pouring more than I needed into my desire to burn these fuckers to death. The goblin slipped from numb fingers and landed on its back in front of me.

I slapped a hand down over the tiny creature, trapping it under my palm. Pressing down, I slowly dialed my energy back. This would all be so much easier if I knew what the heck I was doing. Fortunately, my age meant I had plenty of experience to know better than to pull all my energy back and keep it close to my chest.

I was heaving as I tried to catch my breath, and my heart was close to giving out. The exertion was almost too much for it to handle, but if I did that, the flames would die, and I would be shit out of luck.

I crawled to Violet and pressed a finger to her neck and felt a steady if slow pulse beating back at me. My shoulders dropped a fraction at the same time the flames dimmed by half. A dog jumped over the lower fire a second later but never made it to me.

Big muscular arms reached out and knocked the hound off course. "Sebastian." His name fell from my lips as he stepped in front of me. I collapsed and released the word. It was as if his presence signaled to me that I was safe.

An absurd notion. He'd done nothing but scowl at me and try to drive me away. This man wasn't my friend exactly, but he was the sweetest sight I'd ever seen at that moment.

He caught one goblin around the neck and snapped it. Opening his fingers, he dropped the creature to the ground in a heap. It landed amidst the flames sputtering across the forest floor. Without me fueling the fire, it was dying a quick death.

A goblin ran through Sebastian's legs heading toward me when the other two leaped at Sebastian. He lifted one booted foot and slammed it down on the creature, crushing it beneath his heel. A burned dog hobbled toward him with its red eyes glowing brightly.

Bas cursed when the goblins in his hands sunk their teeth into the back of his hand. He shook them in his fist and crushed them. Blackish-green goo oozed through his fingers before their heads popped off and rolled away.

Bile rose in my throat, making my gag reflex do push-ups at the back of my throat. Pushing myself to my knees, I gasped when pain shot through the joints. "Bas, look out," I cried out. My discomfort made my voice louder when I warned him to watch out for the dog he'd kicked a moment before.

Bracing himself with his feet shoulder's width apart, he shook his hands free of the goblin bodies, then swiveled and bent as he turned. I could barely follow his movement, but I saw when he grabbed the stick I'd dropped earlier.

Never stopping, he cracked the makeshift weapon against both skulls before coming to a stop facing me. His chest was rising and falling rapidly while I stared into his bright brown eyes.

A howl sounded to his left, and my gaze fell to the massive black dog that was baring its teeth at him. Sebastian turned and kicked the dog. A loud snap was followed by the dog's head twisting all the way around before it slumped to the forest floor.

The burned dog was left and tried to scamper away, but Bas was on its heels and swinging the stick through its back. It cut through the beast, and brown blood flew through the air, spraying everything within a four-foot radius.

As much as I wanted to collapse to the ground, I channeled all my remaining strength into getting to my feet so I could thank Sebastian. I wasn't sure what would have happened if he hadn't come along when he did.

He held up a hand as he turned to face me. "Don't. I can't allow these creatures to destroy my home. And, I couldn't leave Violet to be sacrificed by them. It wasn't for you."

I crossed my arms over my chest and narrowed my eyes at him. He was an asshole. I didn't like him at all. Even if he was the sexiest guy, I'd ever seen. He had a bad attitude and was rude.

"What is your problem?" I limped over to Violet and contemplated how I was going to get her home. No way was I leaving her here. There might be more of those things out here. "What were those creatures anyway? One looked like a goblin, but I've never seen a dog that big."

He walked over to me and shoved me out of the way with his shoulder before he bent down and picked Violet up.

"They were goblins and Grimm. The creature marked you and Violet for death. Otherwise, there would have been no Grimm here tonight."

"What?!" My voice was shrill as I hurried to catch up with him. "That can't be right. I'm just starting my new life."

"Someone doesn't want you coming into your full power."

I shook my head as I jogged to keep up with his long strides. "I'm a middle-aged widow and mother of three with bad knees and a serious case of hot flashes. Why would anyone want me dead?"

Sebastian stopped so suddenly, it jostled Violet in his arms, and I ran into his back. "Ooomph." That was going to leave a mark. The guy was solid as a brick house.

"You have no idea the power you possess." His lip curled up in one corner, and there was a growl in his voice, displaying his unmistakable disdain. "Learn from your grandmother's mistakes. She made many enemies and is no longer here to usher you into this life. There's no time for you to work through your feelings."

My jaw hit my chest as I struggled to accept what he'd just said. I snapped it closed and pushed past him as I continued to my house. "You're just as bad as my late husband, who refused to stop and ask for directions when we were lost."

I was mad and thinking of every time Tim refused to admit his faults. A gasp left me as I recalled more incidents of me wielding my magic. Anytime Tim and I were lost and arguing about asking for help, something happened to the car. One time it was a flat tire outside a gas station. Another time we ran out of gas, while a third time, the vehicle overheated, despite being brand new.

How had I been so blind before? That was way too many coincidences. I shook my head and paused outside the back door to glare at him. "There is nothing wrong with asking for help. I don't know how you expect me to know everything when I have never been told I have magic. I'll be sure to find a spell that downloads all the information I need directly to my brain, so you won't be bothered feeling like you should help me."

A growl rumbled in his chest. "Are you keeping Violet here, or should I take her home?"

I opened the door and gestured inside. "She can stay here. I don't want to leave her alone tonight. She was helping me, and I feel responsible that she was hurt. And, before you tell me it is my fault, I didn't allow those dark Fae to cross through the portal. I might not know much, but I'm not that stupid."

He grunted as he passed me and headed for the living room. Apparently, he'd been in this house before. He set Violet down with more care than I would have expected before he turned around and left without another word.

I grabbed a blanket and spread it over my friend while trying to forget the events of the past few hours. An odd sense of betrayal settled in my gut. Why hadn't my Grams told me more about this world?

She knew I would come back, at least temporarily. She should have told me something. A heads up would have been nice if not basic information like the Fae existed, and there was magic in the world.

Did my mom know about this? She would dismiss the stories I shared after returning from Grams's house at the end of summer. *It was her way of telling you about this world.* I never thought about it, but my parents never agreed to send me so far away every year.

The more I learned, the more questions I had. Not just about this world I suddenly found myself immersed in, but about my family. I needed to locate that Grimoire and fast. I refused to be so vulnerable again. There was something out there gunning for me, and I was going to stop them even if my magical new beginning was something of a joke at the moment.

CHAPTER 6

"*K*nock, knock," Aislinn called out from the door. "I brought treats."

Please let it be those delicious almond croissants from the bakery. Setting my mug down, I hurried to open the door. Okay, so I didn't move all that fast. The night before, I had fallen asleep on the chair in the living room shortly after Bas left so I could keep an eye on Violet.

Sebastian had shown far more gentleness than I thought possible as he cleaned my injuries. I expected the cloth to hurt as it moved over the torn flesh and was shocked when it didn't make the pain any worse. I was convinced he did something to make it easier for me. Of course, that might be wishful thinking, and I had reached the point where not much could make it hurt worse.

After he bandaged me, I got up to help Violet, but he put me in the chair while he tended to her. She seemed to pass out while he was working. I didn't blame her. I had been about a second away myself. I tried but couldn't get up to check on her.

I had hit a wall and didn't move for eight hours. I fell

asleep before Sebastian finished with Violet. And remained in the chair all night, so now my back ached, and my neck was sore, but it was the best sleep I'd had in over a week.

I woke up when Violet was complaining under her breath about sleeping on the floor. She wasn't surprised to hear Sebastian left us where we were without thinking of moving us to a more comfortable location. She went home before I could get up and make her some breakfast. She needed to make sure Ben and Bailey, her kids, got off to school okay. Then she would shower and get ready for work. I was still in the same chair twenty minutes later, even though I knew I would pay for it later.

A smile spread over my face when I saw the pink box in her hand as she stood on my stoop. "Aislinn. It's good to see you this morning. I could use a croissant after the night I had."

Aislinn let herself in before I reached her and pursed her lips. "Seems like a lot occurred last night. What happened to you?"

I turned and lead her into the kitchen, where I grabbed the coffee pot. "Want some?"

She nodded vigorously. "Yes, please."

I got sidetracked by the fact that she was at my house so early in the day. "Why are you here? Shouldn't you be asleep right now? Or did you have last night off?"

Her smile vanished, and her expression turned somber. "No, I worked last night, which is why I need some caffeine. You don't happen to have an espresso machine, do you?"

I waved my hand through the air before grabbing a mug that Skylar gave me. It said, *'I'm a Nightmare Before Coffee'* and had Jack Skellington's face on the front. "I wish. Tim promised to get me one for my birthday as soon as he had regained his strength after his first round of chemo, but he never got a chance to go shopping before he passed away.

Now, I just can't see spending the money on that, especially since I have stopped working."

Aislinn accepted the mug with a smile. "Are you doing okay? Do you need a job? There are plenty here in town we can arrange. We can't have you move away. We need you."

I'd decided to move here to start a new life centered around me taking care of myself. For longer than I wanted to admit, my life had been about the needs of others. First my husband, then my kids and my job, then my husband and job again. Now was all about me, yet I didn't feel like my needs were neglected when she said that.

"I'm good financially." Between my husband's life insurance and my grandmother's inheritance, I had plenty of money to support myself. "It helps that my bills are minimal, and I have no mortgage or car payment. I just can't see spending that much money on coffee. Anyway, as much as I enjoy your company, you didn't stop by just to bring me pastries. What's up?"

Aislinn sat in one of the chairs at the small table in my breakfast nook. I brought the pink box over and lifted the lid. I was going to need to run an extra ten miles today if I ate all these. I grabbed a pastry and slid the rest to her.

"Please tell me you found something that helped you discover the ins and outs of being Cottlehill Wild's Guardian."

I swallowed the bite in my mouth, and it sank to my gut like a stone. "No. Violet even came over last night and helped me. I nearly got her killed, but I didn't find anything that will help me. Why? What happened?" I hated to ask, but sticking my head in the sand helped nothing if I learned one thing in life.

"Crap. That was what I was afraid of. You need to fix the ward, and now. Dark Fae are coming through in increasing frequency. If we don't do something, there won't be anyone left in our town." Aislinn was picking at her croissant and eating the almond slivers from the top even though her face had gone pale, and she looked sick to her stomach.

"Violet and I discovered that firsthand last night," I admitted. I gave her a brief rundown of what had happened, leaving out the part where I wanted to throttle Sebastian then kiss him senseless. I didn't understand what that was about and had far more important things to worry about than some guy I both loathed and lusted after.

When Tim died, I decided that I had experienced enough love for one life and didn't need the drama finding another man would bring. Someone or something wanted me dead. That outweighed anything else.

"Dammit. I wondered why they risked coming into town last night. Now it makes sense. With Bas helping you, he wasn't around to catch the evil Elf that had slipped into the bar." Aislinn wiped a tear from her cheek and lifted grief-stricken green eyes to me.

My chest ached for her. "What happened? What evil Elf?"

She sniffed and resumed the picking of her croissant. "I was closing Phoenix Feathers shortly before midnight and telling Zed it was time to go when the doors burst open. Before I knew what was happening, the Elf had buried a knife in Zed's back and was coming after me."

"Holy shit. How did you get away?" My heart was pounding in my chest, and I couldn't catch my breath until I reminded myself that she lived through the ordeal.

She pushed her red curls away from her face, revealing a large purple bruise on the side of her face. "I wouldn't have gotten out of there if Desmond hadn't come back to grab the deposit. The Elf was so intent on killing me that he never heard Des sneak up behind him and slice his throat. I've never seen so much blood in my life." She hunched over and sobbed into her hands.

Jumping from my chair, I rounded the table and hunched at her side, and wrapped my arms around her slim shoulders. "You survived, Ais. I'm sorry I wasn't there to help you."

She lifted her tear-streaked face and wiped her cheeks with the back of her hands. "You were too busy fighting for your life. And someone is trying to stop you from doing your job and discovering how you can protect our town better. We need to get that information so they don't take us all out one by one."

"You, Violet, and I were targeted last night. That's no coincidence. But who? And how?"

Cottlehill was a small town, and I knew almost everyone. It seemed unlikely someone who lived here tried to eliminate me, but I couldn't rule it out. The dark king might have been sending his minions through the portal. I had no idea where it was or how to stop creatures from crossing.

"I have no idea, but there has to be something somewhere to help. Did Violet find anything in her store?" Aislinn asked, interrupting my thoughts.

I tapped my lips as I tried to recall what we'd talked about the other day when I went to see her. It seemed like another lifetime ago when I sought her out to confirm Aislinn's assertion that I was the new Guardian.

I shook my head. "Not that I know of. When I went to see her, I asked if what you said was true and nothing else. We came here to look for any information my grandmother might have left to help me in my new role. I didn't find anything from my Grams. Not even a letter."

Aislinn pushed back and stood up. "Sounds like we need to pay Violet a visit. Perhaps there's something there that can give us some information."

I shook my head but stood and grabbed the pink box before I followed her to the door. "She told me she didn't have anything that would give me information on my job or anything."

Aislinn opened the driver's side door to her car and gestured for me to climb in. "That might be the case, but there's more now, it seems. More often than not, our focus is narrow. There's never been a reason to look too deep or consider alternatives. We've lived a life of relative safety while Isidora was alive. Now we're facing unknown threats."

I latched my seat belt as she turned the key then took off down my dirt road. "Fair enough. I'm still struggling to wrap my mind around all of this, so I guess I should keep my mouth shut and leave it to the more experienced. Unless it's Sebastian making the suggestion. Then I'll seek a second opinion."

Aislinn snickered as she turned down Main Street. "Bas has always been moody, but he seems to have a little extra for you."

"Understatement. The question is, why? I've never done anything to him." I could hear how petulant I sounded, but I couldn't help it. He unsettled me and brought up every doubt I've ever had in my life.

Aislinn lifted her shoulders as she pulled into a parking spot close to Pleasure Bound, Violet's bookstore. "He's a hard Fae to crack."

I got out of the car clutching the pink box while considering a muffin. "He's as hard as a macadamia nutshell. I wonder if I apply three hundred pounds of pressure if he'd crack, too."

Aislinn chuckled as we entered Pleasure Bound. Violet lifted a hand as she finished checking out a customer. When the young woman was gone, we approached the register, and I set the pastries in front of Violet.

"How are you feeling? You were gone before I woke up

this morning, and I didn't want to call and interrupt your morning routine."

Violet sighed and lifted the lid. "Thank you. I'm starving. I didn't have time to grab anything when I went home and showered, and the store has been slammed all morning."

I waved to Aislinn. "Thank her, she brought them to my place."

Violet turned to Aislinn, and her smile died. "What happened?"

Aislinn managed to tell her what happened at the bar last night without devolving into sobs. "This is getting dangerous. We need to find something that will help Fiona."

Violet set the croissants down and rubbed her hands together. "Gods, sometimes I hate living at a crossroads. I should have moved away when Trent first suggested it. It would have saved me a painful divorce, and my kids wouldn't have grown up without their dad."

Aislinn thrust her hands on her hips and narrowed her eyes. "Nonsense. Trent was an asshole, exactly like Bodin. And leaving was the best thing he ever did for you. He didn't deserve you or Bailey or Ben."

"Trent made a promise to you. And, he broke that promise. You both need to reclaim your soul."

Both women tilted their heads, looked at me, and then said, "What?" practically in unison.

One corner of my mouth lifted. "When you give yourself to someone who doesn't respect you, you surrender pieces of your soul. They don't deserve that much of you. It's time you start to expect something extraordinary to happen and realize the past no longer holds you captive. While you will never truly get what you lost back, you can forge something new. It's why I'm here to start my life over. I wanted something for me."

Violet smiled and picked up her tart, then took a bite.

"You're right. And, I'm starting with this pastry. Now, let's see if we have anything here on portals or Fae magic."

"Or, reinforcing boundaries. The one around town is faltering." Aislinn tossed out before she grabbed a scone.

Violet typed into her computer and read the screen. Leaning against the counter, I scanned the street through the large glass window.

"Did my grandmother fight these things like we did last night?" I blurted into the silence.

Violet's fingers stopped, and she looked up from her computer. "I have no idea. She never mentioned anything of the sort."

Aislinn's head went up and down. "She would have told everyone if she'd been attacked."

"Maybe that's why she gave that small slice of land to Bas," Violet blurted.

"What? She gave him his land?" I couldn't believe he was such an asshole when he'd been given such a significant gift.

"I'm not exactly sure. It was before my time, but I've heard they had some kind of arrangement. Unless you find your Grimoire and Isidora wrote about it, you'll have to ask Bas," Violet informed me, then went back to typing on the computer.

A sigh left me as I pushed the fatigue away that threatened to drown me once again. "I don't care that much. I have more important shit to worry about, like figuring out who's trying to kill us."

"You, I understand, but why us?" I gaped at Aislinn, thinking she didn't like me after all. Why would she understand someone wanting to kill me?

Her hands flew to her mouth, and she shook her head from side to side. "I didn't mean it like you're malicious or something. It's because you're the Guardian here. That makes you a target, but I'm nothing but a waitress."

"And, I'm a bookstore owner that can't seem to find a book to help us. I carry several books on spells, potions, and cooking with magic, but nothing on portals or Fae magic." Violet looked defeated.

"I'll take everything you have on magic. I have no idea how to cast a spell or brew a potion."

Violet popped the last of her pastry into her mouth and came out from behind the counter. "One crucial thing to remember is that these books will give you the basics but being a halfling, they won't work quite the same for you as they do for me."

"Of course not. That would be too easy. I don't know the first thing, so it will be a beginning." I followed her down an aisle and fought the urge to run my fingers over the spines.

Aislinn bumped me with her shoulder. "I'll help in any way I can. It wasn't until Bodin left that I asked Isidora to teach me. I can't brew potions as powerful as Violet, but I can create basic ones."

"Here we are," Violet announced and picked two books from the shelves then handed them to me.

I flipped one open and smiled when I saw drawings of herbs. This would come in handy while learning what was in my garden. A big black pot was on the first page of the second book. "I need a cauldron? I would never have guessed Hollywood got that right."

Violet laughed. "Where do you think they got the idea? Many myths are fairly accurate because supernaturals leak information either to entertain or frighten others. Those stories are beyond anything most can comprehend and capture their imaginations."

"My kids will love this stuff. Skylar especially."

Aislinn's head snapped in my direction, and her curls went flying around her face. "Are you going to tell them?"

I paused and considered her question. "Eventually, I will

have to tell them. They're the ones who will have to take over after me, and I refuse to leave them in the dark."

Violet started back to the front of the store. "That makes sense. You can always start a diary. Doing that will alleviate a lot of the pressure to do it in a certain timeframe. It'll be there for them when they need it."

My head was bobbing up and down. "That's a great idea, but I think I'll type it into the notes app on my tablet. That way, I can easily add and correct information. What do you guys say to dinner and wine one night soon so you can help me make sense of these books?"

"I have Thursday night off. I'll bring the wine. Anything in particular you like?"

"Wino," Violet teased Aislinn. "That Chilean blend you brought to my house last month was delicious."

"Chilean wine is the best. Do you guys like curry?" I hadn't spent enough time with them to know their food preferences, and there were only three restaurants in town. The Sapphire Clam was a fancy seafood place, while Fire and Ice was more casual and served various foods. Salutation was probably my favorite. It served sandwiches and burgers.

Aislinn's face lit up. "I love curry. I usually have to go into the city when I'm in the mood for it."

Violet paused in ringing me up. "And, I tag along. I'd love your recipe. It never turns out when I make it."

"It's all about using the right curry paste. I brought some with me from the States." We devolved into laughter at that, and I enjoyed the brief respite from the world of magic. I hadn't hung out with friends like this since I had Emmie. Life had taken over everything, hence the reason I was now living in England, starting a new magical phase. And, while I loved my children, there was nothing like spending time with people my age. Especially ones that understood my hot flashes, bad-knee, and need for reading glasses.

CHAPTER 7

"Incoming!" I ducked as I shouted the warning, then devolved into a fit of laughter.

Violet's shriek was shrill. "What was that?"

Aislinn's laughter joined mine. "What spell did you try that time?"

I lifted my head as I was bent over, bracing myself on my knees. "Apparently, I'm like that kid in Harry Potter who blows up every spell he tries."

Violet started laughing then. "It's levi*o*sa not levio*sa*. What were you trying to do, and what did you say?"

That sparked another fit of giggles. Wiping my eyes, I reached for my wine. Thankfully, I hadn't sent that flying across the room, too. "I was trying to make the book levitate."

Aislinn and Violet shared a look before Aislinn turned to me. "Let me guess. You didn't think the translation was correct, so you used the terminology from the popular movie?"

My cheeks immediately heated. "Maybe? Okay, I see that was wrong, but that's not the biggest issue here. My magic doesn't work right. I'm all over the place, and nothing happens like it's supposed to. I mean, I created a fire in the forest without even trying, and just a minute ago, water dribbled from my fingers when I actually called on the element."

Violet patted my shoulder in sympathy. "I'm not the best teacher. And you're unique. I've never actually met another hybrid quite like you. I think we need to find better books. It might be time to…"

Aislinn threw out her hand, cutting Violet off. "No. Don't say it. Having her negotiate with Filarion is a mistake."

Violet thrust her hand on her hips. "Do you have a better idea?"

"Who is this Filarion, and why is going to him a bad idea?" Both women just stared at me for several seconds. I fought the desire to fidget while my heart raced, and I clutched the wine to my chest. Being under their scrutiny was disconcerting.

"He's Violet's main competition where our kind is concerned. He has a table at Staves and Stoves and is a known scoundrel." Aislinn's wine nearly spilled as she gestured wildly with the full glass she was holding.

I wracked my brain to recall the store name. Unfortunately, I had no idea what she was talking about. "What are Staves and Stoves? I would have guessed a tobacco store, but if he's in competition with Violet, I'd say he's into books."

Violet sighed and sat on the arm of the nearby chair. "It's not a store precisely. It's more like an open-air market. Only it's hidden from humans, accessible to supernaturals."

"It's more of a bazaar," Aislinn added. "There isn't much you can't find there."

I was hurt for a split second. Why hadn't anyone taken me there before? It sounded fascinating, and I suddenly wanted to go right now. Then I recalled my Grams had kept my true identity from me, and it hadn't been all that long since I discovered who I really am. Violet and Aislinn had been going out of their way to help me learn and adjust.

"Sounds like Diagon Alley. Let's take a field trip and go. I need to catch up. There isn't time to dilly dally. The portal is somewhere waiting for me to do my job. Then there's the whole bubble around town." I turned to grab my handbag when the pinging started up again. This time it was more of a giant gong being hit inside my skull, and I clutched my temples with both hands.

A hand ran up and down the right side of my back. I recognized Violet's soothing energy without having to look. Seeing auras and sensing energy were two things that came effortlessly to me. I wish the rest was as simple.

"Is it the clanging in your head again?"

All I could do was nod in response to Violet's question. I had no idea if either of the women said anything else because I focused on shutting out the sensation. It had gotten to the point that an invisible knife was stabbing my frontal lobe over and over again.

This is not a brain tumor. The pain won't kill you. I chanted those words repeatedly until finally, I was able to take a deep breath and focus on my friends' anxious faces.

"I'm okay," I promised as I lowered my hands. "Are you guys up for a shopping spree?"

Aislinn pursed her lips and opened her mouth but shut it without saying anything. It was Violet who finally broke the silence. "We should have taken you there first, but honestly, I didn't think about it. I've been so focused on you finding some non-existent letter from Isidora that I missed the obvious. Even when you guys came to the shop looking for books to help. For that, I am truly sorry."

"You have no reason to be sorry. My Grams is the one that should have done so much more." Now-familiar anger started rising in my chest when I think about the mess I

MAGICAL NEW BEGINNINGS

found myself in and how she could have made it better. Of course, I was as much to blame. I hadn't exactly been around lately.

Aislinn gave me my handbag and paused at the door. "I'm not sure any of us should be driving. We've been drinking."

My head moved up and down. "I feel fine, but it's better to be safe than sorry."

"Already taken care of. Bailey should be here any minute." Violet was like the mother hen of the three of us.

"Are we like a coven now?" I blurted when we walked out of my house. There was a serene green glow surrounding my property until you reached the cemetery. It glowed with a myriad of colors. Initially, I wondered why, but then I realized my ancestors were buried there. It was likely their auras that created the effect.

Violet shrugged her shoulders. "I've never been part of a coven before. There is one in town, the Coven of Cottlehill Wilds, but my family wasn't invited to be a part of it."

Aislinn's face split into a wide grin. "We can be the Wisdom Circle or the Backside of Forty, even though I won't be forty until next year."

We all laughed and were still giggling when Bailey pulled up two minutes later. Violet's daughter was a younger version of her with blonde hair, blue eyes, and voluptuous curves. Violet was a looker back in the day.

Was? She looked even better now. There was no denying the way Violet's confidence cast the fine lines and dark spots in a different light. Something was enticing about a woman who had lived enough to learn from her mistakes and knew what she wanted and needed.

And then there was the ability to see through any BS thrown our way. Add to that being comfortable in your skin, and the combination was just about perfect. The only things I would change were the aches and pains and faltering vision.

"Backside of Forty it is," I confirmed as we climbed into the dark blue sedan. The drive to town was quick and silent for the most part. Violet and her daughter talked about her university plans. Bailey, it appeared, was nervous about leaving home and planned on taking classes online. At the same time, her twin, Ben, intended to live it up on campus.

Butterflies swarmed in my stomach the second we were standing on the street. I smoothed my shirt, wishing I'd changed when I noticed the curry smeared on the front. The square was surprisingly active this time of the day. Not that it was all that late at eight o'clock at night. It'd just been decades since I was out after dinner.

When Tim was alive, we didn't go out all that much. At first, it was because of my long shifts at the hospital, then it was the kids and their various schedules. Then he got sick. I enjoyed staying home and had needed the downtime. I wanted something different now.

Violet grabbed my arm and led me through the square. My gaze shifted around as I took it all in. "Why didn't you guys tell me it was so lively here. I would have suggested dinner at Fire and Ice if I'd known."

Aislinn leaned toward me and cupped her hand around her mouth. "It's way too freakin' busy to come here on a Friday night. Every human that lives here is out, and it's impossible to have an open conversation about what we needed to discuss."

I winced, realizing I had forgotten the need for secrecy so quickly. "Right. It's surprisingly easy to forget that magic isn't completely in the open here. Is there somewhere Fae and witches go on a Friday night? Or do they all just stay home?" It was odd to forget not everyone knew about magic while at the same time being surprised to discover more of the hidden world.

I was beyond allowing any of it to overwhelm me. That

was one definite perk of being middle-aged. I had been through enough that I rolled with the punches and jumped right back up, ready to tackle whatever came next.

Violet shimmied through a narrow alley between buildings. "Many go to Teatime. Dahlia is usually open to us Friday and Saturday nights."

Stepping into an empty park at night was far eerier than I anticipated. Or perhaps it's because I knew we were about to enter a secret market for magical beings. Violet paused between the stone pedestals at the entrance. The plinths were topped by massive marble gargoyles, complete with wings and sharp teeth.

Violet lifted her hand and placed her palm on the base to the right. There was a loud rumbling sound followed by rocks falling from the gargoyle as it moved. My eyes went wide as I watched it shake its wings.

"We'd like to enter the market," Violet announced.

The gargoyle on the right extended its wing while the left one moved, increasing the sound of rock tumbling down the cliffs a few miles away. When the two wings touched, the air in front of them shimmered.

Aislinn and Violet both grabbed my hand and pulled me down the path. The second we passed under the wings, my skin erupted as if ants were crawling all over me. It was followed by heat in my blood.

Voices and laughter intruded before the sensation got too painful. Between one step and the next, the jungle gym in the middle of the park vanished, folding tables and people appeared. Not just people, but brownies, pixies, and nymphs, as well. I couldn't believe what I was seeing. It was incredible.

A table covered with a purple cloth had dried herbs of all kinds spread out on top of it. The table next to it had muffins, a bright pink punch in a big jar, and fruit. Next to that was one with variously colored drinks in clear containers. Given the crowd around that stall, they had to be selling alcohol of some kind.

"Welcome to Staves and Stoves." Aislinn swept her arm in front of us, gesturing to the market.

Violet's arm shot up next. "There's Filarion." I followed her finger and noticed a big guy with dark blond hair and gold eyes.

"What is he?" The words slipped past my lips.

Violet leaned toward my ear and whispered, "He's a Griffin shifter. When in his other form, he has the body, tail, and back legs of a lion and the head and wings of an eagle with talons for his front feet."

"I've fallen even deeper down the rabbit hole. Let's go talk to him, but then I want to try that bright pink drink."

Aislinn grunted and shook her head. "No, you don't. It's a Fae drink and will get you so wasted you will wish you were never born."

One of my eyebrows lifted to my hairline as I looked over at my friend. "There's a story there I can't wait to hear."

"Later. Let's go talk to Filarion," Aislinn replied and started toward the griffin's table.

"Well, who do we have here?" Filarion's voice was higher than I would have thought, and I had to bite my tongue to keep from laughing. A guy with as many muscles as he had should have a deep voice that made me shiver like Sebastian's.

I crossed my arms over my chest, not affected by his attempt at flirting. "I'm Fiona Shakleton, and I'm looking for a book."

His golden eyes went wide before they shifted from me to my two companions, then around the bazaar before landing back on me. "And, you don't have anything that could help her?" The question was directed at Violet, who glared at him.

"Her magic is powerful and refuses to be controlled. She

needs more advanced spell assistance than I have in stock, and we all know you have a knack for procuring rare tomes." There was no mistaking Violet's disdain for this man and the way he got his hands on the books.

His gaze returned to the various boxes on his table, and he began rifling through them. "I have just the thing here for you. It's a book of advanced spell work written by a powerful witch family. They only printed a dozen copies, so it's difficult to find. It's my last copy, so it'll cost you."

Aislinn snorted. "Let me guess. You ran across it at an Estate sale."

"How much is this going to cost me?" I had no idea of the history between Aislinn and Filarion, but I didn't want that to shift the focus from what we'd come after. I needed to get the book and leave.

The griffin turned a forced smile my way. "Five hundred."

My jaw dropped open, but Aislinn was in Filarion's face before I could respond. "You don't want to try and take advantage of Isidora's granddaughter. She's far more powerful than you know, and when she hones her craft, she will realize you ripped her off and make you regret it."

The blood drained from the griffin's face as he looked up from the box he was searching. "You… you're…" He waved his hands, and I realized he found the book he'd been looking for. At the same time, it hit me he was afraid of my Grams.

"That's right. I'm the new Guardian in town." It was still odd to claim the title, but nothing had ever felt truer. My shoulders went back, and my head tilted up. This was who I was, and I was going to own the shit out of it.

"Umm, in that case, I'll give it to you for two-fifty."

"I've got one twenty," I said, then pulled the cash from my purse.

Screams started on the other side of the market. My head swiveled, and a gasp left me when I saw a cross between a bear and a dog. At first, I thought it was another Grimm but then realized this thing was twice as big as the last ones I faced and had orange eyes plus Ginsu knives for claws.

My head snapped back when the money I had been holding was snatched from my hand. The griffin shoved the book at me and muttered something under his breath before waving a hand over his goods. Everything vanished, including him.

Violet grabbed my bicep and tugged urgently. "We have to go before that thing gets over here."

The three of us were running with the crowd toward the entrance. "What is that?"

"A barghest. They're vicious killers," Aislinn yelled as she ran next to me.

"Why is it here?"

Violet panted and fell a couple feet behind us. "It's after dinner. They feed on life force then the flesh after death." Her words chilled me. I slowed, and it was my turn to encourage her to move faster. That thing wasn't getting my friend.

My legs pumped so fast I got a stitch in my side, but I couldn't slow down. The shouting was getting closer and louder. The thing was tearing through those behind us.

We'd just passed through the plinths when the gargoyles shot into action and flew toward the creature. None of us stopped as we ran through the small alley until we reached Bailey's car.

We were all gasping for air as Violet pulled her phone out to text her daughter. Surprisingly, there was no hint of the attack in the park. There had to be some powerful spells hiding the market.

Part of me never wanted to step foot there again, while another wished I could have seen more. "Does that happen often?"

Aislinn shook her head, and her red hair bounced with

the movement. "It's never happened that I'm aware of. Shit is falling apart. It's one reason it's so important that you learn how to do your magic so you can reinforce the shield around town."

No pressure. I bit back the snarly retort. I couldn't blame Aislinn for wanting me to do something. My family had always handled safety in Cottlehill Wilds. I was just late to the game. Didn't make it any easier, though.

CHAPTER 8

My head dropped into my hands as I sat on the edge of my bed. It'd been four days since my trip to the market, and I was no closer to understanding magic. "I could really use some help, Grams," I muttered out loud in the hopes she was still hanging around in some way.

When I asked Aislinn and Violet if ghosts were real, they told me yes. But there was no way for the dead to communicate with the living. There had been no mention if they could hear and understand us, so I'd taken to talking to myself from time to time.

I picked up the box I found in my search yesterday and went through the contents again. It was mostly family relics. There was an old handheld mirror and brush set, a jewelry box, and photos.

The pictures told me nothing, but I went through them again anyway. I scanned each one looking for a common thread, book, anything that might lead me in the right direction.

I found a spell in the book I got from Filarion about calling teachers to me, but I was reluctant to use it. Violet recommended trying it, so I doubted it would backfire on me.

By the fifth picture, I saw something I hadn't before. All of the women in them wore a necklace. It was an amber charm on the chain. I couldn't get a good look at it, but I thought I saw a pentagram and maybe wings on it.

Picking up the jewelry box, I opened the lid and removed several earrings, three rings, and a dragonfly brooch. I picked up the box and was about to throw it at the wall when I heard something rattle.

Tilting the thing one way then another, I heard an object hit the side. I lifted the tray from the inside and shook it again. Despite being utterly empty, something hard hit the sides. Flipping the lid, I felt around the aged mirror glued to it.

There was nothing there, and the glass was secured in place. The red velvet that lined the sides and bottom was thick and soft. I felt terrible when I slid a fingernail between the fabric and the wood. With a firm tug, it came away in my hand, and I was staring at a tiny door on the bottom.

My hand shook when I lifted the panel. Sitting on the bottom was a silver chain tangled with an amber charm the size of a quarter. It had a pentagram on it along with dragonfly wings.

Power vibrated from it when I reached down to pick it up. It wrapped around me like a warm blanket. With a smile, I pulled it out and slipped it over my head. The second it settled on my chest, something cracked open inside me.

It was as if a door swung wide. Power rushed through my veins, and I had more energy than I ever had in my twenties. I ran down the stairs and outside, wanting to test my skills but not wanting to damage anything inside the house if things went awry like they had been.

I stopped next to the pond and held my hand out. "Levitate." I focused on my desire to have the lily pads float ten feet in the air before falling back into the water.

Electricity zipped down my arm, and blue lightning flew out the tips of my fingers. It hit the water with a sizzle, and the water exploded around me, drenching me. Wiping my eyes with the back of my hands, I cleared my vision and growled when I saw the lily pads lying on the bottom of the now dry lake.

My magic was no better. I lifted a shoe to kick a rock in frustration, but I stopped myself when I noticed it wasn't granite at all. Instead, I was staring at a fish as it flopped around with its gills opening and closing. It was gasping for breath and would die unless I did something.

Racing to the side of the house, I grabbed the hose and turned it on full blast, then dropped it into the empty pond. Dropping to the mud, I scooped up fish after fish and tossed them into the slowly filling pool.

They were going to die, and it was all my fault. I had no idea what I was doing. I needed to use that spell and ask for help. The slapping sounds echoed as the fish around me tried in vain to survive, and I attempted to get them to the pond. There was hardly any water in there, but it did cover about three inches of the bottom.

Closing my eyes, I called water to me, not caring if the skies opened up at that moment. I didn't want to be responsible for killing the fish. Energy built under me as I muttered, "*aqua*," over and over again.

The skies didn't open up, but my feet seemed to sink into the ground. My eyes flew open. The water rose up through the mud. My magic cut off in my shock, and it stopped rising. The incessant pinging started up, and I was momentarily paralyzed. I couldn't turn my head to check on the pond.

All I could do at the moment was breathe through the

agony of the pinging. It seemed to go on forever. When it finally faded, I was kneeling on the ground covered in mud. A quick scan of the pond brought a smile to my face.

My magic was out of control, and I was a hot mess, but I wasn't a fish killer. The pond was two-thirds full. Pushing myself to my feet, I limped to the door and removed my tennis shoes.

I hated the idea of tracking mud throughout the house and considered stripping down before going inside. No one lived close to me, so it wasn't like anyone would see me. I was about to remove my top when it hit me that I had a mudroom.

My body heated as I ran inside and stopped in the tiled room off the back of the house. I removed my dirty clothes and ran naked through the house and up the stairs. Once inside the bathroom, I flipped on the water and jumped in the shower.

Squirting soap into my hand, I ran it through my hair and over my body. This wasn't working. It was time to use the spell and ask for help. I finished cleaning the mud off and turned off the water.

After drying and throwing on some sweats, I grabbed the book and paused in the middle of the kitchen. I was about to go outside and cast the spell, but it was a mess out there.

I really needed a place to practice magic. Somewhere I wouldn't cause too much damage and have space to work. The one thing that stood out to me was how many implements witchcraft called for—cauldrons, herbs, jars, knives, spoons, crystals, and so much more.

With a sigh, I set the book down and cleared off the island. I needed a candle for this one, so I went into the living room, grabbed a vanilla-scented one, and then hurried back.

I went out the side door directly into the garden and grabbed some thyme, thistle, and lavender. Back in the kitchen, I put it in a mortar and ground them together with a pestle. Once I created a sticky mixture, I scooped some out and smeared it in a circle around my feet. It was supposed to be dried herbs, but I couldn't find any.

I grabbed a lighter from the drawer behind me and a knife from the butcher block. I hadn't gotten around to purchasing an athame yet, so this would have to do. I pricked my finger and added drops of my blood to the herbs, then focused on the candle.

"Witches and Fae course through time, I need assistance. Come, I beckon you. Share your wisdom and enlighten me." I changed up things a bit since I was a hybrid. The intent was the most critical factor, and I focused on my desire to learn and become a better Guardian.

Next, I lit the candle then drew my knife through the herbs, and put it in the window above the sink. I waited for several minutes listening to the wind blow outside, and the branches hit the house.

Finally, I realized it wasn't an instant spell and cleaned up the mess on the floor before putting water on for some tea. Taking my favorite mug from the cabinet, I decided on green tea and put a teabag in the cup.

The kettle started whistling the second there was a knock on the door. My heart started pounding in my chest as I hurried to see who my spell called forth.

The smile fell from my face when I opened it to see Sebastian standing there with a scowl on his chiseled face, and his stunning blue eyes narrowed. "You rang. And, rather rudely at that. I don't appreciate being forced to come here."

My mouth opened and closed when his head snapped around. I glanced over his shoulder and rubbed my eyes. A woman with silver hair that was cut into a stylish bob was climbing out of her car. She had on leggings and a long, teal sweater.

The woman lifted her hand in a casual wave. "Hello, Bas. How are you this evening?"

"I'm good, Camille. Did she call you here, too?"

The woman smiled and shifted her blue eyes to me. "Seems like she did. Although, I must admit I'm surprised to see you here."

I lowered my gaze and twisted my hands together. "I need help learning my magic and how to be a Guardian. Violet and Aislinn told me I was part Fae too, so I modified the spell a bit."

The woman chuckled. "You used fresh herbs, too, didn't you?"

I gasped as my head snapped up. "How did you know?"

"Because I was forced to drop everything I was doing and come right away. There are reasons we use dried herbs. You're lucky it didn't blow up in your face this time, but it's clear you need a lot of help."

Bas crossed his arms over his chest. "I'm not needed here, seeing as you are here to help her." The dismissal burned, and my heart raced in my chest. That should destroy every ounce of attraction I felt for the guy. I looked at him, hoping to see an ugly toad now. Unfortunately, it did nothing to quell how good-looking I found him.

Camille held up her hand, stopping him. "Not so fast. I can help her with the proper use of herbs and incantations. However, that will only do so much. She's a hybrid, and her magic works differently than mine. Besides, I have a feeling the most pressing issues she needs to address revolve around becoming a strong Guardian, which means she will need us both."

Sebastian only grunted at that and headed inside the house. "Would you like some tea?" I asked the witch. Her presence was comforting and eased a lot of the worry I had been obsessing over.

"That would be lovely. It's been a rough few nights trying to reinforce the wards around Staves and Stoves."

I held the door open for her as my breathing quickened. "Were you there when the barghest attacked?"

She nodded as she passed me and entered the messy mudroom. My face flamed. I hadn't cleaned up the evidence of my disastrous spell. "I was. I have a booth there where I sell herbs, potions, and soy candles."

"I feel like it's my fault. I had no idea about any of this before I moved here after my Grams died."

She went straight for the mugs and tea and handed one to Bas before she poured hot water into the cup in her hand. "None of this is your fault. Isidora talked about needing to bring you in for weeks before she passed, but she worried about ruining your life. She said that you've had a hard time after your husband died, and she didn't want to add to that."

I sighed and picked up my drink. It was lukewarm now, but I didn't care. "She had to know how bad things would get if I wasn't told. What if I never came here? Shit would have really hit the fan then."

Sebastian shook his head. "You don't give this power enough credit. The magic wouldn't have allowed that to happen. It stepped in to ensure you were where you needed to be and enticed you to stay."

My initial instinct was to deny that I was forced to accept this position. The second I arrived at Pymm's Pondside, I knew this was where I belonged. "That's reassuring. I'm not ready to tell my kids, but it helps knowing one of them will be drawn here if something happens to me. Speaking of. Where do we start? I know I have a lot to learn and don't want to push you guys this late at night, but I need something I can do."

Camille set her mug down and blew out the candle in the window. "Have you found your family's grimoire yet?"

I shook my head from side to side. "Not yet. I have searched this house from top to bottom, but I haven't come across anything. Is there some trick to finding it? Does it hide when someone dies or something?"

Camille chuckled. "Not that I'm aware of. Your family might have cast a spell on the thing to keep it safe. They are the most powerful witches I've ever known, and that knowledge would be highly sought after. You can find out rather easily. That necklace is imbued with your family's magic and something extra. Hold that and recite the word, *'revelare'* while thinking about the desire to find the tome. Witchcraft is all about the intent behind your spell."

When Camille mentioned the charm, Bas's gaze drifted to my chest, and my heart started pounding. It was a relief to know my instincts were right about the thing, but unnerving to have so much attention focused on it at the same time.

I closed my eyes and took several deep breaths, then wrapped my fingers around the necklace. "*Revelare*." A tingle spread through my body but was gone by the time I opened my eyes. "Did it work?"

"What do you think? You need to trust your instincts and pay attention to tiny details all around you."

I did as Camille instructed and took in the room, then the feel of the house in general. "There's something outside." I was moving out the door before either could respond.

The cold night air cooled my heated skin, and the energy surrounding me invigorated me. But nothing was there. The garden, cemetery, and pond all looked the same. "Ugh!"

Camille placed a hand on my shoulder. "Just because nothing jumps out at you doesn't mean there's nothing here. I can't tell you what pulled you out here. The energy surrounding Pymm's Pondside is powerful and makes it impossible for me to see every detail. What about you, Bas? Do you see anything?"

The guy glared at me without responding for several seconds. "I can't tell her what it is either, but it's not the book." Why the hell did my spell bring him to me? He was as helpful as bladder problems in the middle of the night.

"Don't get discouraged. This will take time, but show me your ritual space before I can teach you much more. You can work on maximizing it for you rather than how your Grams had it set up."

That got my attention. "You mean like a workroom? I just thought I need to create one."

Camille rolled her eyes at me. It made me feel like I was a child in school and had just blurted the wrong answer in front of the entire class. "There's no reason to recreate the wheel. Show me Isidora's space."

It hadn't dawned on me where that might be until that moment. When I realized I had misinterpreted the attic, I turned and hurried for the stairs. Once inside the top floor, I paused and saw it through different eyes. Grams didn't have a table for working or a cauldron over an open fire.

Instead, there were shelves and shelves of books, herbs, jars, and liquids. Her cauldron was on the top of one bookshelf. "I thought she stored the things she canned for winter in here. I had no idea this space was her ritual room."

Camille turned in a circle with a look of awe on her face. "There should be a switch to open the ceiling somewhere. All good witches want to access the power of the moon."

I glanced around, looking for something. There wasn't even a light switch up here. Bas stormed past me and went to one end of the room. He grabbed a crank and turned it. Creaking echoed through the space, and dust fell from the square, lifting in the middle of the ceiling.

"Your chore until we meet again is to get this space organized. Think about how you will easily find herbs when you need them. And you might want to have a basket handy. It'll make hauling your cauldron and various supplies downstairs easier when you need to make a potion."

"Have you found the portal entrance yet?" Sebastian's voice filled the attic, and I was embarrassed to admit it sent a shiver of arousal through my body.

Gritting my teeth, I turned to face him. "Not yet."

"Then that's your other assignment." With that, he turned and left my house.

"I might end up killing that man," I muttered.

Camille chuckled. "You haven't seen his good side yet."

"I'll have to take that on faith since I've never seen one hint of a good side. When can we get together again?"

My heart slowed, and the tension riding my shoulders lessened. For the first time since I unknowingly accepted the position, there was light at the end of the tunnel. Let's hope an eclipse didn't come along and blot it out.

CHAPTER 9

Mae walked into Pleasure Bound with a grim look on her face. I didn't know the older siren all that well, but it was chilling enough that my gut immediately started churning. I looked to Violet behind the counter and lifted one eyebrow in question. The owner of the bookstore, and my long-time friend, lifted one shoulder.

Mae approached us at the register with her hands fluttering around her chest. The movement brought my eyes to the wicked scar across her throat. I internally winced at the poignant reminder this woman was tough as nails and had survived having her throat slit.

"Did you guys hear? Philbert was found dead this morning in his kitchen!" Mae's words registered, and I gasped along with Violet.

Violet's hands shook as she brought them to her mouth. "Philbert? How did someone manage to kill a dragon shifter? Granted, he's a big teddy bear, but his animal could eat most creatures whole."

"Exactly! The police have been tight-lipped with the

details, but I'd say it's witchcraft," Mae said in a loud whisper as she glanced around the store.

When I thought I rolled with the punches and had accepted crazy, something new like this happened. "First off, dragon shifters are a thing? Second, maybe whoever did that is also responsible for the decay in the forest and failing protections."

Mae's midnight eyes went wide, and her mouth formed an O. "The protections around town? Why didn't you tell someone? We all need to leave. Now!"

Violet leaned across the glass counter and grabbed hold of Mae's pink top. "No, Fiona was talking about Pymm's Pondside. Isidora never told her about her heritage or what it means to be Guardian. The good news is that no one is getting through the portal while she learns her new job, but she does have a lot to catch up on."

Mae's eyes narrowed and went from Violet to me and back. "I'm not surprised Isidora never told you anything. She believed she could handle anything. Look where that arrogance got her in the end?"

My ire rose, and I lifted one corner of my mouth in a snarl while thrusting my hands on my hips. "My Grams allowed me to live my life. She was the most thoughtful, giving woman I've ever met. And, there wasn't anything she couldn't handle. She'd be here right now kicking the ass of whoever killed Philbert if age hadn't gotten to her first."

Mae reared away from me and pursed her lips. "You don't know everything. Isidora didn't die of old age. Someone killed her. And, you'd be wise to realize you need others in your life. They might not be able to decide who crosses and who doesn't or be able to help you block Fae from forcing their way through, but they can be there for you in countless ways that will save you."

Grams was killed? Why had no one told me? Who the heck

would hurt a sweet old lady? Okay, she had a sharp tongue and no problem telling you if you'd screwed up or made a massive mistake, but she was my Grams, and I couldn't understand why someone would hurt her.

Violet looked at me with sympathy and regret in her eyes. Yeah, she should have told me, but that didn't change my predicament. I was well aware there was a creature gunning for me.

I took a deep breath and reached for as much calm as possible. "You're right. I don't know everything, and I appreciate you letting me know. And, I know far more than you how much my friends and allies can help me. I wouldn't be sane right now without Violet and Aislinn."

Violet lifted a finger in the air as she nodded. "Or Camille and Bas. They're helping with your magic."

The lines around Mae's lips disappeared, and her arms dropped to her side as if she'd been waiting to hear those words. She was back to the gossipy woman I'd come to know as her ruffled feathers settled. "You girls need to watch out. There's something foul in Cottlehill Wilds."

Violet and I nodded our heads. "Keep us posted on what you learn," Violet told her before the woman turned and left the store.

The second she was gone, our gazes met, and I had to swallow the lump in my throat. She sighed and ran a hand down her face. "This is bad, Fiona. Dragon shifters are very difficult to kill. I fear Mae is right, which won't bode well for those of us in Cottlehill."

My heart was hammering, and I was huffing and puffing like I was in the middle of a marathon. "That is the opposite of what I wanted to hear right now." I can't let this be the end of my journey. Or, worst-case scenario, my life. "I'm trying as hard as I can with Camille, and I am making progress. I lit a candle this morning without burning my house down."

MAGICAL NEW BEGINNINGS

"Have you found the portal? Or, discovered how to handle that side of things? If you have a firm grip on the Fae, it will go a long way to calming people down."

"I have my first meeting with Bas in a couple hours. He's been reluctant to work with me, but Camille finally forced him into it."

Violet chuckled as she started counting the cash in her drawer. "That sounds like something she would do. Just be careful when you work with him later. We don't want you coming under the Chief Constable's radar right now. Lance is always suspicious of newcomers. And while he's investigating Philbert's murder, he's likely to look at you with extra scrutiny. The last thing we need right now is for you to end up in custody."

I waved a hand in dismissal. "I highly doubt Bas will be of much help. He's an ass most of the time. I'm more likely to learn something from Aislinn as I am him. I still don't know why my spell brought him to me in the first place, but that's a question for another time. I'll see you later."

Violet said goodbye and was finishing her closing routine when I left a second later. Her bookstore, Pleasure Bound, was on one corner of the square on Main street, and it had parking spots right in front. This late at night, I was able to park in front of the door.

I was in my rusted Mustang in no time and speeding down the road. The old car was the second purchase I made the day I went into the city. The first was a new mattress the day after the kids left. No way could I get any rest on the lumpy one in Grams' bedroom.

The car had more dents and divots than my backside, but I loved it anyway. It was a classic that my son would love to fix up when he visited. If only the tune-up and paint job it needed could wait until their summer break. It might. After all, I rarely went anywhere.

Cottlehill wasn't all that big. Nearly everything was within a ten to fifteen-minute drive. As if to prove my point, I was sliding under the portico next to my house ten short minutes later. A shiver shook me the second I stepped out of the vehicle. I nearly dropped the pink box of goodies as I stood with my hand on the door while I scanned the area.

There was a strange energy in the air. It was heavy and oppressive. Unfortunately, I couldn't find anything that would explain the feeling. Slamming the car door, I hurried inside my house and set the pastries on the island.

I filled the teapot with water and contemplated what kind of tea I would fix for Bas. Part of what I had been learning was how to make my own brews. Apparently, I had a knack for it.

Yeah, I was shocked to discover that one, too. During Camille's first session with me, she walked me through the garden and pointed out what many plants were and their uses.

Immediately, my mind started putting leaves together. I thought about easing the pain in my knees or the intensity of the hot flashes that had been keeping me awake. The next time Camille was over, I offered her an energy-boosting tea, and she told me I could give her a run for her money at Staves and Stoves selling my blends.

In thinking about facing Sebastian and actually working with him, I put some together in the hopes it would lift his spirits. A crash upstairs startled me while I was mixing St. John's Wort with some ginseng and a pinch of lavender.

My heart started galloping in my chest, and sweat broke out on my brow. Could whoever had killed the dragon shifter be in my house? I considered calling Violet or Aislinn but dismissed it, not wanting to put them in danger if the killer was, in fact, in my house.

Instead, I tiptoed out of the kitchen and into the living

room. *Creak!* Damn this old house. The floor was original to the centuries-old house and had as many squeaky boards as my crackly body.

"*Silentium*," I whispered and prayed the spell would take effect. When nothing blew up, I continued to the stairs. I wanted to fist pump the air when I didn't make any noise.

I was halfway up the steps when I realized my folly in rushing headlong up to the second floor. A loud screeching roar shook the walls right before a creature that looked like a frozen man-demon mix appeared right above me.

The thing had three-inch fingernails that seemed to be made of ice. And they were coated in red and green goo. Then there was his face. His eyes were completely white, and his teeth were razor sharp.

His bluish-gray skin tone was matched in eeriness by the sound he made. It was a cross between metal scraping metal and a high-pitched scream of a motor in desperate need of some oil. I read something about these creatures but couldn't call up the information.

I turned tail and meant to run down the stairs, only I ended up on my face when I fell. A scream left my throat when I scrambled on my hands and knees to get away from the thing.

Right as I reached the sofa and braced a hand to climb to my feet, the pinging started up in my head. "Oh no! Not now." This was it. I would never escape now. I couldn't even concentrate on pushing the pain aside, so I was able to track the beast's movements.

My head snapped back when icy daggers plunged into my temples. The blood froze in my veins, and the few breaths I managed to squeak out puffed out in white plumes in front of my face.

Fight, dammit! This was not how my story ended. I'd just begun my magical journey. Adrenaline dumped into my sluggish system, and I pushed it to my limbs. One hand managed to reach back and smack the beast. I latched onto one of his arms and tried to pull the fingers he'd dug into my skull.

My weak attempts were unsuccessful. Flopping my arm through the air, I refused to give up. My heart stuttered and slowed its frantic pace. Just when my vision dimmed, the creature was ripped away from me.

My body fell forward as my heart picked up the second the ice was gone. I was still wracked with shivers, but I was able to move. Turning, I saw Sebastian had saved me. He was holding the creature in a chokehold and dragging it outside.

I ran to follow. It was more of a stilted lurching motion, but I was outside before I knew what was happening. "Reinforce your protections," Sebastian yelled at me.

I ran back inside, happy to note I was moving easier. Up two flights of stairs, I grabbed the bag Camille insisted I pack with herbs and potions and hurried back to the lawn.

Pulling out dill, lavender, oregano, and parsley, I mixed them in my palm and chanted, *"praesidium."* It was next to impossible to focus on my intent to create a bubble around Pymm's Pondside with the sounds of Bas cursing and fighting the creature. After repeating the spell for the third time, I blew the herbs into the air.

Energy exploded out from where I stood on the lawn. It was forceful enough that it blew me on my ass. My skull bounced off the grass. Pain ricocheted around my gray matter, and my stomach revolted. *Well, that went well. You didn't look like an asshole at all.* I wanted to roll my eyes at the snark running through my aching head.

Groaning, I turned to my side and pushed the bile back down my throat. For several seconds, my vision wavered. At least I thought there was something wrong until I realized there was, in fact, an odd glow coming from the crypt in the cemetery.

MAGICAL NEW BEGINNINGS

Why had I never seen this before? I pushed onto all fours and rocked until I got to my feet. I weaved in a zigzag to the first headstone. There was something magical about being on sacred ground. Or perhaps it was being so close to my ancestors.

I wanted to check and see if Sebastian had seen my drunk-but-not-actually-drunk stagger. *Who gives a rip if he sees it? It's not like he's any better.* My thoughts scattered in a hot flash. My body heated to a million degrees in a second, and energy rushed through me. It was better than what I imagined it was like when you were high.

I was embarrassed to admit I used every headstone on my way to the small building. The stone door was warm under my hand. That was odd, considering it was cold outside. I pushed the panel, but it didn't move. Using my shoulder, I shoved my way inside.

For the hundredth time that night, I found myself stumbling, only this time I was tripping over my own feet. There was nothing inside to brace myself on, and I hit the opposite wall before I stopped moving.

My jaw fell open, and my eyes flared. "What the…" I cut off my question, unable to believe what I was seeing. The walls and ceiling inside were comprised of skulls and bones, while outside the crypt was made of stone. All of them. Skulls, femurs, arm bones, ribs.

I lifted my hand, intending on touching the wall but stopped short. I had no desire to touch the decayed bodies of dead people until my instincts screamed it was okay because they were my flesh and blood. My head lowered, and I saw my amulet glowing brightly. It filled the room with amber light.

I placed one palm on a skull, and light filled the room. Turning, I plastered myself against the wall and watched the lights shift, and the wind started up. Energy washed through the room like a wave crashing against the shore.

The pinging that had never really gone away increased in intensity, adding to the nausea bubbling in my stomach. *This is the portal.* I watched the cyclone in the middle of the room, wondering where the heck that thought had come from.

"Fiona!" Sebastian's voice broke the spell, and the light died along with the wind. The energy was still present, but it was far less.

Hurrying to the door, I expected it to be just as heavy and was pleasantly surprised it was easy to open. Sebastian was standing on the crushed granite path that surrounded my family's graveyard.

"I found the portal!" I wanted to jump up and down in glee. I'd finally managed to do something useful. And, I was happier about that than I had been when I got my degree in nursing. The situation suddenly didn't feel so hopeless anymore.

Bas tilted his head, and the corner of his mouth twitched. Just when I thought he was going to be friendly, he opened his mouth. "It's about damn time. Do you want an award or something?"

I rolled my eyes and walked past him, then stopped in my tracks. "You killed it. What it is anyway?"

"It's a Dark Fae called a hrimthur. It has power over ice and freezes the heart, killing its victims." That's why I was so cold and felt like I was dying. My body shuddered when he explained how it killed. "I'll take care of this while you get cleaned up, then we can get to work."

I opened my mouth to tell him I didn't need to clean up, but he was halfway across my yard and had the corpse slung over his shoulder. Lifting one shoulder, I went back into my kitchen, put the kettle on the stove, and then checked the tea I had been putting together.

While I was waiting for the water to boil, I cast another protection spell inside, directing it toward the building. I had to be sure nothing could enter here and hurt me while I sleep. Otherwise, I'll never get any rest between bathroom visits.

I almost stopped the spell but didn't. With my luck, it would bounce back at me. Energy snapped into the walls, and they glowed brightly for a second. Too late now. I'd just have to take tea out to Sebastian.

My head snapped around at the sound of the door opening and closing. "Ah hell. I failed again. We need to reschedule because I need to call Camille and ask for her help. I'm not going to sleep tonight before I make sure nothing can enter these four walls."

Bas shook his head. "For once, you managed to cast a successful spell. And, you managed to use both sides of your heritage to do it."

A smile spread over my mouth. That was the nicest thing he'd ever said to me. And, damn, if that didn't make him even more attractive. I couldn't go down that road. There was too much at stake here. "If that's the case, then how did you get in here?"

A sigh left him in a rush, and he pinched the bridge of his nose. "That should be obvious. I have no ill intent toward you, so it didn't keep me out. Did you feel anything different this time when you used your magic?"

The kettle whistled, and I poured both of us a mug and placed his steeper in his water, then handed it to him. "I didn't notice anything different, but it was easier to cast. What's that look for? You'll like the blend, I promise. Just taste it." He looked up, and the wrinkle disappeared from between his eyes. It was too hard to tell if he didn't like tea or if he didn't trust me not to poison him.

He lifted the cup and took a tentative sip. His eyes went

wide, and he looked down at the mug again. "You're right. This is good."

I chuckled at the surprise in his tone. "Watch out. That was almost a compliment."

The look he shot me next was part desire and part exasperation. He held my gaze for several seconds before taking another drink. "Making tea isn't what you should be focusing on right now. You don't even know basic information about Fae or magic. That is going to bite you in the ass sooner rather than later. For tonight, let's cover how you will know when someone is trying to cross the portal now that you know where it's located."

I wanted to go back to the sexy looks. Instead, I set my mug down and rubbed my hands together. "About time. I haven't been able to do my job for a couple weeks, and it's been killing me." I was ready to dive right in and get my feet wet. This was the turning point. I knew it in my gut.

CHAPTER 10

"I know I sound like a broken record, but I need your help. I can't face Sebastian again without gaining some basic knowledge." The coffee I brought to my lips suddenly wasn't enough. Last night had been excellent and awful all at the same time. I wondered if I'd ever not feel like I was back in high school and struggling to get the Pythagorean Theorem right.

I gasped and smiled at Violet and Aislinn before they had a chance to respond to me. "But before that. I found the portal! I know where it is, and I know how to tell when a Fae wants through."

Aislinn let out a woot, and Violet squealed. It brought far more attention than I wanted at the moment. Perhaps meeting at Teatime had been a mistake. I craved one of Dahlia's scones when I asked them to meet me at the popular café in town.

Violet leaned forward. "Well, where is it? Was it in the worn-down shack in the back of the garden? I've always thought that building had a bigger purpose than housing tools and fertilizer."

I chuckled at her excitement. "Nope, it wasn't there. Get this. It's in the mausoleum in the cemetery. Someone along the way took the bones of my ancestors and made the walls with them. It was so freakin' unreal. And that pinging I've been feeling in my head. That's a Fae asking for asylum!"

Aislinn's gasp eclipsed the chatter in the restaurant, and her eyes went wider than the saucers under our jumbo teacups. "It looks nothing like it does outside. It's actually made of bones. Why would they do that? I couldn't imagine digging up my grandparents and taking their bones to make walls." Her shoulders shook as she shuddered.

"That actually makes total sense. The structure isn't built out of the bones. It's obvious they used marble slabs in the construction from the outside. They must have lined the walls inside with them. It's brilliant." Violet's awe was evident in the reverence with which she spoke.

"Yeah, brilliant." I wasn't sure I agreed with Violet. I was on Aislinn's side. I can't imagine digging Grams up and pasting her bones to the walls inside. "Is that a witch thing? Will I have to add Grams to the walls? My knowledge of the halves of my heritage is painfully minimal."

Violet tapped her lips as she looked off into space while she contemplated my questions. "We will help you learn everything about who you are. As for having to add Isidora, I would say no. The spells are already active. They used the magic inherent in your line to add an extra layer of spells to keep the location hidden from anyone outside your family. There's no need to add to it now."

"Unless the structure gets damaged somehow. Just make sure that doesn't happen, and you won't have to dig anyone up," Aislinn added.

Violet nodded in agreement. "Good point. Now, to tell you a little about witches. We are connected to Gaia and the four elements. Fire, water, earth, and air. We draw upon and use those elements and their powers to create potions, cast spells, and the like. We're also mortal."

All of that made complete sense, even if I hadn't yet been able to put it to words before. "Do we have any weaknesses?"

Violet picked up her tea and took a sip. "Like any human, our bodies are fragile, but we tend to heal faster and age slower than our non-magical counterparts."

Aislinn picked at her orange scone. "If you're cut off from the elements, you can't access your magic. Thankfully, that's next to impossible to do. At least one element is around you at all times."

"She's right about that. You might be weakened if you're cut off from earth and fire, but the air is always there." Violet confirmed and popped a piece of a chocolate chip muffin into her mouth. "Now, the Fae live close to nature. You will notice that their homes are often hollow hills or mounds. Oh, and they dance in rings of mushrooms or stones. Brownies do, at any rate. Some haunt overgrown ruins and tangled green places."

Aislinn waved her hand across the plate glass window they were sitting near, gesturing to the square on Main street. "Do you notice a theme here?"

My gaze scanned the various businesses, taking note of the shop with handblown glass and wood carvings. Then there were the two art studios. On the other corner, I saw the ceramics store where you could pick up handcrafted pieces and even paint your own.

"They spend a good deal of time devoting themselves to the arts. They like creating, as you can see," Aislinn said while I was looking out the window.

If all I had seen of the Fae were the arts and crafts in the square, I would have thought the Fae were a peaceful people. I recalled the icy creature Sebastian had killed the night before, and my heart skipped a beat. There was nothing gentle about how he tried to kill me. "How can I tell if one is good or bad? Bas refused to give me any information last night. I'm terrified I will be summoned when I get home and have to decide to let someone across or not."

Aislinn tilted her head to the side and pursed her lips. "That's not cut and dry. Fae can hurt or help, and there seems little evidence of why they choose to do one or the other. Some are tricksters and enjoy playing awful pranks on the unsuspecting, usually humans. In contrast, others' sense of honor wouldn't allow them to do anything harmful. The best I can say is to trust your gut. I have always been able to tell when a Fae is downright evil."

Violet lifted a finger into the air. "But you don't always know if they simply have a nasty side. Remember when Wistari planted a fungus that killed all the plants in Camille's garden?"

Aislinn gasped and sat forward. "I'll never forget what that fucker did. She's not entirely evil. She also helped clear moles from Isidora's property. It's like she gets a cruel streak at that time of the month."

"Or if you piss her off. I heard Camille refused to give her a discount on some thistle," Violet added.

"Got it. Trust my gut but be wary. I hate that there's no clear answer, but I should have known better. I don't believe people, no matter their heritage, are all good or all bad. There's the potential for both in us. We make the choice of how to behave constantly. I have no idea what I will face when I finally respond to requests for permission to cross over, and I am sure I'll make more than one mistake, so how do I protect myself?"

Aislinn reached across the table and gave my hand a squeeze. "Full-blooded Fae fear iron which is why there are iron fences around most homes here. You have one surrounding your property's outskirts, one around your garden, and one around the pond. Your grandmother already left some protection for you."

"You two should write a Fae for dummies book. I don't know what I would do without you guys." I tossed down a tip for Dahlia and climbed to my feet while they both laughed in response.

Aislinn linked her arm through mine as we headed out the door. "It would be a best seller in this town."

Violet chuckled and held the door open for us. "We should include information about how giving a Fae a gift of clothes will frighten them off. But seriously, Fiona, the most important thing to remember is that they can appear as many natural world elements. That means they can look like a human, animal, or flower."

I lifted one eyebrow at that. "I've seen the flowers at Pymm's Pondside come to life, but animals? From what I have seen, there is nothing natural about most of them."

Aislinn tsked me. "You've only seen the tip of the iceberg. Some creatures are bird-like, fox-like, and insect-like. Then there are the ones that have seal skin and others that look like fish."

A couple walking past gave Aislinn odd looks. I cringed and hastened my steps. The last thing I wanted was to be seen as crazy.

Violet slapped her forehead and turned to us. "We've missed the most obvious. Fae are highly lusty creatures and some of the biggest whores alive."

A choked laugh escaped me as my lower jaw dropped to my chest. "Apparently, I didn't inherit that trait."

Violet shook her head. "Not true. You took care of your husband when he got sick and haven't been with anyone since. Years of no sexual activity will blow anyone's pilot light out. But the heat flowing between you and Bas is enough to start a bonfire. I think your fire's been relit."

My cheeks flamed, and I shook my head. That was a one-way street. No way did that man find me so much as attractive. "You might be right about me, but you're not about Sebastian. Just because he kinda gave me a compliment last night doesn't mean he likes me."

Aislinn let go of my arm and waved her hands animatedly through the air. "Wait a minute. You never mentioned a compliment. I didn't think he knew how to be nice."

I smirked at her and rolled my eyes. "I wouldn't go that far. All he said was that my great-great aunt Shelby made almost as many mistakes as I did when she became Guardian. It made me feel so much better because she was raised with full knowledge of magic and the existence of Fae. Which reminds me. How the heck old is he? You mentioned witches are mortal. What about Fae?"

The first thought I had last night was that I was hot for a guy more than twice my age. I'm not sure how I felt about being with someone so much older than me. On the surface, it was like being with my great grandfather or something. In reality, all I could see was a good-looking guy in great shape with a bad attitude.

Aislinn's voice brought me out of my head and away from thoughts I had no business thinking. "Some Fae are immortal, some are long-lived, and some are subject to harm and death as easily as mortals are. It depends on their power level."

"I wondered when you'd show up this morning." My head shifted from Aislinn to Mae, who was standing outside Violet's bookstore. I lifted my hand in a wave, wondering what she was doing there.

"I left a note that I'd be opening an hour later this morning. I met these guys for breakfast," Violet replied. "Did you come for something specific? Or are you trying to put me under your spell?"

My eyebrows went up at that. Was she talking about those bright pink candies in Mae's hand? They looked like some kind of saltwater taffy or something.

Mae thrust one hand on her hip and glared at Violet. "I would never do such a thing. And, these aren't for you anyway."

Violet gave the town gossip a dubious look and turned to me. "True Fae food and drink are harmful to humans." She must have seen the confusion on my face.

Aislinn crossed her arms over her chest. "Am I to assume you're trying to manipulate Fiona then?"

Mae shook her head from side to side. "I am not going to harm Fiona. Isidora could eat Fae food with no problem. I heard the protective bubble around town is more powerful than ever, so I wanted to thank you. Even if that didn't keep *Iymbryl* safe."

Violet's face lost all its color, and Aislinn gasped. I had no idea who or what *Iymbryl* was, but both my friends were clutching their chests as if they ached, so I knew it wasn't good, and I kept my mouth shut. It was Violet who broke the silence. "What happened? And, why didn't Dahlia say anything? We were just there."

Mae sighed and handed me the clear bag of candies. "She was killed last night in her house. Lance has kept a tight wrap on the news. He doesn't want to panic, people. Anyway, I need to get to Mug Shots to meet up with the girls. Thank you again for whatever you did, Fiona. Enjoy the *agiope* candies."

Violet opened the front door to the store, and Aislinn and I followed her inside. "This is bad, isn't it?"

Aislinn's head nodded and her forehead furrowed. "It's horrible. I'd bet someone is trying to take over Cottlehill Wilds."

"What does that mean?" I lifted the cellophane bag and

poked the candies inside, unsure I would ever eat them. Perhaps I'd give them to Sebastian. He was Fae and could eat them without issue.

Aislinn went to the counter and picked up a pen that had a fuzzy end. "I believe someone is using Fae magic to take the portal from your family. From what I understand, such a switch in power would require the blood of every species and a power practitioner."

"You're likely right," Violet agreed as she went about her routine when opening the shop. "That would take balls, and I can only imagine one being with that much gall."

"King Vodor." Aislinn and Violet blurted at the same time.

"I'm going to go out on a limb and say that's the evil Fae King."

"Sure is," Aislinn replied.

"That changes nothing. We knew someone was after me. I'm making progress with my magic, and I know where the portal is. What do I need to do to keep him from getting his way?" My confidence was shaky at best, and I hoped they didn't see the way my knees shook. I refused to lose my family's legacy. Not on my watch. I wasn't some young woman that would be easily frightened.

I've faced the death and loss of the man I loved most in the world. And I survived. That changed a person on a fundamental level no matter how old you are. You stopped sweating the little things in life and focused on what matters most.

"KEEPING PEOPLE in Cottlehill safe is the only place I can think of to start," Violet murmured as she started the tablet that acted as her register.

Aislinn set down the pen she'd been twisting between her

palms. "I agree with Violet. It's not like we can go out and hunt whoever has been killing Fae."

I tilted my head. "Why not?"

Violet shook her head. "You have to remember that everything the Fae do is driven by base behaviors which makes them very dangerous. We need to tread carefully."

Aislinn's face broke out in a smile. "You need to start making friends in town."

"That's been my plan regardless, but why's that important?"

"If you respect them and their sacred spaces, the Fae can be one of the best benefactors to the natural magic practitioner. Isidora always said she wasn't as powerful outside of Cottlehill. I didn't understand until just now. By showing them the reverence you have for them, you will win their hearts. Mae's gift is proof enough of that." Aislinn crossed her arms and smiled in satisfaction at her advice.

I would do my best to win over the townspeople, but I knew that wasn't going to be the answer. That would just mean a lifetime of trying to stay one step ahead of the killer and ensure he didn't have the opportunity to follow through on his plans. My gut told me I would have to find this Fae and eliminate him. And, there was only one person I trusted to help with that.

I needed to focus on winning Sebastian over rather than the entire town. He was more than capable of having my back. I wanted Violet and Aislinn there, too, but I couldn't put my coven mates in danger like that.

CHAPTER 11

"First things first. I need to find my family Grimoire," I told Aislinn, who had come over after dinner to help. Having the tome would make my job so much easier. Having checked the entire house many times before, I figured the best place to start was in the attic.

Aislinn cracked her knuckles. "Tell me how I can help."

I paused at the base of the stairs and glanced back at her. "Look through the attic with me. Honestly, I'm hoping you will be able to sense its magic."

Aislinn bit her bottom lip and furrowed her brow. "I doubt I will be able to sense it because I'm not connected to it, but I have two hands and can comb through the morass like nobody's business."

My heart sank hearing she wouldn't be able to pick up on its presence. "That's okay. I'm just grateful I don't have to do this by myself."

We climbed to the second floor, then the third faster than I had when I arrived a few months ago. All this activity was getting me in the best shape of my life. "Can I ask you something?"

Aislinn walked to one side of the attic and lifted the lid off a box. "Sure. Anything."

"You mentioned the other day that some Fae were immortal and some long-lived, and it depended on their level of power."

"Yeah. What about it?"

"Well, you also mentioned I was quite powerful. Or maybe that was Violet. If I'm higher on the scale, why did I find three more gray hairs this morning? And what's with the age spots on my hands and face?" Seriously. Being a hybrid should have some benefits. My first choice would be no aches and pains, and the second would be not finding any gray hair in my light brown locks. It would also be nice to not have to get up fifty times a night to pee. I'd love to lose the hot flashes, too. Honestly, anything would be nice.

Aislinn chuckled. "You're a hybrid, Fiona. You won't age like humans, but you aren't immortal either."

"I guess that was too much to ask for. Wait a minute," I called out excitedly as I crouched down and swiped some dust away. "What's this?"

Aislinn rushed to my side and knelt beside me. "It looks like the remnants of a spell."

"Could it have to do with the Grimoire?"

Aislinn's shoulder lifted and fell. "No idea. Anything is possible. All I can say for sure is that this is Fae in nature and leftover from someone casting in this space."

"Crap. That could be from my grandmother then. Or anyone else in my family. So much for thinking I found something." It was crushing to get my hopes up only to have them dashed so quickly.

"Don't give up just yet. This isn't from Isidora. I didn't know your other ancestors, but there would be familiar elements if it came from your family line. It's not something to dismiss entirely."

The pinging started up, sending pain arching through me like wildfire. My hands flew to my head. "Gah."

Aislinn's frantic voice echoed close to my ear. "What's wrong? How can I help?"

"Portal," I managed to say on a gasp.

Aislinn's slender arm wound around my back, and she helped me to my feet then down the stairs. The agony had never been this bad before. Thankfully, it eased some as I got outside. Enough so I could walk into the cemetery on my own.

Aislinn paused by some headstones ten feet from the crypt while I continued to the door. My hand sizzled when I pushed against the panel. I had to ignore the discomfort and force my way inside.

My hair blew around my head in a whirlwind of light brown locks. The lights spinning in the center blinded me momentarily. I stood there gaping at the tornado in the center for a couple seconds, unsure what to do next.

"Enough. Who wants to pass?" My words were swallowed by the winds, but they seemed to work as it died down, leaving my hair in a tangled mess.

The lights dimmed and formed an oval that was fifteen feet high. The center shifted, and another world became visible as if I was looking at a television screen. It was nothing like I expected.

The grass was lime green, and there were brightly colored flowers throughout. In the distance, crystal clear water fell over a stunning waterfall. The water wasn't blue but iridescent. But the major draw was the woman in the middle of it all.

She was skinny as a rail with pointed ears and long, blue hair. She lifted her hand and bit down on a fingernail. It was such a human thing to do despite the butterfly wings at her back and wide turquoise eyes.

"Are you the Guardian? I need to come to earth right away." Her voice wobbled, and she kept looking over her shoulder.

"Why? What's going on?" I wasn't picking up any red flags, but I needed to know more before I just let her through.

Tears filled her eyes. "The uh, I am being hunted. I've tried at every portal I've passed on my flight from the capital city. Please. I mean, your kind no harm. I just need to get away before he catches me."

I gasped and approached the light. Instincts told me to extend my hand to her. "Of course, you can come through. I have an idea who you're running from." The second our skin touched, the oval shimmered, and the Fae woman was stepping through.

"I'm Fiona. Do you have somewhere to go here?"

The female was shaking as she fell into my side. I held her up while her legs shook. The instant her entire body was through the portal, it vanished with a loud pop. My ears were plugged like they got when I flew. Sticking a finger in one ear, I shimmied it around, trying to clear them.

"I'm Kairi. I'm a mermaid princess, and back home, I have a palace, but it's no longer safe for me there. Here I have nothing." I glanced down at her legs then at her wings. She followed my eyes. "I had to shift forms to escape the king's Guard. This is my other form. I haven't spent much time on land, though.

"I thought it had to be something like that. And, I'm sorry if my staring was rude. I meant no offense, but I just discovered supernaturals existed." I guided her through the door and watched her shrink back from Aislinn.

"This is my friend, Aislinn," I said, changing the subject away from my ignorance. It still bothered me that I didn't know much. "The ocean isn't far from here. I can take you there." I hated seeing how frightened the poor thing was. I wanted to ask her a million questions. Who wouldn't? She was a mermaid!

Kairi's head shook rapidly from side to side. "Not the ocean. He can find me there. Well, his minions can."

I rubbed circles on her back and helped her walk through the cemetery. Aislinn fell into step with us. "Not the ocean then. I have a pond. It's not very big, but you're welcome to stay there. It's right over there, close to my house and completely private."

The tears wobbled on her lower lashes and fell to her cheeks. "Oh, thank you. That's perfect."

Aislinn swung her arms as she walked a few feet away from us. She couldn't hide her curiosity as she kept looking over at Kairi. Finally, she broke the silence. "Won't it be too shallow for you?"

Kairi's head stopped swiveling all around as she scanned her surroundings. "In its current form, yes, it will be, but I will alter it to fit my needs. I'll remove dirt, so it goes deeper and add some tunnels for rooms under the water." The mermaid's eyes went wide, and she turned to me. "As long as that's okay. I won't do anything if you would rather me leave it alone."

"Are you kidding me? I don't mind at all. I enjoy looking at the pond, but no one wants to see all this in a bathing suit, so I don't use it for anything. Wait. There are fish in there that I would like protected. And, it might take a while for my hose to fill up what you dig out."

Kairi waved a hand in dismissal. "I will call the water to the pond."

"Won't relocating that much water weaken the surrounding land?" Aislinn asked as she headed to my back door.

Kairi paused and tapped her lips. "Good point. I'll make

sure to draw from a hundred-mile radius, so there isn't a problem."

I smiled big as I brought her into the house to offer her some tea. I'd allowed my first Fae through the portal. She was a beautiful mermaid that was going to live in my pond. My chest swelled with pride like it did when I was part of saving someone's life at the hospital.

* * *

"Thanks for coming over. I wasn't sure who else to call. I don't trust anyone in town enough yet to ask their opinion," I explained as I let Sebastian inside the house.

His grunt was low and did funny things to my insides. Why was I so attracted to this guy's grumpy demeanor? He was the opposite of how Tim was. "What is it that you need?"

A sigh left me as I turned and started for the stairs. "I found these markings in the attic, and I have a feeling they are a clue about my family's Grimoire."

"And you think I can help you. Why?"

That time the growl in his voice made me shiver for a different reason entirely. He wasn't happy about being called on for such a menial task. No doubt he thought I should know how to solve it on my own.

"You're the wisest Fae I know."

He snorted as we entered the dim space. "I'm one of the few Fae you know."

I wagged my finger at him. "Not true. I've met a dozen over the past few days. I rather like Mae, even if she's a busybody. She gave me some agiope candies I'll share with you after we're done here."

He simply looked at me with one eyebrow raised. Apparently, offering sweets wasn't the way to his heart. Lifting one shoulder, I pointed to the marks on the floor. "Do you recognize these?"

Bas bent and held his hand about a foot over the floor. "They're from a summoning spell. It seems Filarion was in your attic recently."

My eyes went wide at that. "You mean that griffin with all those muscles was in my house? But why?"

Sebastian narrowed his eyes at me. "You know Filarion?"

I swallowed past the guilt. Why I suddenly felt guilty, I had no idea. I'd done nothing wrong. "Yes, I bought a spellbook from him. Why was he in here, though?"

Bas stood up and put his hands on his hips. "Likely to steal your family's grimoire. There'd be nothing else Isidora would have hidden in her home. But that she wouldn't want to fall into the wrong hands."

"Dammit. I knew he was an asshole when I met him. How do I get it back?"

"How else? You take it. By any means necessary."

"Will you help me get it?"

Bas shook his head. "No. I'm not going to do your job for you. But I will give you a weapon to use and be there when you take it back."

Jerk! I wasn't asking him to do my job. Why did he have to be such a pain? I mean, it wouldn't kill him to make the griffin give it back to me. I've faced far more than most in the last few months, and I just wanted space to breathe and learn.

"Follow me," Bas commanded. He was past the second floor before I snapped out of my anger and followed suit.

I had to run to catch up when I hit the first floor. He was already outside. When I joined him, I noticed he was already at the tree line and wasn't stopping. "Wait up!"

"Move your sexy little ass."

My mouth dropped open, and my stomach flipped over.

Did Sebastian just call me sexy? Maybe Aislinn and Violet were right, and he was attracted to me. A smile bloomed across my face, and I felt giddy.

His low growl startled me. He was standing at the edge of the woods with a pinched expression. He didn't tolerate fools, and I was acting like a teenaged one at the moment. Trying to lose the grin, I picked up my pace and reached his side in seconds.

The silence was thick as we walked. I wanted to ask Bas why he said that. Asking would be a mistake, though, so I didn't. My gaze kept traveling his way, but he remained focused on the forest ahead of us.

When I thought my heart was going to explode out of my chest, I broke the silence and changed the subject. "I have a mermaid living in my pond now."

"You managed to figure out how to do your job?" The dubious look on his face made me want to throat punch him.

"Don't look so surprised. I just needed to find the damned thing. I may have fumbled through the rest, but I managed."

"What was the story she gave you?"

"Kairi was running from someone. I think it was King Vodor. My guess is he was trying to force her to give him something she didn't want to, and she took off."

The way he looked at me next brought a grin to my lips. He lifted one eyebrow. "Someone's doing her homework. Here we are."

He stopped next to a small house set in the middle of a grouping of trees. "Where are we?"

"My place." That had my head snapping in his direction. "I told you I'd give you a weapon. Follow me."

Heat wafted out the second he opened the wood door. I blinked, unsure what I saw the second I stepped inside. Along one wall was a fireplace that was big enough for me to stand in. Off to one side were shelves with various tools.

Three tables stood around the space, as well as a stone pedestal with an anvil on top.

"What is all this?"

He walked over to one of the tables and picked up a tiny shovel. "These are tools I'm making for a family of gnomes not far from here."

"So, you're a blacksmith?"

He set the tool down and lifted one shoulder. "I'm not an ordinary blacksmith."

I crossed to a table that had what looked like charms on it. "You're anything but ordinary. Hey, this looks like mine." I pulled the necklace I'd been wearing since I discovered it in the house from under my shirt.

He stopped an inch from me and reached for the charm around my neck. His masculine scent surrounded me. His cologne was outstanding, which was odd because I usually hated the stuff. It was too strong, but not whatever he was wearing.

"I made this over two centuries ago." Something passed over his face as his blue eyes lifted to mine. "Do you feel that?"

My throat went tight, and my lady bits started tingling. "Ye…yeah. What is it?" Desire!

One corner of his mouth lifted. It was the closest I'd ever seen to a smile on him, and damn did it do things to me. My mouth went dry, and I suddenly wanted to feel his lips on mine. I lifted onto my tiptoes, closing some of the distance between us.

"It's a spell I imbued into the silver. It recognizes your family line and opens the path to your ancestry of magic. I added the amber to repel negative energy."

That was why I'd been stronger since putting it on. "You do this for every family?"

His head shook side to side. "Only the special ones." With

that announcement, he lowered his head and pressed his lips to mine.

Electricity exploded in my bloodstream. It was like being electrocuted and given an injection of adrenaline at the same time. My body turned languid, and I melted into Bas's body. His big hands landed on my hips, pulling me close to his body.

His tongue traced my lower lip, and I groaned. He took advantage and slid his tongue into my mouth. Arousal shot through me in an instant. The kiss went from gentle to heated in a heartbeat.

His mouth surged over mine, his tongue tangled wetly with mine, and his hands grabbed my ass and lifted me. My legs wound around his waist and my core pressed against his erection. I couldn't help but writhe in his arms.

One of his hands moved from my backside to tangle in my hair. All I could think about was getting this man into bed. I'd never been a forward woman. It had been decades since I was last kissed like this, and it made me want so much more.

All too soon, he broke away and stood there panting as he stared at me. I licked my lips, tasting him. "That was…"

"Fucking perfect," he growled.

"And unexpected. What now?"

He set me on my feet. Not what I was hoping for, but the distance allowed me to take a breath and calm from inferno to smoldering. "Now we get your Grimoire back." He turned to the table he'd been standing at and picked up a knife.

I accepted the weapon when he handed it to me. My palm tingled, and bolts of lightning shot out of my skin. They didn't travel more than a couple inches from my body as they wound down the blade. I wasn't sure if that was residual arousal or something else.

My mind refused to focus on the matter at hand as I

followed him outside. All I wanted to do was push Sebastian to the ground and climb him like a mountain. I had no idea how he continued walking back to my house as if he hadn't just kissed me like he was dying of starvation and I was his first meal in a decade.

And I'd been lost in the desert for months, and he offered me a drink of water. It was both addicting and frightening. But I couldn't think about that at the moment. I had an elf to talk to and a knee to ice.

CHAPTER 12

"I still can't get used to the fact that there is this hidden market right in the middle of the park." I was babbling, but nerves were getting the best of me. Bas had come with Violet, Aislinn, and I to Staves and Stoves, and all I could think about was how hot his kiss had been.

Aislinn snorted. "That's because you see humans as being open and accepting because that's how you are, but that's not reality. People would freak out over our version of a Farmers Market. Can you imagine trying to explain why Dave is only two feet tall? Or that he sells toadstools as houses for his kind who look more like French bulldogs than anything human."

I chuckled at that and thought of not only the people that visited and sold items at Staves and Stoves but the things they hawked. My gaze turned to Sebastian, who looked like he'd just sucked on a lemon as he crept with us.

"Do you ever sell your tools and weapons here?"

Bas turned his gaze to me. The look he shot me was full of disgust. I lowered my head, and my cheeks filled with heat. Was I having another hot flash? As if I hadn't already embarrassed myself enough. Ugh!

He lifted one eyebrow and the same corner of his mouth. "No. I don't." He didn't say anything else or try to explain in any way.

"Okay. So why would Filarion steal my family's grimoire?"

Sebastian growled, and Aislinn's gaze shifted from him to me. I could see the question written in her expression, but thankfully, she didn't say anything about that. "If I had to guess, I'd say he was trying to steal your family's power. It's the only thing that's passed down from person to person and carries a piece of your line."

"It's not the only thing." The words were out of my mouth, and my hand flew to my neck. The amulet sat underneath. I never took it off. Hadn't since putting it on. It wrapped me in warmth and was reassuring.

"What else holds your power? And, why haven't we heard about it before?" Violet gave me a pointed look, but we passed between the gargoyles and through the entrance before I could respond.

Energy sizzled over my skin. The next thing I knew, we were standing in the same park, only now we were surrounded by tables full of various items for sale and Fae, witches, and hybrids. I saw Camille and waved before continuing to peruse the area. Filarion was on the opposite side of the bazaar from the last time I visited him.

I was able to see so much more this time as we made our way through the area. I pulled the amulet from beneath my shirt. "This necklace holds some kind of power. I'm not sure if it has anything to do with the portal or not, but the first time I touched it, I was able to use my magic."

Aislinn and Violet both looked at the charm for a second before I tucked it away. "That's gorgeous," Aislinn observed.

"And you have an unbreakable connection to it. I can see why it fueled you." Violet's description surprised me. I hadn't thought of my connection to the necklace, but she was right.

Filarion stood fifteen feet away, talking to Theamise, the nymph that lived in the tree near the pond. I wondered what she wanted from him. I'd needed to make a note to ask her if I could help in any way. My steps faltered, and I grabbed Aislinn's arm, stopping her. Violet and Bas paused a few steps from us.

"What's the plan, exactly? Do I just walk up and demand he give me the book back? That seems ridiculous. He's going to deny having it."

Aislinn bit her lower lip. "That's the approach I had in mind, but you have a point. Is there a spell she can use to force him to talk?"

Violet shook her head as her eyes took on a faraway look. I'd gotten to know her tells well enough to know she considered other options. "It's difficult to force someone to do something. Let alone act against what they would normally do."

"We could ask Camille," I suggested.

Sebastian was quiet while my friends nodded their heads. We took a detour to the right and approached Camille's table. The scent of herbs was heavy in the air as we got close to the older witch.

Herbs of all kinds, both dried and fresh, were scattered on a purple silk tablecloth. I was proud that I was able to pick out a dozen different types of plants. And, I knew the uses for most of them.

Honestly, that had been the most difficult for me to remember. Each herb had various roles in potions and spells. Nothing jumped out that would help in forcing Filarion to admit the truth. I could destroy his sexual drive with hemlock. That would be highly satisfying but wouldn't help me get my book back.

"Fiona, so good to see you tonight. What brings you here?"

A heavy sigh left me. This entire situation weighed a ton and was exhausting. I didn't get more than a few hours of sleep per night, and I couldn't stop obsessing about learning enough magic to do right by the town.

"It seems Filarion broke into Pymm's Pondside and stole the family grimoire sometime before I arrived, and I need to get it back. However, I don't think he will be honest with me or give it back. Is there a spell I can use to force his hand?"

Camille picked up some sage and brought it to her nose. "It's impossible to override a person's natural inclinations. And, Filarion is a crooked thief that only considers how he can benefit from something."

"What if I threaten his life? Would that be enough of a motivator for him to give it back?" I was serious, so when Aislinn started laughing, I realized my folly.

"Somehow, I can't see you sounding scary enough." Aislinn lifted one shoulder with a slightly furrowed brow and the barest hint of a frown. She sees me about as frightening as a poodle. Or maybe a big fluffy teddy bear.

"Threaten those I love, and you'll see mama bear attack," I bit out. "It was worth a try. I want my damn book back. Let's go." My anger rose as I turned to head to Filarion.

Violet hurried to catch up with me. "I agreed with Aislinn until you said that. Now I'm terrified. Just pretend he threatened your children."

"That's not a bad idea." I focused on the fact that he put my children in danger by taking what belonged to my family and me.

"Hey!" A low voice startled me as I marched across the grass. I stopped in my tracks and glanced down. My leg paused in its trajectory to the ground. I gasped and jumped back, bumping into Sebastian. The feel of his warmth behind me was highly distracting, but I couldn't miss the angry gnome I had almost stepped on. *Note to self. Watch where you're going!*

I bent down, so I wasn't hovering over the little guy. "I'm so sorry. I need to pay better attention. I was caught up in my annoyance with Filarion."

"It's okay. That elf pisses me off that much, too. Just watch it. Many of us won't fare well under your boot."

"Thank you," I called out as he stepped around me and walked away. I brushed my knee off to hide the grimace as I got to my feet. Getting old really sucked.

"You need to recapture that fire," Violet murmured as we started walking again.

One look at Filarion and his smarmy smile, and it was back. "No worries there. I don't think I will ever look at that guy and not get mad. I can't believe I thought he was attractive before. There is nothing good-looking about him. He has no morals if he's going to steal from a dead old lady like that."

A low rumble sounded behind me, and I turned, thinking I had upset one of Filarion's friends, but it was only Bas. His eyes were narrowed, and his lips were pursed. What the hell had I done to piss him off now? I didn't have time to deal with his mercurial moods at the moment.

I focused on approaching Filarion and forced a smile on my face. "Hello, Filarion. Or should I say, thief?"

Filarion's head shot up like a bullet from a gun. "Oh! Fiona, right? How can I help you this evening? I have the other spellbooks you passed on last time. I can give them to you for a deal seeing as you're becoming a regular customer."

My jaw dropped at his audacity. "Actually, I had something else in mind. My family's grimoire."

His eyes widened for a split second before he tilted his head and blanked his expression. "I wouldn't know anything about your family's book of magic. I suggest searching Pymm's Pondside. Isidora would never let it out of her house."

A growl left me at his words. "See, that's the thing. I've searched throughout the house. What do you think I found?"

The elf lifted his shoulders and shot a look to my left where Aislinn was standing. "I'm sure I have no idea."

"Yeah, you're definitely a liar. I found your magical signature, asshole. You took advantage after my Grams died and broke into my house and stole the grimoire. And, I want that book back. Now!"

Filarion flinched when I shouted at him. Everyone in the area around his table stopped and stared at us, as well. His hands started shaking as he pushed himself out of his chair. "I did no such thing. How dare you accuse me of stealing from Isidora."

Violet snorted. "Yeah, because you're such a stand-up guy."

"We all know what you did. You need to return my property."

Filarion crossed his arms over his chest and stared at me. I wanted to smack the smug look off his face. "I have nothing to give you. Not that you can prove your accusations anyway."

"You like pain. I should've known that too. Sebastian?" I called over my shoulder.

It was the right thing to say. Filarion's face went pale as all the blood drained away. "Wh…what can I do for you?"

Bas didn't move from where he stood three feet behind me, but he didn't have to. The way he stood there with his arms crossed over his chest and his eyes narrowed was enough to have me practically peeing my pants. It was funny that Filarion had been standing in the exact same position, yet I wasn't afraid at all.

I smiled at Bas. "Can you confirm what we found in the attic?"

The wrinkles in Sebastian's forehead doubled and one corner of his mouth lifted. "I don't need to tell this bastard anything. He knows what he's done. Just like he knows, he will never get away with it."

The wind whooshed by the side of my face and blew something into my arm. I turned to see Filarion muttering under his breath and his table packing itself up. For a second, I stood still, gaping as the book rose into the air and floated to a chest behind the elf. Damn, I need to use that spell to dust the house this weekend.

I needed to ask Aislinn or Sebastian how he'd done that. I was beyond tired of cleaning at my age. I'd spent a good portion up until then cooking, doing laundry, and washing toilets. This was my time which meant no more dusting the million tchotchkes Grams left behind.

"I don't think so, you piece of shit." I lunged before the words were out of my mouth. My body went sailing over the table, but I lost my momentum when my knee smacked into the side.

I reached out for the elf as I started going down. Unfortunately, all I managed was to rip part of his shirt off. Aislinn was in motion right behind me, only she jumped on top of the table instead of trying to throw herself over it.

Violet ran around the edge in pursuit. Filarion barked something over his shoulder, and the chest floated after him as he made his escape. Bas picked me up and set me on my feet before he took off after the elf.

I was in hot pursuit a second later. My legs felt like noodles, and my knee still hurt, but I gave it all I had. Violet was right beside me, but Aislinn was younger than us and in far better shape, and she passed us in no time at all.

I was huffing and puffing as I watched Sebastian throw himself into the air. He was a couple feet from Filarion. He was going to get the fucker. "Make him pay!"

Violet barked out a laugh next to me, then started coughing. "I don't think he takes orders, Fi."

"Shit," I huffed and puffed when Filarion disappeared a split second before Bas's hand landed on his shoulder. I expected Sebastian to stop and turn back to us, but he continued running.

Aislinn slowed, then stopped and turned back toward us. My chest was on fire, and I couldn't catch my breath. "Did he just disappear?"

Violet nodded her head as she braced herself with her hands on her knees. "Yep. He sure did. Asshole's on the run."

"But Sebastian will get him," Aislinn added. It was nice to see she was breathing hard, as well. She wasn't bent over like she was barely holding her guts inside like I was, but she wasn't unfazed.

"I'm going to be banned from S&S, aren't I?" Everyone was staring at us as if we were aliens from another planet. This was the second time shit went south at the market while I was there.

Aislinn clapped me on the back. "You might. We usually don't see this much activity here."

Violet shook her head. "No, you won't. But you might want to buy some things to appease them."

I headed to a table filled with jars of variously colored liquids two feet from us. "You sell potions, right?"

Everyone was still watching us. I wanted to leave and find Filarion, but I needed to live in this town, and the best way to do that would be to make them forget I caused trouble when chaos had broken out the last time I was there.

The slender woman sitting in the folding chair nodded her head. "Brewed them myself. Not as powerful as Isidora made them, but effective, nonetheless."

"Do you have an energy potion? I need to locate someone, but my body is begging me to go home and take a nap. And ibuprofen." I smiled at her.

She looked over her shoulder at Violet and Aislinn then picked up a small bottle with vibrant blue liquid inside. "That'll be ten pounds, please."

I paid her and continued toward the exit, stopping at three more booths to buy a scone, some incense, and a candle that would help me sleep. I was antsy and needed to get moving. I couldn't stand taking so much time to get out of there.

Every second I wasted made it that much more likely that Filarion was getting away with the grimoire. I wouldn't put it past him to skip town after seeing Sebastian come after him. Speaking of, I had no idea where Bas went and refused to assume he had gone after the elf to help retrieve my book.

After stopping by Camille's booth to say goodbye, we were finally able to head out. Either the energy potion was working, or I got my second wind because I had some pep back in my step.

CHAPTER 13

"I have to grab a bite before we continue. I haven't eaten for over twelve hours, and I need all the energy I can get." Not to mention I didn't do well when I skipped meals. I became cranky, easily sidetracked, and scattered.

"I could eat," Aislinn agreed.

Violet nodded and shifted direction to head across the square. "Let's grab a sandwich from Mug Shots. Bruce is still open."

We were at the café and heading inside two minutes later. I might still be out of shape, but I was improving. Typically, I'd be falling on my back after my earlier exertion, but I was crossing the space in no time. Perhaps all this exertion was helping get me in shape.

Bruce was a short man. His dark hair and long, dark brown beard screamed dwarf to me. "What can I get you?" His golden eyes were unique. It seemed fairly obvious he was a Fae of some kind, but they weren't all that foreign.

"I'll take a pastrami on rye with mustard and a diet coke,

please." Violet and Aislinn placed their orders, and Violet paid for the food, refusing money when I offered it.

I stood several feet from the counter and leaned toward my friends. "Do you know where Filarion lives?"

Aislinn and Violet's heads went up and down rapidly. "Yeah, but we need a plan."

Violet sighed and pushed her long, blonde hair out of her eyes. She was beautiful, but I could see how tired she was. I felt bad about dragging them further into this. "He will be expecting us, so we need to pool our magic."

"You guys can go home. I just assumed you'd be coming, but it's going to be dangerous, and I would never forgive myself if anything happened to you."

Aislinn held her hand up with pursed lips. "Nonsense. We're a coven now, remember? That means we have each other's back no matter what."

"We're, as Bailey would say, 'ride or die.' There is no other place I'd rather be than with you kicking his ass. He needs to be put in his place once and for all." Violet's eyes darkened as she spoke.

"Your order's up," Bruce called out. Aislinn grabbed the bag while I snatched two of the drinks, and Violet took the last cup.

We headed out the door and crossed the street to my Mustang. Adrenaline dumped into my system as I put the drinks into cupholders and buckled my belt.

Aislinn held out the pastrami. "Here's your sandwich. We won't be able to eat once we arrive at Filarion's house, so dig in."

I took the sandwich and had a big bite. "Mmmm. God, this is good. What is Bruce anyway? I can't tell if he's a short human or some kind of Fae creature."

I turned the ignition on and backed out of my spot. Violet was in the backseat chewing when she leaned forward between the seats. "He's a dwarf. It's a Fae creature that lives below ground. No one knows how he runs Mug Shots because he's supposed to be turned to stone during daylight hours. But I will say he never goes near the front windows."

I took another bite when I stopped at a red light. There weren't very many in town, which had been a shock to me. But now, I could hardly remember my time in the States. It was funny how the previous forty-five years felt like another lifetime, and the past few months seemed like years.

"Turn right up here," Aislinn pointed out. I made the turn, taking us away from the cliffs and further inland.

I finished off my sandwich and thought better of eating when my stomach roiled. I wasn't going to be sick or anything but having butterflies with a full belly was uncomfortable.

Violet's arm shoved between the seats, and she called out, "He's up there on the left in the green house."

I parked the car down the way where he wouldn't be able to see us. "Do you see Sebastian anywhere?"

"No. He might not be here," Aislinn pointed out.

Violet's head popped between them again. "I don't know. He was pretty angry earlier. Filarion never should have run from him. He'll never stop looking for the asshole."

"You mentioned pooling our magic. How the heck do we do that? I'm so freakin' tired of being the lame duck of the group." The growl that left my throat was guttural and full of frustration.

"When we formed a coven, we established a bond between the three of us. We can send each other energy when needed. All you have to do is concentrate and open yourself to us. We will take what we need. And, if you need the help, grab hold of our bonds before your power runs out," Violet explained while we climbed out of the vehicle.

The night was quiet as we stood on the street. Glancing

around, I wondered who lived in the houses on the road. The last thing I wanted was for harm to come to anyone if things got nasty with Filarion.

Creeping through the shadows, I wished I was wearing black clothing. It would make it less likely that I'd be seen sneaking into the house. We paused in the shrubs closest to the neighbor's house and scanned Filarion's two-story.

There were no lights on downstairs, but the entire second floor seemed to be lit like a Christmas tree. "I think he's upstairs. Probably packing his shit so he can take off."

Aislinn braced herself on the side of the building. "Even if he leaves, he won't be gone forever. There aren't many places where our kind can live comfortably."

"I never considered that. Why would Filarion steal from me then? He had to know he would be discovered."

Violet stood on her tiptoes to see over the hydrangea bush and looked back at me. "I'm sure he assumed you didn't have magic and would never know. After all the last time you were home, you were well past sixteen, the age when our kind usually comes into our powers."

"Speaking of, why didn't I come into power at sixteen? Why now?"

Aislinn waved a hand through the air. "I think you did. You mentioned making stuff happen. We aren't capable of much more until we gain an understanding of how to control it."

"Yeah. My mom always told me it was nature's way of ensuring we don't destroy the planet. I mean, could you imagine a moody teen capable of blowing an entire continent up?" Violet laughed at that.

I chuckled at the idea. It was so true. Teenagers were reactive and knew everything. "I don't know. Bas is that moody, and he hasn't blown anything up yet. At least not that anyone's told me about. Alright, I think the coast is clear."

Violet and Aislinn followed behind me. Somehow, I had become the de facto leader of our ragtag group. I had a fraction of the knowledge they did, but they looked to me for direction. Not that I minded. I was a lot like my mom, always stepping up and taking shit into my own hands.

That confidence faltered as I crept up to the front porch. Walking through the front door seemed a bit too brazen, and I turned between the houses and walked through the dark, praying I didn't run into anything. The moon was bright but didn't reach between the buildings to offer any illumination.

I took a moment to connect with my magic. It was getting easier to call it up like Camille had taught me. It buzzed beneath the surface of my skin with an electric vibration.

The window above my head was dark, but I lifted to my toes and peered through the glass, hoping to catch a glimpse of something. The inside was a hoarder's dream. Stacks and stacks of crap filled the room, and I barely saw the floor through it all.

The stuff made it difficult to see much inside, but if Filarion was in there, he would be moving shit, and something was likely to fall. No way could you pick anything up without causing an avalanche.

With a shudder, I lowered myself and continued to the backyard. Unlike most areas I've been to, there were no fences here. It made getting to the back door easy peasy but didn't offer any cover from the neighbors.

The back of the house had two windows and sliding glass doors on the first floor. The sound of glass breaking from inside startled a yelp out of me. With wide eyes, I looked back at Violet and Aislinn. I jerked my head to the area behind us.

Both women scanned the yard while I looked through the glass. I saw into a kitchen that wasn't even close to as cluttered as the other room I'd seen. In fact, in comparison, the room was spotless. A kettle sat on the stove, and a bowl of fruit on the small butcher block island, but not much else was around.

I tested the handle and groaned when it refused to budge. A hand landed on my shoulder. I managed not to yell this time and turned to see Violet gesturing at the panel. I stepped aside, and she placed her hand over the lock and muttered, "*Recludam.*"

A second later, she pushed the sliding glass open, and we tiptoed into the kitchen. The second we were inside, I heard shouting and yelling. There was a loud crash followed by the shaking of the walls.

"It's coming from upstairs." I pointed to the ceiling, where dust was falling on our heads.

Aislinn held up both hands. "Be careful. Could be a trap."

I nodded, letting her know I understood, and turned to the door on the other side of the kitchen. I put my ear to the panel and listened to see if anyone was on the other side. The shouting above us continued along with the sound of items falling to the floor.

My heart hammered in my chest, making me slightly dizzy as I pushed through the door and found myself in a short hallway. We passed two rooms. The one that represented my personal hell and the second that had a cozy fireplace and reading nook.

I was pleasantly surprised that I didn't have to maneuver through piles of crap. I made it to the stairs and continued up without pausing. The voices at the top were masculine. It had to be Bas and Filarion.

Worried Sebastian needed help, I took the steps two at a time. "Fiona." Aislinn was trying to stop me, but I was at the top and heading toward the ruckus before she got my name out.

There were five doors along the hall—one at the end and

two on each side. The panel was shut at the end, but that wasn't where the sound was coming from. It was the last door on the left.

"Asshole!" Sebastian growled. I raced past the other rooms and paused in the doorway.

Bas was standing next to Filarion, and his fist was pounding into his skull repeatedly. Not that Filarion was just standing there taking it. He had a blade in his hand and was swiping toward Sebastian.

My feet carried me inside without thinking things through. I jumped on Filarion's back and wrapped an arm around his neck. He shouted, and the knife stabbed into my forearm.

"Ow! Shit." Instinct told me to let go and take off at the same time it said to fry him. Blood dribbled down my arm. Before I could come up with a path, Filarion raced backward, and my back slammed into something with sharp angles.

My head swam, and the breath was knocked out of me. A second later, a box fell on top of my head with a crack. When another followed quickly after, I realized the room was packed full of crap, as well. My vision turned red, and I wondered if it did that when I became outraged. It was wet and sticky, and I realized a second later I was bleeding.

"Take from us," Aislinn shouted out to me.

Sebastian caught up with us and wiggled his hand under my arm right as I became slightly dizzy. I shifted my hold higher and felt Bas's hand wrapped around Filarion's throat below. I tightened my grip, and so did Sebastian.

I reached for my friends and pulled on our bond. Suddenly there was so much electricity traveling through my veins I felt like I was going to burst. I looked down and saw that my hands were dancing with electricity. "Where is my book? I want it now."

Filarion choked out a cry. "I don't…" His words were cut

off when I zapped him. The smell of burning flesh made me gag.

"Don't lie to me."

Sebastian lifted the both of us together and snarled at Filarion. "If you want to live, you will give her the grimoire. Then I will leave your fate to the town council. Otherwise, I will drag you to my property where I can tear you limb from limb."

"O… okay. I'll get it. Let me go." Filarion's voice was hoarse, but I let go and dropped to my feet. Aislinn and Violet helped steady me when I landed on some books and nearly fell on my ass.

Bas kept hold of the guy and jerked his chin in the air. "Where is it?"

"It's in my safe. Over there." The elf pointed across the room to another pile of what looked like old books. How the hell many tomes did he have? I scanned the room, not trusting him, to be honest.

"Do you see anything?" I whispered to my friends. Both were looking everywhere but shook their heads.

Bas picked Filarion up and carried him to the section he indicated. The elf was turning purple, and his eyes were bulging out of his head. Sebastian shoved the tower over when they reached the area, revealing a large painting of a landscape.

Filarion's hand shook as he felt along one side of the frame. It swung out a second later. Behind it was a metal safe embedded in the wall. The elf placed his palm on the door. It glowed brightly then popped open.

I was transfixed as I approached the pair. All I could see was the biggest book I'd ever seen. The cover was dark brown leather, and there were runes engraved along the spine. What drew me was the tug in my gut.

Something about it confirmed this was my family's

grimoire. Violet had been right. I'd know it anywhere. I snatched it from the safe and sighed as I hugged it to my chest. There was a hum that vibrated from it and into me. It was followed by heat and sizzling.

"Why did you break into Grams's house after she died and steal this?" My words were like razors, and the elf flinched with each word.

"It was wrong. I see that now, but I had a buyer offer me a hundred thousand pounds if I got my hands on it."

"What buyer?" Bas's demand was followed by his hand closing around Filarion's neck because he turned purple again.

I lifted a hand and touched Sebastian's muscular forearm. "Umm, he can't talk to me if he is unable to breathe. Can you let up a bit?"

"I don't know. They sent me a fire message and instructed me to reach out when I had the book."

I lifted one eyebrow as I stared Filarion down. "I don't believe you. You've had the tome for a few months now, yet you haven't sold it to this mystery person. Why?"

The elf tried to take a deep breath but ended up choking and coughing. The elf turned red as he hacked for several seconds before it died down. It made me wonder if Sebastian damaged something. "I figured if he was offering me that much, I could find someone to buy it for more. But I couldn't look for a buyer unless I knew what it had to offer."

I got up in his face as anger surged through me. "There was nothing for you to offer them. The knowledge in here is for my family and my family alone, you piece of shit."

Filarion held up his hands. "I see that now. I should have given it back weeks ago. It's not like I can read it anyway. No one can."

I took a step back, flipped open the page, and stared at the intricate handwriting indicating the book belonged to Fiona

Shakleton. Why would it say my name? I just inherited the thing and haven't ever laid eyes on it. *Magic, dumbass!*

I flipped through several pages and heard Violet and Aislinn come up behind me. I felt them looking over my shoulder but didn't mind. These women had my back no matter what.

"He's right. It's completely blank." I looked over my shoulder at Aislinn.

"You can't see the writing?"

Both she and Violet shook their heads. Sebastian let go of Filarion and glared at him. "You will find the name of the one that contracted you to get the book, and you will give it to me. Understand?"

For a second, it seemed that Filarion was going to deny Bas. "Of course. I assume you want a meeting."

"Don't assume, asshole. Contact him and let me know when he gets back to you." Sebastian turned away from the elf and crossed to us.

He paused at my side, and his eyes darkened when his gaze landed on the injury on my head. He lifted a hand then lowered it. "Let's go. I'm not leaving you in his house unprotected."

I headed out of the room and downstairs while considering the significance of having the grimoire in my hands. This was a game-changer for me. I was going to be the best damn Guardian this town had ever seen.

CHAPTER 14

I brought the muffins I made earlier that morning out and sat at the metal bistro table close to the pond. Lifting the mug, I sipped the coffee. My body still ached from the race through S&S the night before. Being tossed around that mess of a house was hell on my middle-aged body.

To be honest, I thought discovering I was some hybrid would make the aches and pains go away. Sadly, that was not the case. Although, I had to admit I didn't look my age. The fine lines around my mouth and eyes hadn't increased since I was in my early thirties.

Unlike most of my friends who had to dye their hair to hide the copious amounts of gray hair, I had found less than a dozen strands on my head. And, yes, when they start to appear, you count them until they overwhelm you. Seemed I took after my Grams in that respect. She never looked her age. Even when she died at eighty, she looked like she was a couple decades younger.

My symptoms were all about my body. Hot flashes, loss of muscle tone, aches and pains. You name it.

I laid my head back and soaked in the rays of the late morning sun. Fall in England was crisp and cool. I loved it because walking outside could invariably lower my temperature when the hot flash hit, making it less likely that I'd pass out from heatstroke.

Shivers wracked my body. It was suddenly much colder. I cracked an eye open and noticed dark clouds were covering the sun. The skies might open at any moment. The rain here was something I hadn't gotten accustomed to yet. It seemed like it was constantly drizzling. I refused to let the threat of rain send me inside. Once the water fell, I'd have no choice. I didn't like my clothes soaked through.

A snap echoed from the forest across the road leading to Pymm's Pondside. I never went over there and explored. Perhaps Grams had moved a family of kobolds or pigwidgeons.

Deciding to check it out, I rose from my chair with a groan and crossed the yard and dirt driveway to the forest. The chill increased as I walked, and I wrapped the sweater I was wearing closer to my body.

There was nothing evident along the trees edge, so I passed between two massive sugar pine trees. The instant I was off the road and into the trees, the ground cover became thick. Ferns and other plants were everywhere.

The scent of dirt and mold increased as I walked. It was colder under the canopy of trees, and I started shivering. My stomach roiled, and I battled nausea. I had one leg over a fallen tree when a creature stepped out from behind an oak.

I fell off the tree, landing on my ass when I tried to turn and run. The newcomer gave off an evil vibe. It looked human for the most part. Except its skin was white-blue, and its hair was as white as snow. Its eyes were scary as hell. They were black with no whites around them like those of a shark.

And he was tall. Easily seven feet, but he wasn't as muscular as Sebastian.

I scrambled backward on my hands when I noticed the fog coming off his fingertips. It reminded me of dry ice when a liquid was poured over it. It was like some ice giant.

"I'm so glad you came to me." The creature's voice was rough and gravelly, but not in a sexy way. "You're going to do me a favor and bring me your family grimoire."

Ah, so this was the fucker that tried to buy the book from Filarion. Was he the one killing others in town? "Yeah, I don't think so. I'm not giving you a damn thing." Using the fallen tree, I pushed to my feet and started backing away.

"I think you will." He tilted his head to the side and pointed a finger at me. I had no idea what he intended, but I wasn't going to stick around.

I'd just turned around when ice hit my back. A scream left me as I arched, and my vision blinked in and out. Agony was a living being inside my body. I'd never felt anything so excruciating.

I stumbled forward and made it two steps when a band of cold wrapped around my throat. My hands flew up, and it felt like shards of ice sliced through my fingers when they landed on Ice Giant's arm.

I had to make it to my house. My gut told me the family protection spell I had added to would repel him. My skin stuck to his when I pried my grip free. Ignoring the blood that trickled out of the wounds, I formed a fist and punched behind me. I wanted to claim victory when I hit his face, but it was like smacking a block of ice. Hurt me more than it did him.

Ice Giant chuckled in my ear, letting me know I was doing no damage. It was infuriating. I just needed to make it to the driveway. I crouched as much as possible and managed two steps before he stopped me again.

There was a stick in front of me that was covered in frost. He must have stepped on it to lure me out here. Reaching down, my fingertips scraped over the branch. After three tries, I managed to pick it up. Shoving it over my shoulder, I poured all my strength into forcing it through his skull.

I didn't hit as much resistance as I expected. His shout of pain bolstered my confidence, and I let go and ran for my house. He hit the back of my head and sent me sprawling to the ground. I was less than ten feet from my driveway at that point. *Just a little farther. C'mon you got this!*

Rolling to my back, I kicked out and immediately wished I hadn't. He cast some spell or did something because my foot froze when it made contact with his body. The branch sticking out of one eye was highly satisfying, making it easier to deal with the discomfort.

"I said get me your family grimoire. Now!" He was shaking with his fury.

"Why do you want it? What's in mine that isn't in any witch's?" I had to assume every magical family had such a book.

"That's not of concern to you."

I had been inching my way toward my property the entire time. I was now less than seven feet. Could I lunge and reach it? On the cover of trying to get up, I crawled toward a tree next to me. "Ow!" I yelped when the area missing flesh scraped over the bark.

Once on my feet, I panted as he watched me with a confident smirk on his face. I was even closer now and could definitely dash for safety. My foot was defrosting and went numb, which was a problem, but I wouldn't let that stop me.

"Enough stalling. We are getting your grimoire now." When he reached for me, I jumped toward my driveway. It was awkward, and I ended up stumbling rather than executing a graceful dive for the dirt.

When my face hit the drive, and I got a mouthful of sand, I wanted to cry out in victory. Instead, I cried out in agony when his hand latched onto my frozen appendage. My gaze shifted, and I snarled while kicking and screaming—the heel of my tennis shoes connected with his face. I saw a fine line appear in his skin, but he didn't let go.

Think, Fi. There has to be some way to hurt him. A smile spread over my lips as I calmed my frantic mind and stopped fighting. He was dragging me back into the woods, but it was obviously difficult for him.

"*Liquescimus.*" The second the words left my mouth, the grip on my foot disappeared. Without hesitation, I tucked my legs to my chest and moved every inch of my body through the protections around Pymm's Pondside.

The Ice Giant howled, and his skin darkened while the fog turned to smoke. He glared at me and tried to step through the trees and grab me, but he wasn't able to cross the edge of the forest. When his skin bubbled and blistered, he turned and took off.

My head was pounding as hard as my heart, but my foot was no longer frozen. I needed to get up and get inside. Violet and Aislinn were due for lunch soon, and I should text Bas and let him know what just happened.

Every cell protested the movement, and I worried I would have to crawl to my back door, but Theamise hurried to my side and helped me to my feet. "Are you okay? I heard the noise and saw the ryme attack you."

I tried to catch my breath and settle my racing heart, but nothing was working. "That's what that is called? A ryme?" I shook my head. That didn't matter at the moment. "I'm okay now. I shouldn't have gone into the forest when I heard the branch snapping. I assumed it was another of Grams's friends living in our forest. Thank you for helping me."

Theamise kept her arm threaded through mine and

walked with me as I headed toward my house. I was so scared I was shaking. I had almost been killed just now. There was nothing as jolting as that.

My life was no longer recognizable, yet I wouldn't want to give it up for anything. I felt like a new woman now. Gone was the heartbreak. I was no longer a walking corpse. But that shit I could do without. While the adrenaline rush was undeniable, I didn't want it if it meant being attacked and nearly killed.

"Will you be okay on your own?" Theamise's dark skin was regaining its color, but she was still chewing on her lower lip.

I moved my head up and down once, then patted the wood nymph's arm. "I'll be fine. Violet and Aislinn are on their way. You're welcome to have the muffins I baked. Oh, and why don't you offer some to Kairi. Wait. Do mermaids eat regular food? Do you?" I was learning, but there was still so much I didn't know.

Theamise laughed, and it blew away the lingering evil that surrounded me. I still needed to scrub my skin, but it was better already. "Yes, we can eat your food. I haven't talked much with Kairi, but I know she will enjoy the treats. If you need me, just call out, and I'll be here."

"Thank you, Thea. You're a true friend. It's reassuring to know I'm not alone at Pymm's Pondside. I'm not sure I would be able to stay if you guys weren't close." The wood nymph smiled and bounded over to the table and picked up the plate. It wasn't until then that I realized the set wasn't wrought-iron like I believed. Aislinn told me Fae were afraid of iron or something, and Theamise showed no hesitation or fear. I should have known. Grams would never have anything that would hurt her friends.

I went into the house, picked up my phone, and then sent Sebastian a text warning him a ryme was nearby. He lived in a house not far from my home, so he could be in danger.

I had showered an hour ago, but I needed another one. My skin was sensitive as if I'd gotten a windburn, and my fingertips were raw. Fortunately, my foot seemed to be unharmed.

The adrenaline vanished completely about halfway up the stairs, leaving me wasted. A nap sounded great, but the girls would be there soon for lunch. The hot water felt great, but I didn't linger in the shower. Once dressed, I decided to put my thick-soled boots on before I went downstairs.

"Ah! What are you doing here?" My hand shot out and braced me before I fell when Sebastian startled me.

He was standing in the living room. For a second, all I saw was a figure that was too large to be one of my friends, and I panicked. I thought the ryme had discovered a way to enter my home.

"I got your message. What happened?"

I took a deep breath and let it out. "Do you want some tea? I'd rather tell the story when Aislinn and Violet arrive."

He watched me for a couple seconds before shaking his head. "Do you have any scotch? I have a feeling this day is going to require one. Or ten."

"I think Grams left some above the fridge." I grabbed the step stool then placed it in front of the appliance. I had to go to my tiptoes to reach the back of the cabinet. My fingers curled around the bottle, and I picked it up.

When I went to step back, I slipped and fell. The air rushed past me for a split second before steel bands wrapped around my shoulders. My face was inches from his, and I suddenly wanted Bas to kiss me and make me forget the awful experience with the Ice Giant. This man could make me forget my own name when he kissed me.

The clearing of a throat broke the spell. My head

turned, and my cheeks heated instantly as Bas let me go. I wasn't entirely steady and ended up stumbling off the step stool.

I smiled at Violet and Aislinn even though I wanted to sink through the floor and die. They would never let me live that down. "Hey. What have you got there?"

Aislinn held up the bag she was holding. "Lunch. I was craving tacos."

"Yum. Thanks."

"Now tell us what happened with the ryme," Bas demanded before anything else was said.

Setting the whiskey down, I grabbed a short glass, then ice from the freezer, and poured him a drink. I leaned against the counter and told them what had happened while I got a platter for the tacos.

"Why did he want the grimoire so bad? My mom never warned me I needed to guard ours with my life." Violet selected two crispy shells and brought one to her mouth.

Sebastian nodded. "I never gave the magical tomes a second thought. I mean, all Fae know a witch's grimoire has power, unlike anything we've been taught. Lore is that the most powerful of your kind have spells we can use, as well. I don't think it's that though. Your family is special. It must have something to do with the portal."

"Unfortunately, that's what I was thinking." I walked into the pantry and moved a sack of flour aside, and grabbed the massive book. "One of my ancestors along the way must have suspected the danger and spelled it so no one but my line can read the thing. Let's see if I can find what they are searching for."

Aislinn finished a taco and wiped her hands. "Do you really think there is a spell in there that has to do with the portal?"

Sebastian crossed his arms over his chest. "They had to

have documented something in the event your line dies out. They wouldn't want to leave the thing unguarded."

I noticed most of the early pages had to do with witchcraft, and at some point, there was a shift, and it started mentioning how to call on the elements to balance the magic. Fae were fueled by nature and the elements found within. I wondered when Fae blood entered the line.

"This book is so freakin' big. When did my family take over the portal?" I looked at Violet then Aislinn. Both shook their heads.

Bas poured another drink and took a sip. "It was many centuries ago. The previous king fell in love with one of your ancestors, and they had a daughter. It was difficult to travel between realms at that time. There were two maybe three sites, but none close to Cottlehill, so he created this portal."

It was fascinating listening to how life worked back then and the events that lead to my existence. "Let me guess, he and this ancestor of mine decided they didn't want just any Fae crossing, so he made her the Guardian."

Sebastian shook his head. "Not exactly. They didn't worry much about it until one of his enemies crossed and killed her in her sleep. That event weakened the king and eventually led to his downfall."

Looking up from the book, I gaped at him. "Holy shit. That's awful. Losing a spouse is one of the hardest things you can go through. Especially if you loved them. Losing a child is a close second. But your husband or wife is the person you decided to spend your life with. Every plan you made for your life includes them, and when they're gone, you have to refigure your entire existence without your best friend by your side."

I lost my appetite and set the half-eaten taco down, then went back to my search. "I see the change when Fae magic mixed with ours. The spells and considerations changed. But

I don't see anything…no, wait. Here's a spell to shift the portal to another being. We were right. They are trying to take control of the thing. It says here the spell requires the blood of all Fae."

"We need to protect that book at all costs," Violet announced.

Aislinn grabbed a glass and poured herself some iced tea. "Can the ryme get to Fiona here?"

Sebastian looked at me, and I swore he was gazing into my soul. "Not with the layered spell surrounding Pymm's Pondside. But, just to be safe, you and I will reinforce the protections together."

I swallowed and fought back the desire raging through my blood. This man was addictive, even with his grim expression. *Maybe the spell will require it to be cast sky-clad.* There will be no naked times. It was a distraction I didn't need at the moment.

CHAPTER 15

I leaned against the door for a few seconds after Violet and Aislinn left with a promise to meet at the bookstore the next day. I should go with them. I was alone in my house with Bas, and he was too sexy for his own damn good.

The energy of the house had shifted during the lunch I shared with my friends. Ever since he caught me, the tension between Sebastian and I was sizzling. And nothing had made it better. Now we were supposed to cast a spell together to protect my property so the ryme and any other dark Fae couldn't get through and take my family grimoire.

Focus on that. You can't let it fall into malicious hands. That should help calm me and keep me centered, but it didn't. Footsteps made me lift my head to see Bas staring at me with one eyebrow arched.

"You doing alright? We can wait to do this another time. You aren't completely vulnerable. They'd have to use powerful magic to breakthrough, and that would alert you and me."

I opened my mouth to latch onto that promise but didn't

say anything. "Let's do this. I don't want to risk the others that live here. Theamise and Kairi escaped torture and were given a safe place to stay. I won't risk that."

Bas closed the distance between us and placed his arms on the door by the sides of my head. His body caged me in. Being surrounded by him was nothing short of alluring. His heated blue eyes tracked my movements as I licked suddenly dry lips.

He lowered his head and paused with his lips an inch from mine. His breath smelled like whiskey, yeasty and cereal-y. That's not an actual word, I know, but it's the only thing that came to my desire addled brain.

I silently encouraged him to press his mouth to mine when I realized I didn't need to wait for him. I was a grown-ass woman, not an insecure twenty-something. Lifting my chin, I closed the distance and pressed my lips to his for the second time.

My arms slid over his shoulders and wound around his neck. The groan he made was punctuated by him picking me up with his arms behind my back. My heart picked up its pace, and I swore it would burst from my chest.

His lips were soft and firm and full of electricity. The zing turned my blood to champagne in my veins. My legs wound around his waist, and I gasped when his erection hit the sensitive area between my legs.

Desire flooded my panties, and I started writhing while his tongue traced a path over my mouth, seeking entrance. I opened and let him in. His arms tightened on me—everything but getting this man naked fled from my mind. I'd never wanted anything so much in my life.

I spent the first decade of my marriage to Tim hiding what I didn't like and what I wanted. I didn't want to hurt his feelings. Ten years later, I was tired of not having an orgasm every time we had sex. That was my fault. I kept my mouth shut rather than talking to him. Once I opened my mouth, I unlocked a world of pleasure.

I thought your port of call dried up after Tim died. Ugh. I hated that inner voice that constantly intruded at the worst moments. I pushed it aside and tried to remain in the moment, but I'd lost the urgency.

My hips were no longer moving over his cock, and my mouth wasn't as desperate. Our tongues tangled, and just as I was about to get lost in unrelenting desire again, he broke the kiss.

We were both panting and breathing hard. I opened my eyes and looked into his. His desire stole what little breath I had. "Not like this. When I get you in my bed, I don't want you thinking about anything else."

I lowered my legs, and he let me go. Taking advantage, I stepped around him, putting space between us. "So sure I will end up in your bed?"

He lifted one corner of his mouth. "There's no denying how much you want me. Women don't kiss a man like that unless they want more from them. Besides, we're fated."

His tone was casual, confident, and dominant. Usually, I hated controlling men, but Sebastian's version drove me wild.

"True. If I had to guess, you might not make it to that moment. Unless I misinterpreted the desperation in your kiss. Right now, though, we have a spell to cast. Try to keep your hands off me, will you?"

Bas chuckled and twisted the knob, opening the front door. "Grab your herbs and meet me by the pond."

I grabbed the bag I hadn't taken back upstairs after he left. *Time to focus on learning as much as you can about your new position as Guardian.* Right. I'd been docked for winter and needed to figure out a way to prepare for sailing again, but there was no time right now. It was slightly more important to keep whatever asshole was killing in my town from getting to me and my book.

Sebastian was standing next to the pond with the sun setting behind him. The orange-pink glow gave him a halo behind his head. He looked like some kind of God. Apparently, Theamise and Kairi agreed. The pair were giggling on the opposite shore of the pond.

I slipped the strap over my shoulder and crossed the lawn. The night was cold, but when an icy breeze blew over me, I shivered and glanced at the forest where the ryme had attacked me.

"He's not here. He wouldn't dare face me."

I turned and tilted my head. Sebastian wasn't bragging. He was stating a fact. "I'd say you're full of yourself, but I suspect there's more to it than that. Why won't he face you?" Perhaps I should just move him into the house. That would solve several problems at once. *Nope. Not happening.*

Bas lifted the bag from my shoulder and sat cross-legged on the grass. "Because I have the power to melt his core. Without it, he can't connect with his magic. Without that, he will die. There's a reason I'm a blacksmith. My core element is fire."

I joined him on the grass when he made no move to get up. Lowering my body wasn't as easy as it had once been, and crossing my legs was next to impossible. My bum knee refused to bend certain ways, so my legs almost touched his.

"Makes sense. But why doesn't he freeze you and blow out your core of magic? It seems like you would cancel each other out."

The corner of his mouth twitched, and he gave me the closest thing to a smile he ever had. "Because I'm higher ranked than him, which means he can hurt me, but never kill me. If he tried, we'd be forced into hand-to-hand combat.

There I'd kick his ass. I've trained for centuries and fought more battles than he ever has."

"Got it. You're a badass. Now, what are we doing?"

"We're both going to cast the protection spell you did a few weeks ago. Doing it together will compound the power. It'll be another layer to what surrounds your property."

"What about yours? Should we do it again at your place?" My cheeks heated at how dirty that sounded. I lowered my head, wishing for a hood to hide under.

"Oh, we'll do it at my place in good time. Right now, we're sealing up your vulnerabilities. Your safety is what's important."

I nodded and watched as he removed dill, lavender, oregano, and parsley. He poured them into his big palm using more dill than the rest. Using a finger, he mixed them together then glanced at me.

I grabbed the bottles and tried to put identical amounts in my hand but wasn't sure how I measured up. My palm was far smaller than his. "Less oregano next time." His instructions were always short and to the point. I could use more explanation.

"Why's that? What does it do?"

The sigh that left his lips almost made me smile. I enjoyed needling him far more than was good for me. "Oregano is known as a happy herb. If it grows on a grave, it's because the deceased is happy. Aside from embodying joy and love, it aids in protection. I'd bet your grandmother planted it closest to the house to offer even more protection."

"Thank you. I'll get this eventually, but it helps to learn the uses so I can create my own mixtures."

That time Bas did smile, and it completely transformed him. Absolutely gorgeous. "Of course, you'd be thinking of making your own when you haven't mastered the simplest spells yet."

I had no idea if that was a compliment or not. Tossing the herbs aside, I grabbed more. "We cast it together?"

He nodded. "Yes. Three times."

Keeping my gaze locked on his, I muttered, *"Praesidium,"* at the same time he said the enchantment, as well. His voice drowned out mine, and looking at him made it difficult to concentrate on my desire to reinforce the bubble around Pymm's Pondside. After repeating the spell two more times, I pursed my lips and blew the herbs into the air a second after he did.

Energy exploded out from where we sat next to the pond. The strength of it sent a spray of water into the air. I was just glad I didn't end up bouncing my skull off the ground again.

Instead of pain, a high voltage raced through my veins. It was the first time I felt like every watt of power traveled through my body. It took away every ache and pain. And, I saw the world clearly. Each flutter of the pixie's wings was visible, and I saw every dust mote falling to the earth. It was as if time was suspended for one blissful second.

I held my breath and let the magic fill every cell. Beneath it all was a connection to Sebastian. It was a bright blue net flowing from him to me. I had no idea what it meant, but it outdid the bond I had with my coven.

When I released my breath, the electricity traveled with it. It rippled out of me in waves. I wanted to cry out a warning, afraid the magic would singe my friends, but it rolled past them without issue.

The ground swelled and receded as it gushed out of me. Green and blue lights came next and washed the world in a healthy glow. A laugh bubbled out of me as my flowers perked up and the leaves became greener.

I lifted my hand and waved it through the energy traveling through the air. "This is what happened the first time I cast this spell. Is this pure Fae magic?"

Sebastian was watching me with an odd expression on his face. It was like he'd never seen a woman like me, and I didn't think that was a good thing. "It's never happened like this before. I would say it's you, but I saw how it worked last time."

For the third time that day, my cheeks heated, and I wanted to crawl into a hole. "That wasn't my finest moment. It was the first time I used my magic without any instruction or assistance."

His shoulders lifted and fell. "Then this might be the result of you knowing more. Although, Isidora's magic never acted like that. I felt the energy rippling from me." His expression took on a faraway look.

"If the rolling doesn't happen, what usually happens when you use your magic?"

"It kinda explodes out of me. Like a blast all at once." He flared his fingers and pushed his hands out.

I had to look away from him before I did something stupid like jumping on him, tackling him to the ground. A gasp left me when light flared a half-mile or so away from us. "Was that the border of my land? I didn't think it went that far."

Bas climbed to his feet and thrust his hands on his hips. "No that included my land, as well. It shouldn't have included that area."

"Maybe it did because it used to be in my family."

"Or it could be because of whatever made the magic react like it did. Some nuances are as different as individuals. It's hard to say, but you can rest easy tonight. No one is getting to you."

My shoulders lowered, and my back loosened. "Has this happened before? Did my grandma have to deal with crap like this?" I couldn't imagine Grams fighting creatures like the ryme.

Bas ran a hand through his hair. "No. She faced trickster Fae that managed to hide their true identities from her, but nothing like this. She had no problem stopping a goblin from stealing milk from porches or a puck stranding cats up in trees. And, we never had someone hunting our kind and taking us out methodically like this."

Fear flashed through me. "Why are they making a play for the portal now? Is it my presence? Am I causing this to happen?" I would never forgive myself if I brought this to the town. Cottlehill was my home now and had always held a special place in my heart.

"I doubt you are the reason for any of it. If I had to guess, there's been a shift in Eidothea. There are power plays and games ongoing in the Fae realm, and sometimes one goes further and manages to threaten the king's position. If Vodor can offer the dark ones of the Fae a place to play, he will win their loyalty. As it stands, they shift their allegiances from person to person depending on who can offer what. It's what fuels so many grabs for the throne."

I shook my head. "That sounds like a timebomb waiting to go off. Is there anything we can do to establish consistency and stability in your realm? I'd like for the problems there not to leak over to earth where innocents like my children could be killed."

Bas stared off into the distance while a muscle jumped along his jaw. "It's not my problem to fix. And it's no longer my realm. I chose to come here. This is my home now."

There was a story there. My question shouldn't have elicited so much anger, but it had. "I meant no offense. And, I'd love to hear the story there someday. But I am serious. I think we need to find a way to stabilize Eidothea, so their problems don't cause us more. We have enough here and don't need more added."

"You need to focus on what's in front of us first. There's a

Fae out there hunting others of our kind to sacrifice to gain control of the portal. That is what we need to address right now. The bigger picture is not something we can overcome at the moment. Besides, it might calm down once we eliminate our current threat. The problems have never been as bad as in Faery. When I came to earth, there was the random goblin taking babies and leaving changelings behind or a puck stealing livestock, but it was nothing widespread."

"You said my Grams gave you the land. What did you do for her?"

"She gave me more than just land. She gave me friendship and purpose. As for what I did for her, she couldn't do the house and property upkeep when your mother moved away, but she wasn't the one to grant me my initial homestead. I helped the previous king protect his family. Your family."

"So, we survived because of you. I know shit didn't really hit the fan until now, but there's been danger around. I read about Fae that mastered the art of manipulation and how my great, great, great grandma was killed as a result."

Bas waved a hand through the air. "I helped when needed. They did the hard work. I acted as nothing more than a deterrent."

I chuckled, imagining him glowering as Fae passed through, forcing them to move on. "So, it's not just me then. You're a grumpy ass to everyone."

"Oh, you're special, Fiona. You bring out a part of me I thought died centuries ago. Never forget that."

My body heated with his words. There was so much beneath what he said. I wanted to bask in his words, kiss him and talk to him all night. When I met him, I couldn't imagine having a conversation with him, yet he surprised me yet again.

CHAPTER 16

"Ugh. Not again." I was too friggin' tired for this crap. I rolled out of bed and stood there for several seconds, rubbing my tired eyes.

The pinging from the portal started up for the fourth time that night, and I was ready to strangle someone. I needed an out-of-office notice or something. There was no way I would survive if they kept at me at all hours of the night. It made me wonder if time ran differently in Faery than here. I'd need to ask Sebastian.

If there was no one at the portal again, I might find a way to lock it down so I could get some rest. When I went to grab my robe, I caught sight of the pond illuminated by the moon. Instantly, I felt terrible for even thinking about that. Kairi had been running away from something horrible.

The problem was kinda like the boy that cried wolf. I was starting to doubt. Slipping my feet into my slippers, I descended the stairs without even checking my hair. It was too damn early to care if I looked like a hot mess.

Shivers overtook me the second I stepped outside. It was

even colder than forty minutes ago when I had been out here last. It was the kind of cold that permeated every cell in your body.

Was it the Ice King again? I stopped in my tracks and listened to the crickets chirping and the wind blowing, but there was no other noise. I hurried across the lawn and to the cemetery. The mausoleum seemed so damn far away.

The temperature dropped even more. It was early fall, so I doubted snow was coming just yet, but it sure felt like it was on its way. I'd need a better plan during winter. No way in hell was I coming out here in my terry cloth robe to talk to Fae about crossing to earth.

It messed with my head that I was responsible for deciding who came and who didn't. Sure, I was used to making challenging, life-and-death decisions, but this was different from deciding what to do to keep a patient alive until the doctor could get there.

Hospitals frightened most people, but it was a second home to me. Now, I was becoming accustomed to facing mythical creatures. The sound of leaves crunching had my heart racing in my chest and my breaths coming faster.

Quickening my steps, I practically ran to the crypt while scanning the area for intruders. Bas and I had cast a spell not that long ago to increase the protections around my property, and it had worked like gangbusters. Yet, my nerves hadn't settled even a little.

I'd hoped I would be able to calm down and trust that no one could get to me in my home. However, my mind refused to cooperate. A flash of red raced across the edge of my vision.

My feet came to a stop, and I turned to the left. "Oh, hi." I lifted my hand and waved at the brownie scurrying away from the garden. It wasn't one I recognized. All brownies were tiny creatures, barely over a foot tall, but this one was even smaller. And, was a girl.

Theoretically, I knew female brownies existed, but I'd never actually seen one. This one had long dark brown hair and skin that was a shade lighter than the dark I was used to. Her dress reminded me of doll clothes and was cherry red.

"Eek." She jumped when I addressed her and threw the nuts she was carrying into the air. Shells flew every which way. A wave of energy surged through me. It wasn't entirely pleasant, but there was nothing around to warrant fear.

I held both hands up with my palms facing out in the universal sign of stop and gentled my voice. "I didn't mean to startle you. Are you after a midnight snack?"

"Pah…please don't hurt me. I shouldn't have taken the food, but I was so hungry." Her voice was high-pitched yet not annoying. It had a musical quality to it. Her tiny body shook, making me feel guilty for scaring her. To make matters worse, her head swiveled all around, searching for a way out.

"It's okay. You can have the nuts. I'm Fiona. What's your name?" I crouched down with one knee on the ground and hissed when pain shot through the area. It was sharper than the usual dull ache. I really hoped it was nothing more than age.

"I'm Tunsall. You're the new Guardian, right? I've heard about you."

One of my eyebrows shot up to my hairline. "I'm sure you've heard how green I am. Rest assured, I'm learning fast and discovering new ways to keep the area protected."

Her head shook from side to side sending her hair flying every which way. I was jealous when the locks fell back into place neatly. Mine would never have behaved like that. Lifting a hand, I wanted to cringe at the rat's nest I had going on. "I c...can feel your power. It's growing. Some don't like it."

"What?" I practically shouted at her before lowering my voice. "Who doesn't like it? Do you know who's after me?"

Her hand flew to her mouth, and her shaking increased. I was surprised her tiny arms didn't fly right off her body. "I shouldn't have said that. I don't know anything."

The pinging became louder and more insistent, like someone battering on a closed door. It was distracting and took several seconds for me to be able to focus on Tunsall. She'd taken a couple steps away and looked like she was ready to bolt.

"You know something. You said some don't like it. It's okay to tell me. I'll keep you safe." I didn't want to frighten her away, but it seemed obvious she'd heard something.

A gust of wind blew through the area. Now I was practically shaking as hard as Tunsall. She bit her bottom lip and looked up at me with big, tear-filled blue eyes. "Some think you brought trouble to Cottlehill. Many are afraid to go to S&S now." She looked around and shifted from foot to foot.

I wanted to smack my forehead. I should have expected people to blame me for the disruption at the market. I was present both times there were problems. Add to that the deaths since I arrived, and it was no surprise.

"It's okay. I want you to know I never meant to cause problems when I decided to stay here. I don't exactly know what I'm doing. Hell, I didn't even know I had magic until a few months ago. But I promise I am doing everything I can to make our town safer. Speaking of, I need to do my job. If you ever need anything, you can come to the door and ask. I'm always happy to help you."

Her eyes flared, and she stared at me for several seconds before she scooped up her nuts. "Thank you." I nodded and

MAGICAL NEW BEGINNINGS

stood up, then waved before she scurried under the foliage and was out of sight.

This town was on edge. The temperature warmed slightly when I reached the mausoleum. It was odd, but I hardly noticed the cold while talking to Tunsall. Once inside, I pushed the brownie aside and focused on the matter at hand.

Like I had encountered last time, there was nothing there. When Kairi asked to pass before, some winds blew my hair around my head like a tornado. There were also lights spinning in the center of the room. They were bright enough to temporarily blind me.

There was nothing for me to calm this time. I had no idea if I could call up the fifteen-foot high oval that the lights had transformed into before. I relaxed my mind and tried to connect with the Fae reaching out to me.

For a split second, energy whipped around me, but it was different. Like the wind outside, it had an edge to it that hadn't been there before. I waited for a response for several seconds, but none came.

The pinging hadn't stopped. "Dammit." I felt like I was doing something wrong. I had no idea if it was supposed to work like it had with Kairi. I'd never done it before, and I haven't discovered any information in the grimoire on this part of my job.

My shoulders slumped, and I started for the exit, more than ready to climb back into bed when I doubled over. It felt like someone had taken a knife and sliced through my abdomen.

I crumpled to the floor while trying to catch my breath. I had no idea what was happening. Something seemed to push at me while the pain increased. Sweat broke out on my brow, and my heart was once again racing in my chest. Although for a very different reason this time.

Push this asshole away. He can't force his way through.

Where the hell had that thought come from? I had no idea, but I was positive someone evil wanted to travel through the portal.

Getting to my hands and knees, I shoved energy out of my chest with a refusal to accept the intrusion. I added some force of my own. *You're not getting through this portal on my watch.*

I was locked in a battle of wills for several long seconds. I refused to give up or give in. Something snapped in the air, and the pain was gone. I was able to suck in a full breath and climb to my feet.

Glancing down, I was relieved when I saw no blood. Battling something that wasn't visible with no idea how to combat the unseen force left me more than shaken. I had some learning to do and fast. I made my way back to my house. I needed to find out if there was a way to set some kind of protection inside my mind. That asshole had made his way inside my head and toyed with me. That would never happen again.

* * *

I WAS COMPLETELY surprised when Sebastian showed up on my porch with a pizza in hand. "You eat pizza?"

That eyebrow of his quirked, and one corner of his mouth twitched. "No, I eat children. This is for you and your friends."

I laughed at his version of a joke. He would never be a comedian, but I'd take this as a good sign. "Aislinn and Violet will thank you. There's no food delivery service out here, and I haven't gone shopping. Did you text Sebastian to bring food?" I called out as we headed into the living room where I'd been curled up next to the fireplace.

Ever since earlier that morning in the mausoleum, I

hadn't been able to banish the chills. Aislinn's forehead wrinkled as she glanced at Violet, whose lips were pursed.

"They didn't call me. The energy coming off your property has been off since this morning. I gave you hours to correct the situation, but I couldn't wait anymore. And, I was hungry." Bas's explanation was as surprising as his arrival.

When I sat down in the armchair and picked up my glass of wine, I scanned his face again. There were dark circles under his eyes. "Did I keep you up?"

He ignored my question entirely. "Tell me what happened. I'm certain the fix will be easy once I understand what changed."

"You want some wine or whiskey?" I wanted him to have a drink so he didn't get frustrated with me.

I'd been trying all day to figure out what had happened but got nowhere. I called my girls a couple hours ago, but none of us could figure it out. The grimoire had so much information that my brain was now mush.

I'd discovered that a trickster won't single me out as someone to toy with if I carried iron. However, there was nothing on actually guarding the portal—no mention of auras or anything. I wondered why my ancestors wouldn't have documented colors and feelings to be wary of.

"Since it sounds like it's going to be a long one, whiskey would be great. I'll get it. I know where it is." He waved me down as I was halfway out of my chair.

I plopped back down, and my girls gave me knowing looks. I rolled my eyes at them. "Stop. Nothing is going on."

"Uh-huh," Aislinn murmured as she tapped the arm of the couch. "That's why he knows where your alcohol is."

"And why you're turning ten shades of red," Violet added with a giggle.

I was shushing them when Sebastian returned to the room. "Tell me."

I ignored the heat in my cheeks and gave him a rundown of what happened last night. He sipped his drink and grabbed a piece of pizza while I spoke. "There was nothing in the grimoire on how to deal with the portal. Every reference said the Fae could not force their way through the portal that they needed our permission because it was tied to our blood. Nothing else."

The frustration was starting to build again and to add to that, my stomach rumbled at that moment. Loudly. Bas pushed the pizza box toward us and gestured to the food.

"You haven't eaten today. Eat." The way Bas said that brokered no argument, so I shrugged my shoulders and grabbed a slice. I appreciated the extra garlic and fresh basil. I always added those to whatever pizza I ate.

I took a bite and spoke around a mouthful. Not exactly ladylike, but suddenly I was ravenous. "Do you know why this happened?"

Aislinn and Violet both grabbed a slice and dug in, as well. Sebastian picked up his second piece and took a bite. I didn't think he was going to answer when he finally broke the silence. "And, you said there was an icy chill in the air?"

"Yeah," I confirmed and took another bite. "It felt like it was going to snow. At first, I thought the ryme was close, but I never saw anything. And, Tunsall didn't mention coming across anyone, either."

Bas finished his pizza and set his drink on the coffee table next to the open box. "The key was in your grimoire after all. It said the portal is connected to your bloodline, right? I suspect someone in Eidothea is trying to damage the portal on that end."

"So, they're trying to take it from her and destroy it? That doesn't make any sense," Aislinn added. She grabbed the bottle of wine and poured herself another glass.

I flinched when Bas glared at her. "That isn't what I said.

Listen carefully this time. I think someone is trying to damage the portal on the Fae side."

Violet gasped. "They're hoping to disrupt her bond. She's how many generations removed? I'd bet they assume her Fae blood is weak."

Bas nodded. "And hurting her in the process is an added bonus."

"Okay, so whoever was knocking last night is hoping to leave me vulnerable to attack. I'm safe at Pymm's Pondside. They can't reach me if I stay here. Although, I don't see that as a solution. We need to find out who is killing Fae in our town." I grabbed another slice but never got it to my mouth. The pinging started up again, and it fell from my hands.

"Fiona. Are you okay?" I heard Violet's voice through a tunnel. It was muffled and sounded far away.

Standing up, I stumbled to the door. I needed to find out who was fucking with me. The sensation was so much worse than when Kairi knocked. For the past day, it practically put me on my ass.

When a warm hand landed at the small of my back, I lifted my head and noticed Sebastian was there helping me make my way to the cemetery. His touch gave me strength, and I found my back straightening and my hearing coming back online enough that I heard Aislinn and Violet's footsteps behind us.

The night had turned frigid once again. I was pushing the door to the mausoleum open when I heard snarling. I turned in a circle scanning the area. "Do you see anything?"

Sebastian had wicked blades in each of his hands. They looked kinda like hunting knives, only bigger and with a dark blue glow to them. "There's nothing close. Go inside and deal with the portal. It might be a Fae in immediate danger."

"I'll be right back," I promised before I shoved the stone door open.

When I entered the crypt this time, I scanned the area with a wary eye. My gut told me Bas was correct. There was no way I would allow this bastard to get to me. My heart hammered against my ribs, and my breathing sped up to the point I worried I might start hyperventilating.

There was a flicker of dark light in the corner of the room where skulls tapered down from the ceiling to meet some long bones. It gave me the heebie-jeebies. There was evil behind that light.

I kept my focus on that area. *"Conmostro!"* My spell was directed at making the portal known. Whoever was on the other side was trying to harm me. When I paid attention, I felt blows to my chest.

The wind picked up, and the air shimmered then lights started flashing. They didn't blind me this time, but they were there, unlike last night. Instead of being colorful like the first time, it was dark grey, almost black.

When the light cleared, I saw a tall elf standing in the middle of the oval. His green eyes widened when they landed on me. The snarl he flashed toward me only served to enhance his crooked nose.

"I don't know who you are, but this isn't going to work. You're done hurting me through this portal."

"You aren't strong enough to best me, halfling." The way his lips curled when he called me a halfling told me how much he hated what I was.

I had no desire to debate with this guy, and I didn't want him trying to get through to my side. *"Excilium!"* The spell flew from my mouth, and I directed it at the greasy-haired Fae. He screamed right before vanishing from the window I opened to Eidothea. I saw the bright green grass for a split second before it disappeared.

My gut told me I had just royally upset the King of Faery. That was going to come back to bite me at some point. I'd deal with it when it came, but there was no way I was going to allow him to continue trying to hurt me through the portal. I followed that instinct that had been guiding me all along. Banishing him from the passage was going to help and hurt me eventually. That was a worry for another day.

CHAPTER 17

"What did you do?" Aislinn was rushing up to me the second I opened the door to the mausoleum.

I pulled the stone door shut and joined her and Violet. "I'm not sure exactly." Whatever happened affected the weather. It was warmer now than it had been earlier. And, I was no longer chilled to the bone. Not that it was warm, but it wasn't icy.

Bas scanned the area across the dirt driveway leading to my house. "Let's talk about this inside."

My feet were carrying me in his direction before I gave them the command to move. "What is it? Is there something out there?" My heart had just started to calm, but it was racing at light speed again.

Bas paused and waited for Aislinn and me, and Violet to catch up with him. "Dark Fae are lurking nearby. I didn't expect them to be so close, but they're out there. The aggression is heightened. I can feel their excitement."

"What the hell are they excited about?" Violet bounced on her feet as if she was ready to attack.

Sebastian glared at her, giving her a pointed look before he continued into the house. I went to the kitchen and put a kettle on to boil, then grabbed four mugs and two boxes of teabags.

I opened the pantry, searching for biscuits or any snack I could add to the tray. One of the first lessons Grams and my mom taught me was that I always had to offer a snack with tea. There was nothing in there, so I grabbed the apples from the fridge, put them on one side of the tray, and carried it into the living room.

Violet cocked her head with a smile. "Apples? That's a new one."

I rolled my eyes but couldn't help the heat that crept up. Good manners had been important growing up. My mom and Grams would be upset if they saw what I was trying to pass off with tea.

"In my defense, I haven't gone shopping all week, and I'm out of everything. I can't put out a tray without something." I waved my hand through the air.

Aislinn chuckled. "If I'd known, I would have brought something. Not that I care. I'm going to have more pizza with my tea."

The kettle whistled, and I went to get it. I snatched a trivet on my way back so I didn't ruin the tray or the coffee table. "Does anyone want wine or whiskey or vodka?"

"Whiskey, please," Sebastian replied as he held out his glass.

Violet handed me her wine glass. "I'll have tea."

I grabbed the other two empties and put them in the sink, except for Sebastian's cup. I tossed in some ice and returned with the bottle, and handed them both to him.

"What did you see out there?"

Bas held my gaze for several seconds. The look in his eyes was intense and not precisely sexual. Still, there was something there that had my libido doing jumping jacks and trying to grab his attention. It was almost as if he was laying a claim to me, which was ridiculous. As lovely as this was, we had more important things to discuss. He broke eye contact when I arched an eyebrow at him.

The tension was building to an inevitable conclusion. Not now. You're being hunted! I wasn't sure I agreed, but I put that aside for now. I've been through enough in my life to know I couldn't ignore the situation, or it would cost me considerably.

"There were at least four powerful Dark Fae far closer to your property line than I anticipated. It seemed as if the spell we cast the other day was strong enough to withstand just about anything, but I was wrong. It should have kept these creatures further away than that. They're taking a huge risk with us standing right there with you."

Aislinn snorted and shook her head. "You mean you. I don't frighten flies. No one thinks I'm powerful enough to boil water, let alone do some real damage."

"I am getting sick and tired of things stalking me. Maybe I need to banish them too." I poured hot water into a mug and added a teabag.

Sebastian popped the cork, poured amber liquid over his ice, and then sat back with the tumbler cradled in his hand. "I think you'd better tell us what happened in the crypt."

"At first, it was like it had been last night," I explained, then told them how I opened the portal and encountered the guy on the other side. I didn't know what I would do without these three to help me through this right now. Grams had to be looking out for me and pulling strings behind the scenes. Otherwise, I'd still be working through the fact that I made flowers bloom on lily pads two months ago.

"What was it like when Kairi came through?" Aislinn asked the second I stopped talking.

"The winds weren't cold, and they were untamed. And the lights swirled in a cyclone like a tornado. It wasn't just those factors that were different. The first time I didn't feel threatened. But it was more than that. I felt hits to my gut like I was being stabbed over and over again with a toothpick."

Bas's eyebrow went up at that. I growled and narrowed my eyes. "It's worse than it sounds. At first, it felt like one of those knives you had earlier, but when I refused to allow the portal to be sullied by evil and it became a toothpick. But imagine a small stick being jabbed into you a hundred times or more in less than a minute. It doesn't feel good."

Bas nodded once. "Did this elf have straight black hair and a crooked nose?"

My gut roiled. *Please don't be that bastard of a king.* "Yes, he did. He had green eyes and a pitch-black aura. I've never seen malevolence is such a pretty package."

"And you banished him?" Bas sat forward with his elbows on his knees and hands between his legs while he held his glass between them.

My throat was suddenly dry as paper and clicked when I swallowed. I took a sip of tea to cover the coughing fit I experienced. "Yeah. All I could think of was forcing him away from the portal. Honestly, I was just tired of the way he kept chipping away at me through the damn thing. It was more annoying than anything, but I'll be damned if I'm the one that ruins my family legacy."

Sebastian chuckled at that. Aislinn's lower jaw dropped to her chest. Violet's eyes flew wide, and her hand went to her mouth.

"You do realize you managed to force the king of the Fae from what he should have had dominion over. That's not something even I can claim, " Sebastian informed me.

"Not likely. I'm not powerful enough." The words were out of my mouth before they even registered in my mind.

"Whoa," Aislinn blurted.

Violet leaned forward and fixed herself some tea. "I'll say. You're badass, Fiona. I'm glad you're one of the good guys. We'd be screwed if you sided with the king."

Bas ran his hand along his chin and scrubbed the five o'clock shadow growing there. "How? You shouldn't be able to make him take a step, let alone force him away from the portal altogether."

That seemed unlikely. I understood his doubt. I knew next to nothing about my magic and barely had enough power to make a pencil float. I bit my thumbnail. "Did my Grams or anyone else in my family ever mention facing him through the portal? I mean, maybe it is possible, but they were never faced with the need or opportunity."

Sebastian sat up straight so fast some of the whiskey spilled out of his glass. "That never occurred to me. I guess it's possible. I know Isidora talked about obscuring the portal in Eidothea. She said the spell she cast would leave the portal's presence disguised in Faery to any with ill intent."

That made sense. I would want to limit access to protect the town, as well. "Let's hope that one doesn't need to be touched up. It wasn't mentioned in the book."

"Regardless of whether or not Fiona is more powerful than most Fae, what she did is going to piss the king off. And, I'm going to go out on a limb here and say it will motivate him to pour even more resources into eliminating her." Violet pointed that out as if she were talking about the weather, not discussing my demise.

"That's a given. I'll be staying close to the house for now. I don't want Vodor collapsing the barrier around Pymm's Pondside to get to her," Bas announced.

I cradled my head in my hands as I focused on slowing

my breathing. Hyperventilating in front of the guy I made out with sometimes was not my idea of fun. "When is this going to get easier?"

Aislinn got up and patted my shoulder. "All we can do is deal with things as they come up. There's no reason to go borrowing trouble. We will be here when you need us, but for the time being, we're going to head out. I need to get some rest, and Violet needs to get home to her kids before they burn the house down."

I laughed as I got to my feet and embraced them both. Sebastian followed us to the door, and we walked them to their car. The chill in the air was still there, but it was typical for fall in England.

I stood close to the porch while my friends got in their car and drove off. I hated them going alone. Something could happen to them, and I didn't like worrying about them. My eyes scanned the forest to the left, looking for danger.

"They'll be okay. It's you he's after, not them."

I turned to meet Sebastian's gaze. "You know that's not all that comforting. For them, yes, for me, not so much. At least my kids aren't here and in danger. What do you think are the chances of me surviving what Vodor has planned for me?"

Bas's eyes darkened, and his brow furrowed. He was angry, and the look was terrifying. "One hundred percent survival rate. I won't accept anything less."

"Be realistic. I'm new at this and still have a lot to learn. You can't be here all the time. Don't get me wrong. I appreciate the help, but ultimately this is up to me. And, I'm afraid he will get to me somehow." I walked over and took a seat at the bistro table.

Sebastian stood there for several seconds before joining me. The anger vibrating off him was unmistakable. I saw Kairi poke her head through the surface of the pond, then go right back under when she got a look at his expression.

He sat with his arms crossed over his chest before he got up and went to the woodshed near the garden's corner, closest to the house. Seeing him open the door reminded me I needed to have some wood delivered before winter. Grams had installed a heater when I was a kid, but I loved having fires when it snowed.

He came back with a handful of logs and dumped them on the ground a few feet from the table where I sat. "You're going to practice. Fire and Fae don't mix. Iron is another item I want you carrying at all times."

He was right. I didn't have time for a pity party. Thankfully, shoving how I felt aside to get a job done was second nature.

Squaring my shoulders, I took several deep breaths and got up from my chair. Bas picked one log up from the pile and held it out to the side of his body. "Light this one."

That seemed highly dangerous. "I don't think that's a good idea. I haven't mastered fire."

"Start by focusing the fire in your palm. Once you have it, you can toss it at the log."

I nodded my head and closed my eyes. Looking at him was far too dangerous. "*Ignis.*" I held out my hand, palm up, and pictured a tiny flame flickering to life in the center.

"You need to watch what you're doing." My eyes flew open when I heard Sebastian's voice.

I sucked in a breath and stomped on the flames dripping off my hand to the ground. The leaves had turned and were falling from the trees all around us. The last thing I needed was to start a fire.

Once the flames were extinguished, I lifted my arm again. This time I kept my eyes open on my palm when I muttered the spell. Flames burst from the center and shot five feet into the air.

Panicked, I waved my hand around, and the flames flew

toward the pile of wood. It ignited immediately. Bas sighed and said, "*Mergit*." He waved his hand over the logs, and the flames were extinguished.

There was no frantic waving of arms or barking of curses. Sebastian cast the spell with his usual calm confidence, and it went off without issue. "Your emotions rule you, and that chaos is translated to your magic. You need to blank your mind."

"Easier said than done. I'm a woman, in case you haven't noticed. We're emotional creatures by nature."

"And, yet you handled dying babies without devolving into a blubbering mess." Bas kicked the embers to ensure they wouldn't flare back up.

Go into nurse mode. That I could do. "Got it. Okay, I'm ready to try again."

Focusing on the need to ignite that log, I called fire to my hand. A flame flickered and flared in my palm. *Nope! Not this time*. The fire subsided, and I forced it into the round mold I used for ice.

Bas extended his arm again and held out the log. Keeping my gaze on the rough wood, I bounced the flames in my hand, then pulled my elbow back and tossed it at the target.

The fire exploded when it hit, and Sebastian dropped it to the ground. "Good job. Again."

Cracking my neck, I connected with the energy tingling in my chest while he picked up another log. The second his arm shot out, I conjured another fireball and threw it. Sweat broke out along my forehead, and I had trouble catching my breath.

Sebastian bent and picked up a charred log. "Again."

I did it three more times at his behest and had sweat dripping from my face by the time I was done. "I can't do it anymore. I'm sweaty and exhausted, and I need a hot shower."

"You go shower while I clean this up." The look he shot my way said he'd much rather join me in getting naked.

My body ignited like one of the logs and spread from head to toe, adding more sweat. I was a mess, and all I could think about was grabbing him and dragging him inside the house.

"Fiona," Bas called when I turned to enter the house. "Good work tonight. Your fire will be there when you need it."

I wanted to preen like I'd just won a scholarship for each of my kids. The more I got to know him, the more I saw who he truly was. There was more to him than a bad attitude.

"I couldn't have done it without you. And, thanks for sticking around. The house is open if you need anything."

I practically ran to the door before I did something stupid, like invite him to protect me from the right side of my mattress. I never expected to find someone else after I lost Tim. I was devastated when he died, but then I met Sebastian. He was not a nice guy. There was nothing soft and cuddly about him. In fact, he was the opposite of Tim, whom I loved dearly. Despite all that and my desire to focus on myself and create my new life, I fell for Sebastian.

CHAPTER 18

"What the....ah!" The scream was out the second my hand slipped, and I lost my balance. There was nothing to grab hold of to stop the fall. I glanced down, cursing when I hit the corner of the table a second later. Pain exploded through my hip as I continued to the floor.

I landed with a thump and threw my arms over my head, wincing when crystals fell on top of me. I gave myself a couple seconds after debris stopped falling and lifted my hand to glare at the short ladder. *What did I ever do to you?*

Right, it was my fault I fell off the thing. The moon was bright in the sky, and I was cleaning the skylight so it would charge my crystals. I'd read that it was necessary to do this periodically, so they were ready for you when you needed them, and I hadn't even touched the things since moving in.

I wondered why Grams put one in the attic where she wouldn't get to enjoy it much. It all made sense now. I'd spent the past two days reading as much as possible to prepare myself.

There was some uber-evil creature gunning for me, and I

had to be ready. I'd gone from being a registered nurse in a hospital to a magical Guardian of a Fae portal. I understood life and death battles. And, I once again found myself square in the middle of one. Except this one wasn't going to take my children's only surviving parent.

Rolling over, I pushed myself to my feet and dusted off my trousers. My left hip hurt like hell. No doubt I was going to sport a massive bruise tomorrow. At least I hadn't broken anything.

Bending to pick up the fallen crystals and herbs that had been on the table wasn't an easy task with my back seizing up. By the time I bent for the fifth time, it had loosened somewhat. Of course, that's when all hell broke loose.

The first thing I noticed felt like a slap to the center of my being, where my magic resided. That transformed into ants crawling under my skin. Disturbed, I rushed down the stairs and looked out the sliding glass door. It gave me a view of the garden and my property on the other side. It stretched further than I could see. When I saw nothing out of place, I ran to the kitchen and looked out the window.

I had a view of one section of my pond and the dirt road leading to my house. My property line was a couple feet beyond the other side of the lane. My gut told me something happened to my barrier, so I kept my gaze trained just beyond the trees opposite me where I was attacked by the ryme several days ago.

My heart was racing like a car in the Indy 500. If someone was coming for me, they'd come from this direction. *Grab a weapon, woman.* Right. I shouldn't go out there empty-handed. I didn't own any firearms. I didn't believe in them, so I grabbed the knife Sebastian gave me a while back.

With the sleeve of my sweatshirt, I wiped the sweat from my forehead before it dripped into my eyes. "C'mon, where are you? I know you're there." Yet, when I scanned the trees, I didn't see anything.

A high-pitched scream shattered the quiet of the night and broke the window above the sink. Without thinking, I ran out the door. The blood froze in my veins, and I tried to stop, but my body was moving so fast I had to windmill my arms to catch myself.

"Leave her alone," I yelled at the half a dozen creatures hauling Kairi from my pond. My many years on this earth had taught me that it was better to hide your fear and project an air of authority. That alone scared most people.

Based on the dark greenish-black aura surrounding the half-human, half-selkie, I knew they were, without a doubt, Dark Fae. The one at the front of the group lifted one corner of its mouth and flashed razor-sharp teeth at me.

Remembering Bas's tip about fire, I called flame to my hand. In my panic, I wasn't able to form a perfect ball like usual. I didn't care about the three-foot tower of flames and tossed it at the hybrid selkie. It was the only name I could come up with in the spur of the moment.

The first one dodged out of the way while my fire slammed into the two standing behind it. They flailed their arms, and fire fell off them to the ground. The pair at the back holding Kairi managed to keep hold of her despite the way she fought against them.

I lost sight of the one that stood in front of me because I looked at Kairi and the others. It growled at me and slammed into me. As we tumbled to the ground my head bounced off the grass like a ball.

Ignoring the dizziness, I lifted the hand holding the knife and wrapped that arm around the thing's neck. Its teeth raked across my shoulder, leaving behind a cut.

A choked cry left my mouth as I plunged the knife I held into the Dark Fae's side. With my luck, I wouldn't hit anything that might make it slow down. Stopping it would take a miracle. Keeping that thought in mind, I decided to give fate a bit of help and wiggled the blade around while it was inside its chest.

"Shit." I couldn't pull my weapon free, and when I heard footsteps heading my way, I had to give up and push the creature off me. Luck was actually on my side, and it stayed on the ground with brackish blood gushing from the wound. The ground sizzled, and smoke rose into the air where it hit my grass. *Talk about toxic.*

Kairi was on the ground and bleeding on the pond's edge while two of the selkies kicked her. The other two had finally put the fire out and were heading my way. I lost my weapon but still had my flames.

I held out my palm and called my fire. It burst from me in a massive column. I was too freakin' exhausted to control it any better—the ones I'd burned paused and recoiled. I hurried to Kairi's side and yanked one off her.

I forgot I was brandishing fire, and it engulfed the selkie instantly. I lost track of everything as I heard what sounded like nails on a chalkboard. I turned my head and nearly peed my pants.

There was a Grim Reaper fifteen feet away and heading toward Kairi and me. The recent arrival had a black cloak with a hood on. It was impossible to see anything except a black hole where the face should be, and the cloth reached the ground. The mermaid fought the selkie while I stood there gaping. Fear mixed with anger, and my fire morphed into lightning.

It rolled over my hands and sizzled up my arms. I had no idea how I managed that and knelt carefully, so I didn't lose it. "Kairi, get back in the pond as soon as you can. This new one looks terrifying."

"Ungh." Breaking my gaze away from the reaper, I shifted

focus to Kairi. The selkie had a chunk of her flesh dangling from his mouth, and the mermaid was fighting as best as she could.

I grabbed the selkie with both hands and zapped it with the voltage sliding over my flesh. The creature gurgled and started smoking. The air filled with a pungent odor of cooked roadkill.

"That was a mistake, witch." That threat came from the reaper, but I couldn't tell if it was male or female. *As if that matters. Kick its ass!*

Letting go of the selkie, I had to trust Kairi would get back in the water. The last selkie was coming at me, and the ones I'd burned a moment ago were lumbering my way.

I was surrounded by the most significant threat I'd ever faced right in front of me. I screamed as loud as possible, hoping Bas was somewhere close that he could hear, and unleashed the lightning. My breathing had already been fast. Now I was close to hyperventilating. It filled my head, blotting out my thoughts.

I trusted my instinct since it hadn't let me down yet and pushed the energy out of me, with most of the focus heading to the reaper. The night sky lit as if a spotlight was focused on my yard. When my lightning hit the creature, it sounded like a frozen egg roll hitting hot oil. All I could hear was the crackle. The sound blocked everything else. And, the smell wasn't as rancid as before but wasn't pleasant.

Like a galloping horse, my heart thundered in my chest, and I stalked the cloaked reaper when I noticed it diminishing in size. Was it using some spell to make it look bigger and scarier?

I passed the selkie-like creatures that were now withered husks. "I don't know how you broke through my protections, but you made a mistake." I poured more anger into my hands, and the lightning flared around me.

The reaper shuddered, then turned around and took off into the forest. *Take that bitch!* I stood there and tried to calm my energy. I had no idea if it would come back, but I needed to preserve as much as possible. I was no Energizer Bunny. I would eventually run out.

I wanted to be protected when that time came. I took several deep breaths and turned to go into the house. I needed to call Bas. By the time I made it to Kairi, the lightning had stopped traveling over my skin and shooting from my hands.

"Are you okay? Can I get you anything?" I scanned the mermaid's body and winced at the injuries she suffered.

"I'll be okay. I just need time to heal." Kairi lifted a lily pad from a deep gash, and I could see the skin was already knitting together.

"I'm going to call Sebastian then hunt that thing down. See if we can neutralize at least one threat. You wouldn't happen to know what it was? Or what the other creatures were?"

Kairi looked up at me and shook her head. "I think the robed being was an elf, and the others were sluagh. Although these were missing the shells that usually cover their bodies. It's why they looked like a creature out of water. Their skin is used to being protected. I have a feeling whoever was controlling them removed them to break through your protections."

"She's right. Whoever was just here was an elf. A female." My head snapped up when I heard Sebastian's voice. I watched as he hurried toward us. "I returned a few minutes ago and knew right away the protections have been breached. What was the light I saw in the sky?"

I held up my hands and turned them over. "Apparently, I can shoot lightning from my hands. Don't ask me how. It started as a fire out of control, but when they injured me and

MAGICAL NEW BEGINNINGS

I saw Kairi being beaten, I lost all control. We need to track that bitch."

Sebastian stared at me for several seconds. "Who are you? No one has ever had that kind of power."

I kinda growled and sighed at the same time and rolled my eyes at him. "That doesn't matter right now. I want to get her and make her pay." I started running the way she'd taken off ignoring the curses that exploded behind me. I ducked under a low hanging branch and paused when I came to a thicket of trees.

The path had been obvious, but the footsteps were now hidden in the ground cover. Bas paused next to me. Tilting my head back, I looked at him. "I lost her. Can you sense her?"

His head swiveled around before zeroing in on the right. "This way." He took the lead that time, and I followed. We traipsed through the forest for fifteen minutes, with me growing more anxious by the minute.

Finally, I couldn't stand it anymore and stopped then thrust my hands on my hips. "Have we lost her?" I continued scanning the area, hoping to catch sight of her.

"She can't leave this realm from here, so we just need to pick up on her trail. Do a tracking spell. That'll make this faster."

My eyes flew up to his. "I should have thought of that before I took off half-cocked. Okay." I calmed myself for a couple seconds then thought of the spells I'd memorized.

Once I had the word in mind, I focused my energy on finding her. "*Investigo*."

Energy burst from my chest in bright orange light and spread out through the forest. I kept her flowing black cloak at the front of my mind. Within seconds the light narrowed to a single path with the orange light settling on top of the ground.

"Oh my God, that worked!" I'd been managing more and more incantations lately but never believe they will work until they do.

"You sell yourself short. You're powerful and need to own that. It's time you start recognizing how much power you have. Not to say you don't still need to train and practice."

I beamed at him then started following the orange dirt path. "I didn't think anyone could get through the protections. What do I do now? I obviously need something stronger."

Bas held a branch out of my way while I walked under it. "There's more at play. When we get back, I want to search around the house. The protections weren't broken."

"Kairi mentioned something about the slaugh I fried giving their shells to help her cross to my land. Is that what you mean?"

Sebastian was graceful as he moved through the forest, and I could hardly look away as he walked. God, the man was fine. Why have I been putting off intimacy with him? "She likely used them to save herself from the damage crossing the barrier would inflict. But she wouldn't have been able to manage that without the shells."

The path grew faint a few minutes later. My heart had calmed when Bas showed up, but it was now back to beating like a timpani drum in my chest. I stopped when he held up his hand.

He pushed me behind a tree and pressed in behind me. All I felt behind me was his body heat. My cheek was scraped on tree bark as he leaned forward. It was hard to breathe, but I didn't want him to move.

There were so many emotions flowing through me now, and all I allowed myself to focus on was that I was safe with him guarding me. When he poked his head around the side of the tree, I followed suit.

In between two large pine trees was a pile of black clothing on the ground. The orange light stopped there. I scanned the area, searching for her. The back of my neck prickled, and my breaths were coming faster. Where the hell was she?

My gaze lifted to the treetops. In almost every suspense book I'd ever read, danger lurked above the victim. I saw a large white owl, but nothing else. "Do you see her?" My voice could hardly be considered a whisper.

Sebastian shook his head then took four steps away from me. A chilly wind instantly filled the space, and I was left shivering from the cold. I moved away from the tree and headed to the cloth.

Snatching one corner, I lifted it and cursed. "Dammit. I was focused on the cloak because it was all I could see. She isn't here. I can cast another spell, but I'd bet money she isn't on my property anymore, and I don't have anything else to really focus on. I don't know what she looked like."

Sebastian took the cloak from me. "It wouldn't do any good right now. We need to find out what she did to weaken your boundaries. There has to be a dampener somewhere close to the house where you spend most of your time."

"What is a dampener, and how would she get it on my property?"

"It can literally be anything. All she'd need is something hard and dense to contain the spell. A dampener burns through most objects."

I groaned as I stepped over a small boulder, partly from exasperation and partly from the aches that started to steal my attention. "So, it could be a rock like this or a brick or something?"

"Or a nut. But you're on the right track. And, it can be several smaller objects or one large one."

I replayed the areas closest to my house in my mind, but

it seemed useless. How would I know if rocks were carrying a dampener spell? "How did she manage to pull this off? No one should be able to get close enough."

"She likely manipulated someone that doesn't have malicious intent toward you. Otherwise, they would be repelled by your spell."

"Tunsall! That damn brownie had to have done it. She was shifty and nervous. Her eyes didn't stay in one place when I met her. And she was carrying nuts."

If that little brownie were in front of me right then, I would put her in a jar with a lead lid. Dammit. She put me and everyone else that lived at Pymm's Pondside in danger.

"I'd say it's safe to assume she made the brownie weaken your wards."

"When I see her again, I will make sure she's sorry for what she did."

Bas held up his hands. "Before you go off on a hunt for her, think about this. That elf could have kidnapped her family or a friend and is holding them hostage for her cooperation. I will say Tunsall didn't do this lightly. Otherwise, she never could have crossed the barrier."

I couldn't punish someone that was just as much one of the elf's victims. Dammit. My head started pounding. "Alright, I need to find her and ask her where she put the nuts. I can't sleep knowing there could be an attack at any minute."

And then I was finding that elf and taking care of her. I was done with being hunted and living in fear. This was going to end.

CHAPTER 19

"What are we going to do about this bitch?" Aislinn had her arms crossed over her chest, and her foot was tapping the ground.

Violet ran her hand through her hair. "How do we stop her from getting to anyone else? I mean, she got to Tunsall and kidnapped her father to force her to place the spelled nuts around the house."

I still couldn't believe the small brownie was the reason the elf could attack Kairi and me. Not that I blamed her. If my father had been kidnapped, I would likely do it as well. Tunsall was in a heap in the garden sobbing for her part in what happened.

I kicked the lead bowl that held the nuts. I wanted to toss them in the ocean, but Bas stopped me. He said they might come in handy with the elf, so I kept them. We theorized the lead would neutralize the magic, but no one was certain.

A loud wail echoed through the night. I glanced toward the garden with a heavy heart. "I haven't found anything to suggest we can provide more protection. But I think Tunsall's situation will serve as a lesson no one will forget.

Her dad still hasn't been returned, and one of her friends was injured badly. There's more than enough proof this elf will never follow up on her promises. When shit went sideways, she should have returned her father first thing. Now not many will be swayed to help her."

"You're right. She made no friends here, but we have no idea who she is, so she can hide in plain sight as she works another angle. We need to find her before she can launch another attack," Sebastian added.

Camille got up from the chair tossing the black cloak back on the bistro table. The older witch had been more than happy to come when I called. I had no idea if she could do anything to help, but I needed all the allies I could get. "None of the tracking spells I used on the clothing have worked. If I didn't know better, I would swear she never touched the thing."

Violet's forehead furrowed. "That makes no sense. Bas, Fiona, and Kairi all saw her in it. She was injured with the thing on. There should be more than enough to use to track her. How is that possible?"

Camille shook her head as she toyed with the amethyst charm hanging on a chain around her neck. "Who knows? She might have donned something like a wetsuit or perhaps cast a spell. While I'm not aware of an enchantment that would essentially cover someone in silicone, that doesn't mean she couldn't invent one."

Bas held up a hand. "We have to assume she's powerful enough to create one. Fiona threw enough magical lightning at her. She shouldn't have been able to move, yet she took off and evaded us."

I sighed, suddenly exhausted. "So, where does that leave us? Powerful or not, everyone has weaknesses. Hers is arrogance. And, I suspect I hurt this one's pride. She won't stop until she makes sure I know she's more powerful than me."

Aislinn's eyes went wide. "You're right. We can use that against her."

Violet inclined her head. "We'll set a trap for her. She won't even know she's walking into it. She assumes you're uneducated about the magical world."

"She isn't wrong about that." I hated being a liability. *You're not a burden. Bas stopped looking at you like that months ago.* Since Sebastian was my gauge for many things, I had to trust that the grudging respect I'd earned from him meant something.

And, regardless, it wasn't like I was going to leave my friends and the town in this bitch's evil hands. "The question is how we manage that and how we lure her into it. I would say I'll sit out on the cliffs until she comes for me, but that would be too obvious."

Violet snorted. "Ya think?"

"Shut up," I said with a chuckle. "Your idea is our best bet. Now we just need to come up with a plan that doesn't cost me my life."

"What is it she wants exactly? Your death?" Camille started pacing as she spoke. Her head was down, and her hands were on her hips like they were when she tried to come up with another way to explain something to me. I had spent the least amount of time with her but had become quite fond of her. She was like a surrogate grandmother to me.

I looked at Sebastian with my eyebrows lifted and my lips pursed. He lifted one shoulder. "She wants me gone, and she wants my family's grimoire. I bet she's behind the killings and attempts to shift allegiance of the portal."

"I'd say that's a safe assumption. Using you as bait isn't the best plan, though." Bas looked at me with an intense gaze that had me shuffling my feet and biting my lip. "She knows you're no lightweight. Violet might be right, and she's underestimating you, but I don't think she will fall into a trap if you are present. Or me, for that matter."

"I was thinking the same thing. But there's no way I'm going to endanger any of you guys, so what's the answer?"

Camille gave me a smile that warmed me and made me think of all those summer days I spent going for ice cream or down to the beach. "Just because I'm old, child, doesn't mean I can't conjure fire or hurricane-force winds if needed."

I laughed at that. "You can kick my ass from here to Sunday, but you guys are all I have here. Hell, you're it anywhere. Except, my kids, and I don't want them anywhere near this shit."

"What if we hide you. We can use the grimoire to lure her to the trap," Aislinn suggested.

"That could work. I can leave my book out on the table or something."

Bas shot me a look that said, *'Really? You think she'd buy you're that stupid?'* I averted my gaze and flushed while he added his two cents. "Using such an obvious ploy will not work. It has to be subtle, and she has to think it was her idea entirely."

I threw my hands up in the air. "How the heck am I supposed to pull that off? Place an ad in the local paper saying I am planning a trip to the city and my house and grimoire will be unattended?"

Violet grabbed my hands. "That could work. Well, not the ad or anything, but something along those lines. You and I can plan a day trip to the city. I'll talk about it at the shop with Mae. The way that old siren gossips, the entire town will know of our plans in no time."

Aislinn clapped her hands. "That's brilliant. I'll mention it at the bar to cover all bases."

"Now we know how to get the word out. How do we ensure she will come here?" There had to be more. I doubted having an empty house will be reason enough for her to come here.

Sebastian started pacing like Camille. Only his long stride ate up more room. "We need to get word to her that you have been seen using the grimoire. She might not know for certain you have found the tome. I doubt Filarion announced he lost the grimoire."

"I'll visit the store tomorrow when Mae usually comes by and mention something about using a spell to help heal Kairi. It'll kill several birds with one stone. It will let Mae know I have the book and am using it and about the attack that injured Kairi."

"And, I'll use that as a bridge to talking about our trip to the city. Like maybe you ruined all of your good towels and need to get more," Violet added.

Camille stopped pacing and faced them. "We know the how. Now we need to discuss when. We need time to come up with a spell that will hide you. That'll take both of us." She'd turned to address Sebastian then. "She's hybrid, and shielding her magic will require us both."

"We will also need to conceal her presence completely. If she thinks she can grab the book, she will use an enchantment to make sure no one is home before she enters. A few days should be enough time to work that out," Bas said.

My gaze shifted to the pond where Kairi was lounging on the shore. She'd been there since the night before when she was injured. Her injuries required more time before she could spend more time underwater. "Will she be healed by then? I want to make sure Kairi is healed enough that she can hide in one of her caves."

"If we plan this for four days from now, that should be plenty of time for us to prepare and Kairi to heal," Camille replied, answering my questions.

"You'll be here with me, right?" I directed my question at Sebastian, who shook his head in response.

"I won't be in the house with you, no. It'll take too much effort to hide you and myself. I don't want to be that drained when we face her."

My heart started pounding in my chest, and I couldn't quite catch my breath. "What? I can't face her alone. She'll kill me."

Sebastian crossed to me and grabbed me by the shoulders. "You will not have to fight her by yourself. I will be far enough she won't sense me when she does a scan, but close enough that I can get here in no time. I won't let anything happen to you."

"We will be here, too," Violet added as she pointed from herself to Aislinn, who was nodding in agreement.

I swallowed and tried to shove my fear aside. "Okay. Will the weapon you gave me be useful against her? Something that can stall her until you get here?" My body shook with remembered fear at what I had faced from the slaugh and the evil elf last night. I couldn't beat her, especially if she brings more with her. "I need to be able to fight off several creatures at once. I doubt she will come alone this time either. And, something tells me she will come with more than half a dozen."

Sebastian squeezed my shoulders before letting go and cupping one of my cheeks. "I think she will show up alone. The knife I gave you will inflict harm, but you will need magic, as well, to take her out. Like you said, her weakness is pride. She'll see you and Violet leaving for the city and charge in here without backup. After all, she wasn't after Kairi."

I thought of the spell to transfer the portal to someone new, and a gasp escaped me. "What if we're wrong? What if she is after her? Think about it. She needs the blood of Fae here on earth. How many mermaids are there here?"

Bas's eyes widened, and I heard Violet curse and Aislinn gasp. Camille merely shook her head. "You're right. We have to plan for either eventuality. The lure should remain the same. If Kairi is her target, she will be more likely to come if you aren't home. As for the rest, I will be with the others and help battle any creatures that might accompany her."

"Okay, good. We need to talk to Kairi and let her know she might be in danger." I turned and headed to the mermaid without waiting for them to respond. "Kairi. How are you feeling?"

The princess glanced up at me with a smile. "Much better than last night. I will be able to return to the water by tomorrow."

I crouched down, so I was close to her level. "That's great news. We have a plan to entice the elf to come here, so we can take her out. That will put you in danger in the process. We aren't sure if she was after you or me or my grimoire. We can move you if you don't want to be here."

Kairi lost some of her coloring as the blood drained from her face. She looked from me to the others with a quivering lower lip. "No. I'm staying. If she was after me, she wouldn't come here if she doesn't sense me. I'll be safe under the water. Even if they have a merman, he won't be able to reach me in my domain. This water answers my command."

I held her turquoise gaze. "Promise me you won't come out and try to help. That would put you in more danger."

Tears pooled in her eyes. "If she is after me, I can't allow you to be hurt because of me, but I will stay under the water. I don't have the skill you do. If I can help from beneath the surface, I will."

I understood her desire to help if possible. It was difficult to stand by while those you loved faced the danger for you. I appreciated that she agreed to remain hidden. It would make facing this bitch so much easier.

Violet rubbed her hands together. "We have a plan. We need to add that disguising Aislinn as Fiona, so she sees her and I drive off. That'll really sell the scenario."

"We can use a twin spell to alter my appearance. I just wish it could give me your power, as well." Aislinn sounded excited about the prospect of becoming my clone. It made me feel good.

I stood up and found myself standing close to Sebastian. His proximity was nice. I hadn't thought about men or intimacy after losing Tim. It wasn't until meeting Bas that my body came to life.

Being this close to him now brought all those dormant desires to the surface. If I ignored how badly I wanted to press my lips to his, it would go away. I just needed to keep telling myself this. *Yeah, right. He's everything you've ever wanted.*

He made it impossible to ignore my growing feelings when he cupped my cheek. "I don't like you being in danger."

"We don't have a choice. I don't want to live in fear forever." I forgot my friends were there as I leaned into him. He was solid muscle. Between that and the power vibrating beneath his skin, my fear dissolved. I'd be safe as long as he was with me.

Don't forget you're perfectly capable of fighting your own battles. That's right—girl power. One of the hardest lessons I learned in life was being independent and capable. Ever since I had my kids, I'd been trying to teach my daughters that they didn't need a man to take care of them. They needed to be capable of doing it themselves, even if they eventually became stay-at-home moms.

They didn't have to be alone but going into a marriage or relationship because you needed someone to provide were not reasons that would sustain the connection. You should be with someone out of love.

"Just don't do anything stupid. Promise you'll text me the second she shows up," Bas insisted.

I nodded and stood on my tiptoes, then closed the distance between our mouths. His warm lips moved sensually over mine. Electricity zinged from him to me where our flesh touched. It aroused every nerve ending as it traveled through my body.

I moaned when his tongue slipped into my mouth. My hands traced a path up his chest and settled on his shoulders, and I fought the urge to climb him like a tree. His arms wound around my back and pulled me, so our bodies were flush against each other. His mouth devoured mine like he was starving, and I was his last meal.

Breaking the kiss, I had to put distance between us. We had spells to practice, and I needed to keep my head on straight. The last thing I needed right now was to become obsessed with Sebastian.

"I knew it," Aislinn crowed triumphantly while Violet shushed her.

"Stop, you're embarrassing her. Let her get her groove back without us interfering," Violet admonished.

Bas smiled down at me before he kissed my lips lightly and moved away from me. "Time to get to work. There's an evil elf we have to deal with."

CHAPTER 20

I couldn't stop my hands from shaking. I was in the attic of the house, waiting for the evil elf to appear. I wasn't positive this plan was going to work. The longer it took for her to show up after Violet and Aislinn left, the more I was convinced this wasn't going to work.

Of course, they'd only been gone ten minutes. Usually, I had the patience to share. Right now, I could barely keep from running out the door and hunting through the forest. Speaking of, my gaze shifted to the other side of the property to scan the tree line on the other side of the dirt road.

We decided to hide in the attic because of the magic imbued in the wood all around me. It enhanced the enchantment Sebastian and Camille cast on me. There was only one problem with me being in here. There were only two windows in the place, and neither one gave a good view of the property around me.

The skylight in the ceiling provided a view of the sky, but not the property. The window at the far end of the room looked over the backyard. My land extended ten feet beyond the house, but I'd never had anything come at me from that direction, so I used a window spell to create a way to see through the house walls.

"Do you think she will come?"

I glanced down at Tunsall, who was in the attic with me. She used her own magic to hide her presence as she waited with me. She'd insisted on being here so she could remove the nuts that allowed the elf to cross onto my property.

We kept the nuts in place because we didn't want to let her know we knew how she managed to breach my protections. The plan was for Tunsall to race around the house and carry the nuts beyond my property line when the elf crossed the border.

"Honestly, I'm not sure. Part of me says there's no way she would miss this opportunity to get whatever she's after. Unless, of course, she's after me. Then she won't show up because she will be hunting Violet and Aislinn. Maybe I should call them."

Tunsall scurried over and jumped onto the table that was charging my herbs and crystals. I was leaning against the wall gazing out at the pond. The brownie wrung her hands. "I don't know if that's a good idea. I don't want anyone else to get hurt because of me."

I placed one finger on her shoulder. "None of this is your fault. You were trying to save your dad. I get that. It's that evil bitch who is to blame. And, I promise you, if there is anything I can do to find your dad, I will."

Her chin quivered, and tears shimmered in her eyes. "I don't deserve your kindness. I'm sorry I brought her onto your property."

I jostled her slightly with my finger. "Don't ever say that. You were placed in an impossible situation…shit." My voice dropped to a whisper at the same time I fell to the floor.

"What?" Tunsall blurted before I snatched her off the table.

I held her in front of my face and pointed out the magical window I'd created. Her eyes went wide, and her entire body started shaking. I put her down and removed my cell phone from my back pocket.

After firing a group text to Bas, Aislinn, Camille, and Violet, I crawled across the attic to check the forest near the dirt road. There was nothing visible there which was a damn good thing because she was alone as she approached from the same direction she had days ago.

"Can she fly?" I swear the woman was floating across the ground. Her movements were smooth, and her feet weren't touching the ground.

"Not that I know of," Tunsall replied in a whisper.

I watched as she paused thirty feet from the house and hid behind a big pine tree. I picked up Tunsall and tiptoed down the stairs carefully to avoid every creaky spot on my way.

I'd already closed the curtains so no one would see me walking around the house. Putting Tunsall down, I remained on my knees by her side and mouthed, 'Be careful' to my small friend. She nodded her head and took off toward the mudroom.

My heart was hammering in my chest hard enough I swore it was going to be bruised by the end of the night. My skin was cold, and my breaths were coming faster. *Time to fake it 'til you make it.*

Energy buzzed beneath my skin, and it was challenging to keep from running out the door. I needed to stay put and see what her plans were. She lifted her hands and bent this finger then that and turned her palm over. It looked like sign language. She had to be signaling someone.

My heart stopped for a second as I ran to the mudroom. "Get the nuts and get them off the property," I hissed low at

Tunsall, who disappeared through a crack we left in the door.

I allowed my energy to flood me as I turned back to the kitchen and went back to the window. She was using the trees to hide behind as she made her way to the pond. She was after Kairi.

With my fingers crackling, I flung the door open and stepped outside. "Fancy meeting you here." I made sure my voice was loud enough to carry to the woman prowling around my property.

I heard a scream behind me and chanced a look backward. There were some slaugh trying to cross onto my property, but they couldn't get through the protections. Tunsall jumped out from between two creatures and ran back toward my house. She was going to be okay.

"How?" The evil elf shouted.

A smile spread across my mouth, and I pushed some of the energy down my arms. My fingertips were crackling with lightning flowing between them. "You must own a hundred of those ugly black cloaks. It's not needed. You can drop the disguise. I know you're a vile bitch."

The elf started cackling as she stalked toward me. I was so focused on where she was walking that it took me several seconds to realize she threw some kind of spell to the pond. When the water bubbled and foamed, I prayed Kairi was safe.

Sounds came at me from different directions. There were pounding footsteps in the direction of Sebastian's house and tires heading down my driveway. My heart slowed slightly, knowing my friends were heading my way.

I spread my fingers, then flung my hands up while channeling my anger. I pushed it out of my body and into my magic. A loud boom exploded out of me the second my power left me.

The elf did something similar, except there was no sound

when she tossed something that sparked at me. Her power hit me in the shoulder. "Shit." That hurt like a bitch. But that wasn't all. Under the agony eating through my bloodstream, there was more fuel in my fire.

A laugh bubbled out of me when my electricity slammed into her, and she flew backward. The way she rolled across the ground was satisfying. Sebastian barreled through the trees and stopped on the other side of the pond.

His eyes met mine before he moved up and down my body. Less than a second later, he was chanting something and gesturing behind the elf. "I buried some amplifiers of my own for a barrier spell. She won't be able to get away from us now."

The elf got to her feet and screeched so loud it hurt my ears. Pain lanced my middle, and I doubled over. The slaugh had managed to breach the protections and were running to my friends. Camille was in the car with Violet and Aislinn.

Bas was already running to help with the dozen creatures heading my way. I didn't dare turn away from the elf. She was prowling toward me. Her hood had fallen off her head, and I got my first glimpse of her face.

She was gorgeous, like supermodel pretty. She had long, straight black hair that was shiny in the moonlight. Her green eyes were the most unique color I'd ever seen, but they were lifeless. It took all the appeal from her flawless skin and her perfect cheekbones.

"*Malleus*," I called out with a thrust in her direction. This spell had a mixture of fear and anger behind it.

I saw when it hit her side. She snarled, turning her full lips into a mask of rage. I was too far to hear what she said, but I felt the impact in my stomach. It felt as if she cut it open. My hands went to the area and clutched it tightly.

I couldn't even conjure any relief when I didn't encounter any blood. I had to breathe through the pain and send another spell to her. Despite how much the blows hurt, I didn't feel depleted at all. I just needed to concentrate enough to injure her back.

I took a deep breath. "*Secare.*" I wanted my spell to cut through her vocal cords. Something had to stop the bitch from winning.

She choked, and her hand flew to her throat. Unfortunately, that did nothing to stop her from sending another spell my way. This time it hit me in my left leg. I heard a crack and fell to the ground. Did she just break my femur?

I landed on my side with a face full of dirt. Without thinking, my hands were in front of me, and I shouted, "*praemium.*" Blowing her up was a stretch, but I needed to stop her. When she bent over and blood trickled from the corner of her mouth, I wanted to cheer.

I managed to lever myself onto my knees and face her, only to be knocked down again. My head swam with the world around me, and I couldn't breathe. She tossed another enchantment at me that added to the agony.

I heard my friends fighting behind me for all they're worth. I needed that lightning back. It sent her running the last time I fought her. My head hurt too bad to call up enough energy, so I sent another spell to her instead. "*Stupefaciunt.*"

I was lying on the ground while, in comparison, she held her torso and had a tiny trickle of blood out the side of her mouth. The evil bitch couldn't win. With a snarl, I pooled all of my energy in my core and held it there while I recalled every injustice I've ever witnessed.

When my chest felt like it was going to explode, I rolled over, so I was sitting and pointed both hands at her. One more deep breath, and I released all the power I'd been holding. It mushroomed out of me like a nuclear bomb and headed directly for the elf.

It hit the beautiful but evil creature in the stomach, and she went up in flames. The sounds she made were awful. I sat there watching her for several seconds until water shot out of the pond and in her direction.

Reacting without thinking, I cried out, *"Obice."* I intended to create a barrier the water couldn't go through. I didn't know how big it needed to be, and about half of the water continued on its course and drenched the woman.

I was bracing myself on my hands, and I watched as the evil bitch glared at me before she disappeared. Right before she vanished from sight, I got a glimpse of her burned facial features. She was no longer supermodel pretty.

Tunsall ran to my side a second later. "Are you okay?"

I nodded. "I'm okay. I think my leg is broken." I turned around and saw Sebastian finishing off the last slaugh. Camille had a cut on one cheek, and Violet had a black eye, while Aislinn had a cut on her lip.

After Bas smashed the creature's skull in and it dropped like a stone, he looked up at me. His chest was heaving, and his face was covered in blood and dirt. He'd never looked better.

With a snarl on his face, he charged toward me. "I thought I was going to lose you. You were fighting the Fae Queen. For fucks sake, I can't believe that bitch is after you."

I was fighting a queen! What the hell? "She was going for Kairi first."

He picked me up in his arms. "That's not surprising. She always was a jealous bitch. She's not going to stop. You're in more danger now than ever before. Especially since she saw me rush to your side. That'll set her off for sure."

My heart twisted in my chest. "You've been with her before." As if that was what mattered most. I couldn't help but compare myself to her. *Nope. You're so much better than that evil bitch*. It was true. I noticed it earlier. Her darkness diminished any positive attribute she'd ever had.

"We need to regroup and figure out how we can handle her. I'm not sure we will be able to beat her. She's one of the most powerful Fae in existence, but we have some time. You injured her badly. She will need to lick her wounds for weeks." The pride shining in his gaze erased any insecurity that had surfaced.

"Sounds like I'm taking the fight to her then. I don't accept that I won't be able to beat her at her own game. If she is out of commission the next couple of months, we need to find her now."

"You're astounding," Sebastian exclaimed.

Yes. I was. No one messed with me or mine and got away with it. But first, I needed some coffee and a nap. Then I would tackle this again. My protections had been breached, there was a queen after me, and she was killing Fae in my town. Talk about trial by fire.

What I couldn't quell was the sliver of doubt creeping through the recesses of my mind. This Fae was too powerful for me. She had millennia of experience against my mere weeks. There was no comparison. Fuckity, fuck, fuck!

DOWNLOAD the second book in the Midlife Magic series, Mind Over Magical Matters HERE! Then turn the page for a preview of chapter one in Mind Over Magical Matters.

EXCERPT FROM MIND OVER MAGICAL MATTERS BOOK # 2

"This isn't working. I'm still like that kid in Harry Potter that keeps blowing everything up." I sounded like a whiny teenager, too, rather than a forty-five-year-old hybrid witch.

I couldn't help it. I was failing at everything. I was anxious and on edge while we waited for the other shoe to drop. A few months ago, I faced the powerful Fae Queen and managed to injure her and send her fleeing when she tried to kill me. No one knows how I pulled that off, but we all agreed she would be back seeking revenge for what I did to her.

"You will get the hang of it," Camille reassured me.

My witch mentor had suggested that I try my hand at potions so I could open a booth at S&S, the magical flea market our town held in the park in the town square. I didn't need the money, thanks to my Grams, but I needed the distraction, and all of my friends agreed it was the best way for me to get to know the supes in town.

For me, it was a toss-up between developing relationships with others like me and finding a way to settle my nerves.

Always being on edge was making me jumpy and my magic even more unreliable than usual. I survived on coffee, which might be partly responsible for my jitters, but caffeine overload could only explain so much.

Being addicted to the elixir of the gods for three decades or so meant my body was immune to a large degree.

"I'm not so sure about that. I spent a life as a norm without an ounce of magic. Maybe I lost my connection to my power." I had no idea how any of this worked. I was learning, but my knowledge was that of a five-year-old when it came to anything supernatural.

Camille shook her hand and dumped the sludge out of my cauldron into the trashcan she'd poured salt into before we began. The substance would neutralize any lingering power. It would also keep me safe when I cast my circle of power. Who knew it was so utilitarian?

Camille gestured to the hefty tome sitting open on the long wooden worktable. "That's not possible. I sense something else is at work here; I just can't put my finger on it. Grab your family, grimoire."

That perked my ears. This was the first time Camille mentioned anything of the sort. I wondered what I was missing. Likely a whole lot, given that I had no idea what normal was. "What do you mean? Why haven't you said something before?"

"I wasn't sure until we got into more detailed work like this. I haven't come across anyone quite like you, so I dismissed my concerns at first. Let's see if there's anything to it."

I set the book in front of us and flipped it open. "I've only looked through this thing a couple of times. What am I searching for?"

"Anything Isidora would have written about you or your birth."

"I've never come across anything about me personally. I've only seen spells and potions. I wish the book would just show me what I'm looking for." My fingers tingled and the wind whipped through the room, blowing my hair around my face. The pages fluttered in the book then stopped about three-quarters through.

Eyes wide, I gaped at the grimoire then at Camille. "What's this?" Camille picked up an envelope and held it between her thumb and forefinger.

"I've never seen it before." I took it from her and noticed the way my hand was shaking. Taking a deep breath, I opened the flap and took out a handwritten letter.

"It's addressed to me." I checked the envelop and realized I'd missed my name on the outside.

"I bet it's from Isidora. What does it say?" Camille was right. The signature at the bottom was from my Grams. My eyes returned to the top of the page, and I hesitated in reading it. I suddenly wished Sebastian was there with me. This was one of those moments I knew would change my life —kind of like when I boarded the plane to England to attend my Grams's funeral.

Bas, my sort-of boyfriend, barely left my side for weeks. He'd refused to share my bed with me and had taken up residence on my sofa. He left when Camille told him we would be making potions. I assumed that he returned to his home in the nearby woods, but I had no idea. I could call him but decided against it.

Instead, I typed in a message to Violet and Aislinn, my two best friends. My girls should be here with me. "Violet and Aislinn will be here soon. Let's see what Grams had to say."

Camille nodded her head but said nothing. "My dearest, Fiona. If you're reading this, that means I have passed on from this life." I read aloud, but my voice drifted off as I continued in silence. My heart raced when I read her apology for keeping my heritage from me for so long.

"What's a *nicotisa*?"

Camille's composure slipped, and her jaw dropped open. "Why are you asking? What does it say?"

"It says she and my mother bound my power shortly after I was born because they realized I was a *nicotisa*. That's why my mom moved away from the area, so it would be easier to hide me."

"That explains why she and your father left so abruptly. I never understood why they moved halfway across the world. Your father's career never meant that much to him before." Camille was tapping the table with a finger while she talked. I placed my hand over hers.

"Hellooo," Aislinn called out from downstairs in a singsong.

"We're up here," I called out.

"Okay, so what was so important you had me close the shop early for lunch?" Violet's voice echoed up the stairs before they entered the room.

I quickly explained what they'd missed then continued reading. "It's important that you call upon my spirit so I can assist you in understanding your transition." A little late for that, Grams.

"How does she propose you do that?" Camille leaned over and scanned the page and seemed to answer her question as she nodded. "She's brilliant. Even dead, she's breaking the rules and pushing limits."

I turned my head to glance at my mentor. "What do you mean?"

"Isidora had a knack for doing the impossible, even if it went against traditional convention," Camille explained.

Aislinn crossed the room and read from the other side of me. "And, she didn't know what the word impossible meant.

She believed there was always a way. You just needed to consider a problem or spell from all angles."

Violet held up one finger. "Don't forget the most important part...you have to think outside the box."

Camille turned and started grabbing jars from one of the bookshelves. "I have no idea how she accomplished this, but she details here how we need to brew a potion of eyebright, cinnamon, mugwort, African violet, and Arabic gum, among other ingredients."

Most of the items on the list were familiar, but I never in a million years would have considered putting them together like this. "Witches use eye of newt and the spleen of eels? What happens with the potion? Because this combination sounds awful."

Violet laughed. "I wouldn't want to be you, that's for sure."

"Wait. What do you mean? Why wouldn't you want to be me?" My words came out so fast that I wasn't sure anyone could understand me.

Aislinn clapped my shoulder. "Because you get to drink this once you finish."

My head was shaking side to side before I replied. "Nope. I'll pass."

Camille pegged me with a stern look. "I have no idea what Isidora had to do to tether her soul to this plane, but I can tell you it required a sacrifice to keep from crossing the veil to the other side. I won't let that be for nothing."

I swallowed the lump in my throat. "No. You're right. Let's get to cooking."

"This is all you," Violet exclaimed as she helped grab ingredients and placed them on the table.

"I can't. I'll blow it up. It's what I've been doing for hours today." I looked at Camille, who had the gall to chuckle.

"You have to do this on your own," Camille told me.

"Remember, patience and careful measurements. Establishing the right balance is the most important aspect when brewing."

Aislinn read off the ingredients, and Camille or Violet handed the correct jar to me, and I poured or scooped the requisite amount and dumped it into the cauldron. Next, I added the fire necessary to heat the elements and blend them while stirring counterclockwise.

The liquid bubbled and boiled. I barely held the bile back as I glanced into the pot and saw a dark green formula with chunks floating along the surface. My hand moved the wooden spoon while I tried not to breathe through my nose. It smelled worse than it looked.

I had no idea how I was going to get this crap down. I remembered not wanting to eat Brussel sprouts when I was a kid. Now I liked them. Somehow, I didn't think this was going to be one of those acquired tastes.

"How will I know when it's ready?"

Camille looked over the potion my Grams had left me. "When it turns pink."

"I must have done something wrong. I doubt this murky mixture is changing…" My words trailed away when the chunky pieces melted into the liquid, and it started changing with every swirl of my spoon.

"Damn, I love magic," I exclaimed and scooped a spoonful of what looked closer to a strawberry margarita than anything magical if you ignored the sparks shooting off the top.

"It comes in handy," Violet agreed.

I brought the spoon to my lips and had to breathe through my mouth when the putrid odor hit me. It might look tasty now, but it smelled like crap. Before my mind could psych me out, I poured a large serving down my throat.

My throat instantly closed off, and I couldn't get any oxygen into my lungs. Next, it flooded my esophagus and gushed into my gut like a torrent. Fire exploded and encompassed me from head to toe. At the same time, I noticed the stuff tasted like an earthworm on the side of the road, rotting in the sun.

After several agonizing minutes, I shook my head and saw Violet and Aislinn hovering close to me. "I'm okay." It came out as more of a croak than anything else. I reached for a glass of water, but Camille snatched it away from me with a shake of her head.

"You can't drink anything. You never know how other substances will interfere with a potion."

I grimaced. "Why can't this taste better?"

"All magic requires a price. Potions hurt and make you sick." I blinked and looked at Camille. Couldn't she have mentioned that sooner? How the hell did she expect me to sell shit to people without knowing this? I'd have customers constantly complaining and wanting their money back.

"It's time to recite the spell." Aislinn's voice brought me out of my ruminations.

"Right." I focused on the letter and my grandmother's words when I noticed that I was glowing blue. At least you know you did the potion right.

"Let my voice be heard on the other side,

And reach the one tethered to my side.

Ignore the bounds of physics and give form to the formless

By the laws of our ancient craft, so mote it be."

The wind kicked up and blew out the candles. Outside, thunder cracked, and the clouds opened up. Rain pelted the window as streams of blue energy left my fingers to form a cyclone on the other side of the attic.

I shielded my eyes from the worst of the maelstrom and

watched through the cover created by my arms. The light coalesced into the form of a person. When the wind died down, I lowered my hands and saw a figure I never thought I'd see again.

"Grams!" I rushed to her side and threw my arms around her. They traveled right through her body, leaving me trembling from the cold.

"It's about time you called to me, child. What took you so long?"

I thrust my hands on my hips and narrowed my eyes. "Sorry, but I was blindsided by the whole witch-Fae hybrid thing. Then I was attacked and almost killed by the Fae Queen. And before that, I had to find the portal then learn how to keep Fae from crossing to earth. A little heads up would have been nice!"

I was beyond glad to have her back and hadn't realized until that moment how angry I was for being kept in the dark. That took precedence.

Aislinn cleared her throat. "Don't forget that you had to get your grimoire back from Filarion before any of that."

"That little weasel stole my grimoire?" Grams turned red around the edges. She'd been glowing light blue and transparent, but when she growled in anger, she changed. Her form was solidified somewhat and had a red tinge around the edges.

"I wouldn't call him little, but he is a weasel." I lifted one shoulder. Filarion was a low-life thief. A good-looking one, but still an opportunist at heart.

"All that matters now is you managed the spell, and I'm here with you. Camille, good to see you. I need you and Aislinn and Violet to help cast a spell to dissipate Fiona's energy signature."

Camille leveled a look at Grams that said she was upset. I wondered if it was because it made her mad that Grams hadn't told her who or what I was. Or if it was something else. "I've told you before, Isidora. I'm not an idiot, regardless of what you might think. I was planning on tackling the topic after I taught your granddaughter to make potions. I'd bet that's why the Fae Queen targeted her. She'd like to steal her power along with the portal. But I want to know how you managed to come back without crossing over."

"Yeah, she's all about being the most powerful being alive. Imagine how your fight would have gone and what she would be like if she had an Energizer battery inside," Aislinn pointed out.

"I have no idea what you just said. Please explain this to me. And how I can keep my friends safe. Attacks have happened ever since you guys started hanging out with me and the Fae came to live at Pymm's Pondside with me. I don't want to be the reason anyone is hurt." I had enough guilt riding me at the moment.

"That's nonsense. You're not responsible for that foul being's power-hungry ways. What is important to understand is that right now, you are like a nuclear reactor. You give off a signal that is impossible for supernaturals to miss or resist." My Grams floated around the room as she spoke. That was going to take some getting used to, but I had her back!

"This is because I'm a *nicotisa*, right? What exactly does that mean?"

"And, how did you find out? She moved away when she was five years old? And, don't think I forgot about wanting to know how you are here with us now." There was a biting edge to Camille's tone of voice. It was clear she didn't get along all that well with my grandmother. There was a story there. I didn't have the mental faculties to get into it at the moment.

Grams glared at Camille then turned a smile on me. "We

knew you were different the second you were born. It started when you were born with an energy that helped soothe your mother. And, I knew for certain when you summoned your bottle one day when I was watching you while your mother operated her booth at S&S. And, to answer your question. I wasn't certain I would make this work, but I bound my spirit to Fiona. I wasn't sure it would work. I couldn't find anything about casting a spell while astral projecting. I had to cast a spell on my soul, not my body."

The thought of having my grandmother's body tied to me turned my stomach, but that registered behind the rest of what she said.

"Okay." I wish I could summon things now.

I was in desperate need of a cup of high-octane bean juice if I was going to get through this conversation. Or maybe a shot or ten of tequila. My head was already starting to pound, warning me I needed caffeine. My ability to focus and engage in conversation went downhill fast if I ignored it.

Violet smacked my arm. "You don't understand. This is huge. We don't come into our powers until our twenties. Otherwise, it would be impossible to hide our existence. Can you imagine your kids calling ice cream or toys to them as you walked through stores?"

Grams nodded. "That wasn't due to your *nicotisa* distinction, though. That gives you the ability to cast magic on your own without needing to call on the elements, and your Fae side amplified that. When you were three, I cast a spell on you that diluted your power. Your parents felt you got too much attention from the Fae and decided to move away shortly before your sixth birthday."

That sounded ominous. And fit with what had been happening since I returned to Pymm's Pondside a few months ago. Honestly, my head was swimming, and I had a hard time comprehending everything. The last few months had prepared me for the insane. The mythical was real, and I was part of that world. Otherwise, I'd have checked myself into the loony bin.

"Let's dissipate her signature," Camille interjected as if she read my mind. Violet, Aislinn, and Camille gathered around me. Camille cast a circle of salt, enclosing all of us, then they muttered, "*Sors.*"

Share? I was learning Latin thanks to my new witchy side, but their choice of spell made no sense. "Why not *dissipo* or *dispergo*?"

"Because we are sharing your signature." I gaped at Aislinn's announcement.

Grams sighed and floated in front of me. "That's only the first step. I can see you've already cast protection spells over you and Pymm's Pondside. Those wards will now be far more effective."

"Didn't you hear me? I don't want to put them in any more danger!" I didn't mean to snap at Grams, but I refused.

Grams put her hands on her hips in that way she always did and pinned me with a glare. It was a look that took me back decades and reminded me of what it felt like to be punished by her.

I wanted to squirm under my grandmother's attention. "You aren't placing them in any more danger. I just hope we aren't shutting the barn door after the horse got out. The queen already has you in her targets, but this will stop anyone else from homing in on you. And, you have no choice but to accept their help. Your beacon gets brighter and easier to follow the more you develop your power."

Grams floated over to the window and looked outside before turning back to the group. "We need to get to work. You need more practice with potions and adding Fae runes to them."

"Coffee first, then we can get back to work." I headed for

the door, trusting that I wouldn't lose my Grams again. There was no way I could continue without a boost. And some food.

DOWNLOAD the next book in the Midlife Witchery series, Mind Over Magical Matters HERE! Then turn the page for another preview. Then turn the page for a preview of the first chapter in MAGICAL MAKEOVER, book one in the Mystical Midlife in Maine books.

EXCERPT FROM MAGICAL MAKEOVER BOOK #1 MYSTICAL MIDLIFE IN MAINE

"What do you mean that was an irritated ghost?" I gaped at my patient as she lay on her hospital bed and shrugged her shoulders. Surreptitiously, I checked to make sure I hadn't peed myself a little. Ever since I had my daughter, my bladder control went out the window with sleep.

How was this my life now? I'd gone from being charge nurse at a respected hospital in the triangle in North Carolina, married to one of the country's best cardiothoracic surgeons to divorced and living back home with my mother and grandmother.

Hattie Silva, my patient and current employer stared at me with a furrowed brow. She was a ninety-year-old woman suffering from cancer of the intestines and required full-time care. After being fired from the hospital, my ex-husband ran me out of North Carolina and had managed to ruin my reputation, leaving me no options for work outside of in-home nursing with a hospice organization.

"I mean precisely what I said. Evanora isn't happy about you ignoring her. She's trying to get your attention. I struggle to hear her most days. I'm at the end of my life and running out of time." Hattie looked frail when she spoke like that.

She was older and suffering far more than was pleasant. It was difficult to watch her in so much pain, but when she talked like this it was easy to forget all of that and simply see her as crazy. I thought her doctors needed to add dementia to her diagnoses.

I reached up and grabbed the necklace Fiona had sent to me a few weeks ago. My best friend had moved to England after her grandmother had died and started a new life without me. At first, I kept busy with the kids and Miles, but when my ex informed me that he was leaving me for another woman and proceeded to tear my life apart like a wrecking ball, I missed Fiona more than ever.

We met in college and hit it off right away. We'd been in each others' weddings, got jobs at the same hospitals and did everything together. I was there when her twins were born because her husband Tim had gotten stuck in traffic. And she was there for me through both of mine. Miles had elected to continue surgeries both times saying it was too complicated for him to hand off.

My heart skipped a beat when the bluish image of a woman wearing a bonnet with a tall brim and a floor length dress that was cinched around the waist with big, poofy sleeves appeared in the spot where the remote control had fallen. Startled, I dropped the necklace and reached my hand toward the ghost. The image disappeared and I shivered with the chill in the air.

Great, now she was infecting me with her crazy. Ignoring what I thought I saw, I set the glass of water on the tray beside the bed and raised the head of her bed more. "There's no such thing as ghosts. Let's get you some lunch. I made some chicken soup today."

Hattie was so thin I could see her bones under her flesh. She felt very breakable when I shifted her body's position. She started coughing when she slumped forward to make it easier for me to arrange her support. As gently as possible, I laid her on the pillows and held the cup in front of her mouth then adjusted the oxygen flowing through her nasal cannulas.

After several seconds, she took a sip then sighed. "How is it you have an item of power, but you are ignorant as the day is long?"

This was a familiar argument. She would say something about me having some powerful object and being ignorant of everything important around me. "I like you too, Hattie. You ready for lunch?" At her nod, I left to get the food. The house was massive and most of the time I didn't notice the echo throughout the place, but I was jumpy after that conversation about spirits.

Rumors from my childhood popped into my head. Maybe they had been right after all. It would make sense for her to believe in ghosts if she really was a powerful witch. Although, I could see only brief glimpses of the power she must have once held. Whether or not that was true didn't matter.

She was ill and susceptible to being taken advantage of. I hadn't been hired to consider anything other than her health, but I would never sit by and allow someone to take her for a ride. Hattie was richer than God and had numerous companies to her name. All of which poachers were dying to get their hands on. *Not on my watch.*

Hurrying to the kitchen, I turned off the pot that had been simmering on low for the past half hour since I finished putting it together. I grabbed two bowls and paused when my gaze caught sight of the water beyond the window. The panoramic views of the Penobscot Bay were to die for and cost a fortune.

Hattie's house was called Nimaha. It reminded me of how Fiona had always called her grandmother's home Pymm's Pondside. Their generation must have named their houses or something. I'd heard several friends talking about names of their grandparents' homes. My generation had nothing as refined to lay claim to. We had crow's feet, liver spots and unwanted chin hair among other unpleasant signs of reaching middle age.

Wanting to shove aside thoughts that would only lead me to perseverate on how my life had gone to hell in a handbasket at the most inopportune time in my life, I refocused on the coastline. There was nothing on the more than three hundred feet of shoreline. Hattie had a serene sanctuary here. The waves lapped lazily against the pebbled beach. It was so peaceful and remote. Nothing like the hustle and bustle of the big city hospital where I spent twenty years caring for patients. I watched for several seconds until my mind quieted and I was relaxed.

Turning away from the big window, I grabbed the rolls my grandmother had sent with me that morning and headed back through the five thousand square foot house. Thankfully I didn't have to clean all of the bedrooms and bathrooms, or care for the three acres and its outbuildings. The gardening alone had to be a beast to maintain, although I had yet to see a gardener come and tend to the multi-terraced back yard.

A hiss nearly made me drop the tray of soups I had been carrying. Shifting my hold on the tray, I scanned the area for the little heathen that I swore was trying to kill me. There she was.

"Don't scare me like that Tarja." The tabby cat stuck her nose in the air as if she could understand me and continued past me and up the stairs. She had the most beautiful coat I'd ever seen on a cat. Multi-colored with the oranges and yellows being vibrant and shiny.

The second bowl on the tray was to feed Tarja. I wasn't used to treating a cat like a person, but she ate the same food I fed Hattie. I swear Hattie invented the term crazy cat lady. Tarja was her princess and the only thing Hattie was forceful about during the job interview. I should have known Hattie wasn't entirely together when she told me Tarja was to be fed meals with her and her litter box needed to be cleaned several times a day.

I could deal with Hattie's eccentricities and bed pan and dressing changes without any problems. It was cleaning animal feces from a box that made me gag. Yes, I was aware how little sense that made. But c'mon it was a container filled with excrement that had been sitting for hours.

Shrugging off that unpleasant thought, I continued climbing the stairs and stopped short when I saw a large creature through the port hole window on one of the landings. It was dark green and almost as tall as the closest tree. And it looked like the dragons Hollywood depicted in countless movies. Only I didn't see any wings on this one.

What the heck was that? I swear something new popped up every day in this place. My heart raced and I was nearly hyperventilating as I tried to figure out what the large beast was. My breaths fogged the glass, making me use the sleeve of my top to clear the glass. When I looked back out there was nothing there.

When another scan didn't come up with the dragon, I continued up the stairs and hurried into Hattie's room where I deposited the tray and rushed to the window. Her room faced the side of the house where I'd seen the dragon. I hoped I would catch sight of it. Something that big wouldn't be able to disappear into the forest surrounding her without leaving a trail.

"What are you in a tither about now?" Hattie snapped at me like this more often than not. It was how someone talked to their child when they'd had enough of their odd behaviors.

I turned to my patient and pushed the table with the tray of food over to the bed. "I thought I saw a dragon in your backyard. I'm losing my mind just as much as you are it seems. Must be the stress of the divorce."

Hattie laughed, the sound like dry leaves rattling over a sidewalk. "You aren't seeing things, my dear. That was Tsekani. Oh, that soup smells delicious."

I was too tired to let my surprise show over her having named this imaginary dragon. *Are you sure it's not real? You saw it for yourself.* I was positive it was a bad sign that my mind was trying to rationalize my hallucinations.

I set the bowl I had brought for me on the plate where the rolls were. "Here's your lunch, Tarja."

The cat approached and sniffed the soup then started lapping it up. "She says the bay leaves were a good addition to the soup. That's not something I've ever added to mine."

My head snapped up to meet Hattie's smile. "What?"

"Seriously. Where did you get that necklace from? I'm beginning to sense you aren't magical at all." Everything in me froze with her words, including my heart for several seconds.

"My best friend, Fiona had made it for me as a symbol of my new beginning. Why are you saying it's magical? There's no such thing." Right? I wanted to believe I was open minded, but the past month of working for Hattie Silva and hearing her bizarre comments had me questioning that. There was no way I could jump on board with her and believe in magic.

Although, I had to admit I was beginning to have my

doubts. I'd seen enough in the past four weeks to really wonder. Problem was that I'm a scientist and relied on what I could prove and see. And while I had seen more than a fair share of oddities there was nothing I could hold onto or examine all that closely.

"You wouldn't believe me if I told you. Can you push the tray closer? I'd like to taste the soup Tarja can't shut up about." I shook my head and moved the tray over her bed and adjusted it, so she was able to reach the food easily.

I picked up a roll and tore off chunks while staring out the window. She had windows facing the forest and another on the wall above her head that overlooked the water. I was focused on the gentle waves and the pebbled beach when a dog raced across the area, kicking up rocks as he went.

My feet carried me closer and I watched as he bared his teeth. He wasn't like any dog I'd ever seen. He was big and dark grey in coloring. "Do you have wolves in this area?"

The clatter of a spoon filled the room. "Of course, Layla moved here first, but several others have taken refuge here over the years." I wasn't surprised to discover she named the wolves prowling in her woods. She had named her house after all. Wild wolves wouldn't have been my first choice of companions, but she had enough property to safely offer a place to as many wild animals as she wanted.

Dark coughing made me turn away from the window. I expected it to be Hattie, but it was Tarja. If she hocked up a hairball, I wasn't cleaning it. "When does your maid come to clean the house anyway? I've never met her."

Hattie cocked her head to the side and looked at me. "Mythia comes after you leave. She doesn't care to be around mundies. Why?"

Mundies? "I have no idea what that means, but I assure you I have done nothing to upset anyone. I haven't been here long enough to make any enemies. I was hoping to talk to her about how she gets rid of hard water around the shower faucet. I have never been able to get mine so clean."

I thought moving home would offer me a few perks. Like not having to clean bathrooms anymore, but I'd been wrong. There was no way I could take advantage of my mother like Miles had me for so many decades. Despite working long hours seven days a week I always pulled my weight around the house.

After the hurt of his announcement settled in, I immediately began dreaming about what my life would be like without him. In my naivete I had dreamed of continuing my position at the hospital and staying in the house and hiring someone to do the cleaning.

Reality was an entirely different beast. After being fired I had spent weeks of job hunting before realizing I had no choice but to move home. Miles's little tart worked in human resources at the hospital and made sure I wasn't appealing to anyone interested in hiring me. I could have filed a suit for violating my rights, but after Miles had managed to fast track our divorce and screw me out of what I deserved I didn't bother. He had friends in high places.

"Oh, I know you haven't. I did my research before hiring you. Speaking of, how did you piss off Tara so thoroughly? She had nothing good to say about you when I called. And Mythia won't share her secrets with me, so she won't share anything with you."

My head started pounding and I clenched my jaw then balled my hands into fists. Miles got his little girlfriend to sabotage my only shot at a job in this area, too? "Tara is the jailbait that slept with my husband and blacklisted me at all the hospitals in North Carolina. My ex-husband didn't want to be reminded of what a jerk he is or that his girlfriend isn't much older than our son."

Hattie laughed so hard she started coughing. Tarja

jumped onto her lap and placed a paw on her chest. Their connection was more than obvious. The cat was always close and offering comfort when Hattie had bad moments. I shifted Hattie forward and rubbed circles on her back until she stopped coughing.

"I was right about that one it seems. When I saw the written record of your employment, it made no sense to me that you suddenly started making fatal mistakes after twenty years of pristine performance reviews. She did her best to convince me that you were stressed out and upset over your husband leaving you and could no longer be trusted with patients."

I gently set her against the pillows again and returned to the window. "I was upset that Miles left me like he did, but it never affected my ability to do my job. I can assure you I will not cause you harm in any way."

Hattie waved a hand dismissively. "Oh, I know that dear. What do you say we curse her with premature winkles? Or maybe make him impotent!"

That made me choke out a laugh as I turned away from the beach outside. "I would love nothing more, but that would make me like them, and I will never be so malicious. I believe that you reap what you sow. They will both get what's coming to them one day."

"You've got that right, dear. Fate gets her way, even if it takes years and several unexpected turns." I nodded my head in agreement as I gathered the lunch dishes from her tray.

* * *

I TURNED my Land Rover off and couldn't help but smile. Keeping the nice SUV along with half of the house when it sold were the only concessions the judge awarded me which was why I was forced to move back with my mom and grandmother.

I couldn't afford the house payments on the lake front house and no one would hire me. I couldn't buy a house on the money I would be given whether Miles sold or bought me out. We owed too much on the property.

Looking up at the house I had grown up in, I couldn't help but think about the differences between Hattie's house and the house I left back in North Carolina compared to this one.

My grandparents moved into this modest one-story Cape Cod style home almost seventy years ago. The yellow siding had been repainted half a dozen times and the windows were replaced with double-pained ones last summer. The kitchen had been updated fifteen years ago when my mom moved in with my grandmother but not much else had been done.

The wood floors were scuffed and scarred and the marks measuring my height were still in the doorway to the garage alongside my mother's. Unlocking the front door, I entered to the familiar smell of lemon polish and baking bread.

"I'm home," I called out as I set my keys in the dish on the table in the entrance. "Where is everyone?"

My mother poked her head out of the kitchen. "We're in here, just finishing up dinner. Did you eat with Ms. Silva?"

I headed down the hall and caught the door before it closed after my mother returned to the sink. "Hi, nana. How was your day?" I bent and kissed her cheek while she sat in a chair at the table. She was the same age as Hattie but in much better shape.

She patted my cheek and smiled up at me. "I made some rye bread for you to take to Hattie tomorrow and finished the book I was reading."

"And you got in a good nap," my mother interjected. "Anything new happen out at Nimaha today?"

Both enjoyed hearing about the events, saying the house had been haunted as long as they could remember. I shrugged my shoulders. "Hattie has given refuge to wild wolves living in the woods around her house and she has a dragon named Tsekani."

Grandma nodded her head. "She owns something like five acres, so she probably does think she is giving them a place to live. But a dragon? Is it dementia? Many of my friends have succumbed already."

My mother shut off the water and leaned against the counter drying her hands. "Good thing we have excellent genes, and you don't have to worry about that mom. You might want to start looking for another job soon, sweetie. Sounds like she's going downhill fast."

"Who's going downhill fast?" Nina asked as she entered the kitchen and approached me with her arms open.

"Ms. Silva," I replied and embraced my daughter. She looked a lot like me except her brown hair was longer than my short cut and she didn't have crow's feet around her brown eyes. I had always loved the fact that she looked so much like me. Until I was fairly certain that was the reason Tara didn't want Nina around anymore.

Nina released me and went to the fridge. "She's been cra-cra since the day you started there. You don't have to worry about finding another job." I could hear the panic in Nina's voice. She was by my side when I struggled to find a position and celebrated with me when Hattie hired me to take care of her.

"I am giving her gold star treatment to make sure she sticks around. Do you want me to make you a snack?"

Nina gave me a side smile and shook her head. "No, you sit down and rest your feet. You work too hard. I'll grab you some rocky road."

I sat next to nana and held back the emotion choking me.

I might not have the fancy house or the cushy job, but I had more love than Miles would ever know and that's all that mattered.

When my daughter asked my mom and grandmother what they wanted and proceeded to get them some vanilla ice cream along with a cookie, I realized Hattie didn't have this. She was all alone in the world and had no one to shower her with love and affection.

I made a silent vow to ignore the crazy and show her how much she was appreciated. She was cranky, and adored cats, but she was funny and made me laugh all the time. And there were times when she had these little nuggets of wisdom that were priceless. Like when she told me to stop complaining that my daughter was asking for a car of her own.

Hattie had just finished the cookies Nina had dropped off at the end of my first week on the job when I started complaining about her latest request. I would never forget the way Hattie had scowled at me as she said, *"Be grateful she doesn't want it to go joy riding. She wants to give you and your mother a break from taking her to and from practice, and a way to get to and from a job. Yeah, she told me how much she wanted to earn money to ease your burden. Most children her age are selfish critters with no care for anyone else, let alone how much their parents sacrifice to give them what they have."*

I blinked and shoved the memory aside when Nina kissed my cheek and placed the bowl in front of me. "Thank you, peanut. You're the best daughter ever born."

"Agreed." My mom and grandmother both spoke at the same time while enjoying their dessert. My midlife makeover wasn't what I had hoped it would be when I was twenty something, but I couldn't ask for more.

. . .

DOWNLOAD the first book in the Mystical Midlife in Maine series, Magical Makeover HERE! Then turn the page for another preview. Then turn the page for a preview of the first chapter in PACKING SERIOUS MAGICAL MOJO, book one in the Twisted Sisters Midlife Maelstrom series.

EXCERPT FROM PACKING SERIOUS MAGICAL MOJO, BOOK #1 IN THE TWISTED SISTERS' MIDLIFE MAELSTROM SERIES

DANIELLE

I was standing on the lawn of Willowberry Plantation House. The sprawling property was located just outside of New Orleans - one that my five sisters and I just purchased. A silhouette caught my eye close to what used to be the slave quarters. I took a step closer and noticed the stacks of beehives. They were my favorite part of the plantation and one of the reasons I wanted to buy the place. I loved honey bees.

Shaking my head at my superstition, I told myself I knew better. I was born and raised in New Orleans. My family were no strangers to the supernatural. I believed in ghosts, vampires, witches, and voodoo queens. It didn't matter that I had no personal experience. My mom saw the ghost of her grandfather when she was a kid. When she was little, Deandra saw the specter of a woman wearing a floppy pink hat. That was enough for me.

I focused on the next step in the dream I shared with my

sisters. I never thought this day would happen. We started our party planning business after losing our mother to cancer. It was a way to ensure life didn't get in the way and force us to drift apart. I couldn't imagine losing touch with the five women I loved most in life.

Our four brothers were business-minded but didn't have an ounce of creativity and had no desire to be part of our venture, which is how we became the Six Twisted Sisters rather than Kay's Talented Ten.

STS started small with a party for one of our brother's grandchildren and grew to the point where we now needed a venue of our own. I had dreamed of owning one of the beautiful old plantation homes in the area, but never thought my sisters would go for it, let alone put in money of their own.

"I can't believe this is finally ours." I smiled and held my hands out as I twirled in a circle. "We are living the dream, Lia."

Perhaps that silhouette by the beehives had been a ghost. It would be just like our mom to come back and share this day with us. I went on tiptoes, searching the spot I thought I'd seen the shadow.

My older sister, Dahlia, snorted, making me look her way. She was a few years older than me. We'd reached the middle of our lives, but she didn't look forty-five. I hoped that meant I didn't look forty-two. "The only thing missing is the pool and the hot cabana boy."

I chuckled. "We brought Fred, the gardener instead. And look, he's even sweaty."

Lia lifted one brow and thrust her hands on her hips. "And happily married. That does not count. At least we don't have to live here with the others. No way would we hear the end of the amount of work from Kota and Dre." Dahlia was absolutely right about that. Our two oldest sisters hadn't read the inspection report.

I winced. Dreya was the oldest of us six and Dakota was just under her. They put in their share of money and trusted Lia and me when we assured them that we could handle fixing the house and getting it ready to host events. When they find out how bad the house really was, they'd want to kill us for buying this place.

I wasn't sure what they expected, but you couldn't get a plantation this big for under a million-five in this area. We got it for half that *because* of the problems. "Thank God for Phi, she's already making a list of the first issues we need to tackle. We've got this, sis."

Lia nodded and headed toward the car that was packed so full you couldn't see the interior color. "Let's go play reverse Jenga and get all this stuff out before the tires pop under the pressure."

Standing on tiptoe, Lia stood around five feet, six inches and was able to grab the zipper for the bag strapped to the top of her SUV. With a yank and a pull, black vinyl parted and spilled pillows, towels, and blankets on top of her.

A laugh escaped me before I could stop it. Before I knew it we were both laughing as the cargo bag continued to spew its guts at us. I had to cross my legs as I bent over at the waist. No one could make me laugh like my sisters, and I loved it despite the consequences. When we were together, we devolved into laughter that ended with one or more of us dashing to the bathroom. None of us had great bladder control after having our kids. Mine went to shit after I had twins.

We could hear Dea chuckling as she got out of the car. Her laugh was the loudest and most infectious of us all. It warmed my heart when I heard it. "What are y'all laughing about?"

"Lia played Jenga a little too well. Now we'll have to wash

everything before we can sleep tonight." I hugged Phi as she got out of the car next.

Kota slammed Dre's car door and hurried toward the house. "Do not make me laugh."

That, of course, made us all devolve into another fit of giggles as we each grabbed up towels and pillows and headed to the house. Kota was shifting from one flip flop to another with sweat running down her perfect makeup by the time we reached her. "Hurry the eff up. I gotta go."

I chuckled and set my burden on the porch, praying the wood held all of us at once. I already had the key in one hand and inserted it in the lock, and twisted. Dakota was through the door like a shot. "We don't have any TP!"

"Or water," Lia yelled over my shoulder. "We forgot to have it put into our name. She's gonna kill us."

Dreya rolled her eyes. "Do not take a dump in the bathroom, Kota! Or you will be fishing it out."

Phi set her pile in the parlor, to the right of the entrance, and had her phone in her hand. "I'll get the water, electricity, and internet turned on. Tucker is on his way with the first load." Once again, Delphine saved the day.

She was super organized and one of the reasons we were so successful. Each of us had a different talent and helped the business run smoothly. I liked to call myself the queen bee, but not because I was more valuable than the others. It was to get under Dakota and Dreya's skin. They were the two oldest and most outspoken of the six of us. I'm sure it bugged the others, but they kept it to themselves. For me, I wanted to feel needed. The truth was, since my divorce from Hugo, I had been floundering and worried I would end up alone.

Dahlia was moving into the plantation with me was that her husband Leo died a few years back. He was killed at work by some angry kids in the foster system. Maybe she needed me as much as I needed her. I couldn't imagine what

I would do in her shoes. Losing Leo, then mom, had to be very difficult.

I stopped that runaway train before it led me to thoughts that would make me cry, like the fact that our mom wasn't here to see us celebrate this achievement. "Steve is on his way to your place Lia, to pick up the laser engraver and supplies. He has the boys with him, so between the five cars, they should be able to get all of our products along with the machine over here and into the barn," Dreya called out as she returned with another load.

Dreya and Dahlia are the workhorses of the bunch. They dove right in and got to work no matter what we were doing. I jumped and dumped the stuff. I looked around at the faded and peeling wallpaper. The musty smell was likely from the mold they found in the attic. Or perhaps it was the broken sump pump in the basement.

My heart squeezed as I walked out of the house to go back to the car. I paused and looked at the wrap-around porch and our investment. The front deck was one of Lia's favorite things about the place. That and what she called the perfect spot to put a gazebo under some willow trees in our yard.

The holes in the flooring were laughing at me. They seemed much bigger now that we owned the place. Rotten wood, check. Mold, check. Broken window, check. I had poured every penny I'd squeezed from my crappy ex-husband into this house. My sisters had each put everything they had into the place as well. Laughter rang out through the massive house, making me smile despite the crushing weight of the project we had just taken on. That right there was the reason this was going to work. Moments like this were priceless and part of the lesson our mom had tried to teach us for years. It wasn't until she was gone that I understood why she wanted the ten of us to be close. You could always count on your family to have your back. At least I could. That was the legacy I inherited from my mom. She didn't leave behind a house for us to fight over or jewelry. She left us love and laughter.

With a smile on my face, I continued to the car while listening to my sisters through the open door. I stopped short when something blue darted out of the corner of my eye. My heart started racing, and my breath caught in my throat. My heart plummeted when I turned, and all I saw were the beehives.

Deandra's arm wrapped around my shoulders as her infectious laughter died down. "Whatcha looking at, sis? Your bees?"

"Our bees." I considered telling Dea about the ghost I swore I kept seeing, then decided against it. There was no doubt she would believe me. She had personal experience.

Hell, all of my sisters believed in them. We'd grown up with stories, but that didn't mean they wouldn't be freaked the hell out. The only one I was certain wouldn't run away screaming was Lia. She loved the paranormal, particularly witches, as much as our mom had.

Dea wrinkled her nose. "You're the bee whisperer. I'll eat the honey, but that's about it."

I laughed as we paused by the trunk of Lia's overflowing car. "I'm afraid to touch anything. Lia had to contort her body to get this stuff in here."

"Don't be such a baby. I'll hand boxes to you," Dea said with a sigh.

I smiled at her even though she couldn't see me. She knew me so well. I was a hard worker like all of my sisters. I'd be right there with Lia repairing walls and striping the wallpaper and painting. However, tweaking my back while unloading the car wasn't my idea of fun.

"Thanks, Dea. Or not." I grunted as she added a third box. I took off before she could add another.

I was perfectly balanced with the packages, so when a box disappeared, I practically fell into Dahlia. "You looked like you could use help."

I lifted one eyebrow. "Is that the box with your BOB?'

Dahlia made a pfft noise. "I had to sell my vibrators plus my house. How else do you think we got such a reasonable monthly payment on a house with fifteen bathrooms and almost double that number of bedrooms?"

I chuckled as I followed Lia up the stairs to the side of the porch. Not many appreciated Lia's sense of humor like us. We passed the detached kitchen and headed up the side of the house. It was amazing how having my sister with me made me see the holes in the porch differently. Instead of lamenting my decision to pressure my sisters, I was busy creating stories about those who had lounged there on hot summer days two hundred years ago.

"We made the right choice, didn't we?" I hadn't meant to blurt that out. My mouth had a tendency to get away from me.

Dahlia stopped, set her box down, and gave me a side hug. "I don't know how to explain it, but this is where we are supposed to be. Everything in our life has led us here. Me losing Leo, you divorcing his royal highness, even losing mom. None of us would have taken the risk without the loss. We know better than most know how imperative it is to live life to the fullest and enjoy the little moments."

I nodded in agreement. "Keep that in mind when we are in the hot attic cleaning out the mold and sealing the wood."

Lia chuckled and picked up her box. "Can we sleep in the ladies' parlor tonight? I'm not ready to be in a room alone yet. I swear there's something here."

I glanced over my shoulder, wondering if she'd seen the ghost. "Did you see something, too?"

"What do you mean, too? I haven't seen anything. It's more a feeling that I can't explain."

"Don't tell me you guys bought us a haunted house," Dakota said as we entered the house. "We can't afford for this to fail. We're extended as far as possible."

"Lia and I gave up our homes to make this work. Our kids don't have a home to return to during spring break next month," I replied.

Dakota meant well, but I was irritated. Mostly because I worried this would ruin us. I'd quit my nursing job, and Dahlia gave notice at social services. Between the parties, tours, and personalized gifts we planned to offer online, there was no choice. And that was the biggest risk for us. If this failed, Dahlia and I were out of a job while the rest still had theirs.

Dahlia set her box down and took mine from me. "They're coming here and going to work their tails off. I've already warned mine."

I took the olive branch and kept myself out of the muck. The six of us got on each other's nerves at times at time, but because we had each other to vent to, we didn't fully blow up with one another. That was what would make it work.

"I know I haven't thanked you guys yet, but it means a lot to me that you have sacrificed so much for us to achieve this dream." It helped keep things calm when Dakota showed insight like this.

She was the most outspoken of all of us and never hesitated to say what she thought. I both loved and hated that about her. I kept my mouth shut about far too much in life, which is probably why I just went through my second divorce. It hit me that I envied Dakota's ability to avoid the hardest of the work and say what she thought, as well.

I hugged her and then went back out for more. Another two loads and the cars were all empty. Dahlia's clothing and mine were all in the ladies' parlor along with the air mattresses we'd be sleeping on tonight.

My back started bitching at me the moment I laid my eyes on the plastic monstrosity that refused to be contained. "Let's take a look around. It doesn't look like the previous owner moved anything out since our last walk-through. I want to take an inventory to see if we will need trash removal."

Phi held up her iPad. "I'll take notes as we go through. I bet there is stuff we can refurbish and sell. Who knows, in an old place like this, we might find some real treasures." Delphine was the most organized of the six of us.

She was smart enough to be a surgeon. Could have been if she'd wanted. Instead, she decided to become a professor in biological sciences. She and her husband, Tucker, bought a hundred-year-old house and refinished the entire thing from top to bottom, so she would know better than me.

The layout was nothing like I was used to in my old house. The entrance was massive with a beautiful crystal chandelier and twin staircases that bent toward the two wings of the house. Beneath the section where the two met and became one wide staircase was a wide hall.

The aisle leading from the front door was long, and there were a few doors on each side as you proceeded into the house. The first rooms on each side were the parlors. One side was for women and the other for men. They would serve as dressing rooms for weddings.

The dining room and a butler's pantry which was a fancy name for an area that was used as staging for the servants to place food before serving. The library was across from that, along with an office. We would keep the library and restore it.

We didn't have plans for the office or servants' prep area. That is what excited me. I loved planning themed parties down to the last little detail and I would enjoy doing the same with this house.

It was hard to be patient when I wanted it done now so we could start making money. "They could have cleaned the chandelier for us," I grumbled as we reached an area that had been renovated and turned into a kitchen. When this plantation was built, the kitchen was in a separate building to avoid a fire burning down the entire house if one started and also keep the house cooler in the summer.

Lucky for us the outdoor kitchen had been updated with modern appliances and would be the perfect location for caterers to prepare. The iron stairs were solid and clean as we climbed.

"These stairs weren't made for people as big as me," Dakota complained.

Deandra started laughing. "This house will never survive us."

By the time we got to the second floor, we were all laughing so hard that I had to go low with my legs crossed. As I balanced on my hands and tried to stop, I swear a ghost appeared at the end of the hallway. It was a blue-colored woman clad in a dress with a wide skirt, high neckline, and fitted top with poofy sleeves. The woman's hair was twisted on top of her head, and her face was pinched.

Dahlia turned wide, frightened eyes my way. Deandra wiped her eyes and opened the first door. "Where's the bathroom?"

Lia pointed further down the hall. "Third door on the left." Dea ran past everyone and into the bathroom.

Delphine shook her head with a smile. "Are we leaving this floor open for wedding parties?"

"Yeah. That's the plan. The place is big enough, we could

live in the other wing, but we're good with the third floor." It was likely an attic at one point, but whoever updated the house with electricity and air conditioning had converted it into a space with three rooms and a bathroom.

"I love this old brass bed," Dakota said. I went on my tiptoes and looked into the room Dakota was standing outside.

"It's gorgeous. Looks like we will have a few things to work with. That'll save some money." Dreya was the oldest and like a mother figure to us. She was the first to find a solution to saving money. She was also the only one that had stories about the rest of us when we were kids.

"Wow, I didn't realize how many beehives were out there," Delphine remarked from the end of the hall.

Dakota scowled. "What are we going to do with so many beehives? How do we even take care of them?"

Deandra joined us holding a roll of toilet paper. "Maleko and I looked into that, actually. We will need to make sure the structures remain in good condition and have proper ventilation. Bees also need a way in and out that we can block when needed. It also said something about woodlice and termites."

I shivered as I listened. There was a cold spot where we were standing, yet there was no vent spewing cold air down on us. This was where the ghost had been standing. Was she still there?

Delphine shrugged her shoulders. "We can sell the honey if we open a gift shop in the old carriage house."

I was overcome with excitement. "We have to have a gift shop. Tourists love their souvenirs. And homegrown honey will be a literal gold mine."

Dreya nodded in agreement. "You're right about that. We can sell personalized jars as party favors"

I saw a person round the corner from the slave's quarters,

and I turned and ran for the stairs. My five sisters were running after me and calling my name. I couldn't tell from the window if it was a ghost, but I wanted to make sure it wasn't anyone messing with our property.

I was across the lawn before I was winded. I paused in the middle of the beehives and looked around. The air was sweet from the honey in the nearby drawers. "I thought I saw someone out here," I told them when they all caught up with me.

The six of us were standing in a circle, searching our property for anyone that shouldn't be there. The only people on the property were us. Fred, the gardener, had already left. All of a sudden, the bees went into a flurry as if someone had agitated their hives. I dropped to my knees, and so did my sisters. Keeping my hands over my head, I watched as they buzzed above our heads.

Kota grunted. "I'm not made to do squats."

"I'm more worried about us being stung. What are they doing? It smells like lavender now," Dreya said. I wished I had an answer for her.

Sniffing the air, I smelled the same thing she did. "I don't recall there being any lavender bushes on the plantation." My skin tingled from the energy produced by the bees. It almost felt like it was vibrating through my blood. Looking at my sisters, I was sure that they felt the same thing. I pointed to the left and commando crawled that way, staying low to the ground.

"I'm not sure what that was," Lia said and rubbed her arms as the bees settled and returned to their hives. "But at least we know the bees are healthy and active. Now, let's talk names. Are we keeping Willowberry Plantation? Or changing it?"

Laughter bubbled up as we helped each other stand up and discuss name ideas for our venue. It would take time and some loud discussions for the six of us to come to an agreement on the name, so I steered us to important tasks while we processed.

We had some shelves to put together in the converted barn, where we planned to have our workshop. It had been a major selling point for us. We just needed the electrical and interior updated to accommodate our laser and other supplies.

My heart lightened, and a smile broke across my face. This was going to work. We finally had our own venue for weddings and other parties.

Download the first book in the Twisted Sisters' Midlife Maelstrom series, Packing Serious Magical Mojo HERE! Then turn the page for a preview of the first chapter of SURPRISED BY A SUPERNATURAL START, book one in the Dame of the Midnight Relics.

EXCERPT FROM SURPRISED BY A SUPERNATURAL START

"We're going to the pool, Keyboard King. You've got to stop that or we are never leaving this room," I told my husband.

Arjun looked at me in the mirror with that crooked smile. It won my heart twenty-one years ago and got me every time. "Are you sure you're set on visiting the pool, Firebird? This is the first vacation we've taken just the two of us in five years."

Turning on my stool, I smiled up at my husband. "You know I picked this resort for the pool, babe. I want to get some vitamin D and rehydrate while the sun is up. I promise to make it up to you tonight."

Arjun pulled me to my feet and wrapped his arms around me. My body ignited the second his lips touched mine. With a moan, I wrapped my arms around his neck and went to my tiptoes. His hands caressed my back as his tongue slipped into my mouth. I allowed him to get the both of us worked up, but not too far gone.

Pushing his chest, I broke away. "That's why we haven't

seen anything in Belize yet. I want to go to the pool and take a trip out to Shark Ray Alley and the ruins and..."

Arjun stopped me with a finger to the lips. "Alright, I get it. I'll book the next excursion for the Hol Chan Marine Reserve & Shark Ray Alley while you get us drinks by the pool."

"Deal." I grabbed the neon pink wrap that my girls had helped me pick out and checked myself in the mirror one more time.

I was not sure about wearing the bikini. It wasn't the triangle top that Maisy thought I would look great in but the bandeau that Amelia picked out for me. I had an extra fifteen pounds, stretch marks from carrying my three babies, and saggy boobs. Life had been good to me. My body, not so much.

"You look hot, Firebird. There is nothing to be self-conscious about. You're fit and strong. For God's sake, you carry men, women and children out of burning buildings. That extra weight you think you have is all in your head. You're perfect."

I preened and fluffed my short bob. "It's about time you noticed. It's only taken two decades."

Arjun grabbed his towel and snapped it at my backside. I yelped and jumped away from him with a laugh. Grabbing my pool bag, I danced out the door then paused and looked back. "You coming?"

"Right behind you."

My toes sank into the sand as we walked out the door of our cabana. Lifting my head to the sun, I inhaled the crisp ocean breeze. Ambergris Caye was a beautiful little island off the coast of Belize. Arjun twined his fingers with mine and we headed to the pool.

"Do you think Maisy and Amelia are getting to school on

time?" I asked as we walked. Our girls were great kids who got good grades and trained hard for their cheer leading team. They were the opposite of me. I was as far from a rah-rah girl as you could get. As a firefighter, I was more comfortable getting down and dirty. And I was a plumber on my off days.

Arjun snorted as we walked up the stairs and found two lounge chairs. "There's not a chance in hell. They're going to have at least three make-up hours when we get back. And we'll have to detox them from eating cheeseburgers every day. I'll be right back. I'm going to see about that tour."

Nodding, I signaled a bartender. I ordered two Mai Tais and two Diet Cokes. The formulation for the soda was different in South America and I couldn't decide it I liked it or not. I kicked off my shoes and laid back on the chair. The heat of the sun felt good and reminded me I needed to put sunblock on. I was no longer twenty and able to withstand the UV rays without issue. Fine lines were no joke when you hit forty.

Yeah, I was a vain person and I wasn't apologetic about it. There was nothing wrong with having pride in yourself and wanting to look good. There were some things I couldn't do much about. I had a few burns on my back and arms but that came with the job.

"Good news, Firebird. There's a tour leaving in ten minutes. You ready to head out to see some sharks and stingrays?"

I sat up, dropping the bottle of sunblock in the process. "Damn, I was looking forward to laying around the pool. Someone kept me up last night."

Arjun grabbed my hand and pulled me to my feet. "Too bad. You wanted to do this one. We're going."

"Okay, okay. I'm going to go and change into my one piece. I don't want these ties coming undone while we are swimming with the fishies. Will you get us some of that pineapple and mango to take with us?"

Arjun pressed a kiss to my lips. "Anything for my gorgeous wife."

I grabbed the key from my bag and hurried back across the beach to our bungalow. I threw off my coverup and then the bikini. The one piece was on the table where I'd been getting ready earlier. I squeezed my body into it and got excited about this excursion. It looked like it was going to be a blast. I debated removing my makeup then dismissed the idea. There wasn't enough time and my mascara was waterproof.

Arjun was waiting for me at the end of the dock. He grabbed my hand and pulled me down to the boat. It was so nice to see him relaxed and having fun. Between his high-stress job in computer programming, the house, and the kids we rarely had time for fun. And never like this.

I hate to admit that I was a total cliché and after turning forty, I had a mini-midlife crisis. I didn't go out and buy a sports car, but have been evaluating what I want from life. I love being a fire fighter but wasn't sure it was my passion anymore. It just felt like something was missing. I hadn't figured it all out yet. But the one thing I insisted on was taking a vacation just Arjun and I once a year. We didn't make it happen last year which I made sure didn't happen again.

We climbed on board the boat and took a seat while the guide went over the rules for the trip. The captain left the dock when the last person sat down. I enjoyed the fresh fruit during the boat ride. After the captain anchored the boat, everyone got ready and jumped in the ocean.

My eyes were wide and my heart racing as I got my first sight of the world under the water. There were sea turtles, nurse sharks, stingrays, moray eels, and various colorful fish.

And then there was the stunning coral reef ecosystem. Belize was home to the second-largest barrier reef system in the world, after the Great Barrier Reef in Australia. It was why I selected Ambergris Caye to visit. I'd done research and picked out the brain coral then I found some elkhorn and staghorn coral. My favorite was the fire coral.

I turned to smile at Arjun and a scream left me. Floating next to me was a young woman of about seventeen years old with long, light blonde hair. Her silver eyes were glaring daggers at me while her white dress floated around her body. The style was familiar but I couldn't place it. I was too busy trying to figure out why she was pissed off at me and why she was down there without any snorkeling gear. She waved her hand and bright silvery light practically blinded me. My hand shot up to shield my eyes and I dropped to land on something soft. I held my breath because my snorkel had to be below the water now.

When the glow faded, I dropped my arm and gaped at what I was looking at. I was in the water but not. A bubble surrounded me and inside was the woman, me, and a nurse shark that was swimming next to me.

I lifted the mask and mouthpiece off my face. "What the hell is going on? Who are you and how did you do that? Whatever it was, you need to undo it. That shark is going to die."

The woman growled and flicked her fingers. Electricity tingled across my body and the shark was no longer in the bubble with us. "You're a hard woman to find Nylah Gilbert. I am the goddess Artemis and I am here to make you the Relic Keeper."

My jaw dropped open as I stared at her. "Did you hit your head?"

Artemis, if that's who she was, crossed her arms over her chest and glared at me. "You're standing in a magical sphere that no one can see and you're asking if I hit my head? I don't have time for this. We need to go so I can bring your latent DNA to the fore. It's not going to be pleasant."

I had no idea what the hell this crazy lady was talking about. It felt like my mind had fractured. Maybe I'd passed out and I was drowning. I extended my hand, hoping not to feel anything. I shrieked when my palm hit something that felt solid. Arjun swam by then and was turning in a circle. The way his eyes were scanning frantically, I knew he wasn't enjoying the wild life. I pounded on the sphere and started shouting his name.

"Would you stop that? It's not necessary. He can't see you."

I whirled and glared at Artemis. "Let me out of here you crazy ass bitch. My husband is worried and looking for me. You have no right to put me in whatever this is. I'm not going anywhere with you."

Artemis took a step toward me. "I do not have the patience for this. I have a mission for you. You need to get past your disbelief and get on board. Now." She snapped her fingers and the denial and rationalizing that was running through my head slowed until it vanished entirely.

In that second, I knew without a shadow of a doubt that things that go bump in the might actually existed. The panic I expected to feel never arrived. "What did you do to me?"

Artemis rolled her eyes. "I sped things along. Humans go through too much drama when confronted with the supernatural world. I don't have time to watch you process what I am telling you."

"Right, because you need to make me a Relic Keeper. I hate to break it to you, but I am not going to cooperate. I have no idea who you really are, but I want out of here. Now!" I put all my anger and frustration into my request.

Artemis cursed and said something under her breath and

a second later, I was sucking in water and kicking my way to the surface. I devolved into a coughing fit as I sucked in air the second that I broke the surface. My lungs burned from the salt water and my eyes were watering. I screamed when someone grabbed my arms.

"Are you alright, Firebird?"

Shaking my head, I continued coughing. When my lungs stopped spasming, I opened my mouth to tell him what had happened but stopped. "My mouth piece filled with water. I'm good now."

I put my mask back on and ducked back down, this time looking for the blonde girl in the dress. I searched everywhere, but didn't see her. Had I just imagined that? It felt unreal and my instinct was to deny she had ever been there. Except, thanks to whatever she'd done I knew vampires and witches and shifters existed. I wasn't into fantasy books or movies. It was all I could do to watch Harry Potter with my kids. This was not something I could have come up with in my wildest dreams.

I was shaken to my core and on edge. I jumped when Arjun twined his fingers with mine. He gave me a look and I had to point to a sea turtle to distract him. I spent the longest hour of my life looking at fish and petting nurse sharks and stingrays with Arjun until we finally climbed out of the water.

"Are you sure you're alright? I thought you would have enjoyed that more."

I smiled up at Arjun. "I'm okay. That truly was an amazing experience. I could seriously live here."

Arjun let it go and we rode back to the shore in silence with me tucked into his side. We ordered food to be delivered then headed to our room. I stripped out of my bathing suit and turned on the shower. Before I could get under the hot stream, Arjun stopped me. "Talk to me. Are you really upset you didn't get to lay by the pool? I thought you'd want to go right away since you've been looking forward to that the most."

I nodded then ducked under the water and started talking. I told him everything that happened from the second Artemis appeared next to me. He felt the back of my head and looked into my eyes. "Did you hit your head when you dove into the water?"

Rinsing my hair, I shut off the faucet and growled at him. "No, I didn't hit my damn head. You should know I'd never come up with something this far-fetched." I wrapped myself in one of the resort's fluffy towels.

The knock at the door interrupted our conversation. Arjun answered it and carried our tray of food to the bed. "I don't know what to think of this, Firebird. It's completely insane, you know that, right?"

A bright light filled the room and that same electricity filled the air. Arjun jumped up and put himself between me and Artemis. "She...she just...how the fuck?"

Artemis sighed and snapped her fingers. Arjun's face went slack. "Supernaturals are real. I'm a goddess and I'm here to make your wife the Relic Keeper she was always meant to be."

"What?" Arjun and I blurted at the same time.

"Nylah has witchcraft in her lineage some generations back. Her line's powers lie specifically with the Relic Keepers. We are in need of one of her kind to protect Objects of Power from falling into the wrong hands. Now, can I get on with enhancing her DNA, please?"

Arjun looked back at me as I sank into his back. "No. You can't. Get out of our room."

Artemis grew in size so she towered over us by several feet. "Let me be clear. I am going to bring your weak DNA forward and you are going to become the Relic Keeper. My huntresses refuse to continue recovering artifacts for me unless we have you."

I swallowed the fear down and told my heart to slow down before I passed out. "Why don't you ask another Relic Keeper? I'm sure you're wrong about me. There is nothing magical about me."

"The Relic Keeper line was hunted down and killed for their power which made anyone with a modicum of Relic Keeper power go into hiding. Over the years your magical DNA had been diluted. This is what you were meant to be. The Fates would not have brought me to you if you weren't supposed to go down this path."

I was shaking my head back and forth when Artemis barked at me, "Enough of this. I wanted you to be on board because it makes this process easier. But I don't need it."

I was gaping at her when she shot me in the chest with a bolt of silver lightning. I fell back on the bed, my towel falling open as my back arched and I screamed. Any noise I was making cut off as I couldn't catch my breath. Every cell in my body felt like it was on fire. Agony consumed me entirely. There wasn't any part of me that didn't hurt. Having my legs chopped off with painful slowness would be preferrable to what I was experiencing at that moment.

It was as if something was growing inside each one until it made me feel like I was going to explode. I glanced down to make sure my skin hadn't split open. There was a silver glow worm traveling beneath my skin. It felt as if it was electrocuting every cell as it went, making the pain even worse. The part of my brain able to process was awed at the tiny red fireworks that exploded every few centimeters beneath the surface. It looked like the worm was shitting red as it traveled. The worst part was it felt as if my insides were rearranging themselves.

Arjun's hands roamed up and down my torso as he

shouted at the goddess. I was shaking my head telling him that threatening that woman was not a good idea. She could kill him with a snap of her fingers. My vision blurred and my mouth went dry yet I couldn't say anything. There was no doubt Artemis was a goddess. Whatever she did to me was not normal.

After what seemed like an hour, the pain subsided and I fell back to the bed. "What..did...you do?"

Artemis was back to just under six feet and glaring at the two of us. "I told you what I was going to do. You're welcome." She pulled a stone tablet from nowhere and dropped it on the bed. "That's the Stone of Transmutation. The first artifact you need to protect. You will want to cast a protection charm over that and keep it away from those you love or it will alter them in ways that will kill them. And you should build your vault before long. It's the only way you can ensure the relics under your care cannot be detected. We will have new Objects of Power for you soon."

I opened my mouth and the goddess disappeared. Arjun reached out to grab the tablet that looked like it was thousands of years old and had letters etched into the surface. "No!" I shouted at Arjun instinctually. Blue light shot from my hands and wrapped around the stone tablet until it was completely encased in it.

My shocked gaze lifted to Arjun who was looking at me with horror in his eyes. "What the hell are you now?"

My heart cracked in half when his expression turned to one of disgust. Arjun had been my best friend and partner for over twenty years. One visit from an insane goddess and I was going to lose him. There was no hint of the desire for me he'd had there only hours before. With one flick of a finger, Artemis had turned me into a Relic Keeper. That wasn't what was upsetting me. There was truth to her words that I was meant for this role. It was the fact that my husband was backing away from me with fear and revulsion. It didn't feel like there was a way we could get through this like we had every problem we'd ever encountered. I wanted to rip Artemis a new one for taking the one person I had always been able to count on.

Download the first book in the Dame of the Midnight Relics series, SURPRISED BY A SUPERNATURAL START HERE! Then turn the page for a preview of The Prime of My Magical Life, book one in the Shrouded Nation series.

EXCERPT FROM THE PRIME OF MY MAGICAL LIFE, SHROUDED NATION BOOK #1

My head snapped up, hitting the shelf as I straightened to see who was entering my store. Placing a bell above the door might have been a mistake. *No, leaving the door unlocked was.* Rubbing the back of my skull where a lump was forming, I walked into the aisle and froze.

This was supposed to be my start on a fresh path in my life. Instead, my ex-husband stood there with a sneer on his face. The disgust rolling off of him was unmistakable. I wasn't ready to face him. Honestly, I hoped I would never see him again.

Crossing my arms over my chest, I forced my facial expression to remain neutral and refused to check my long, brown hair. He could suck it if he didn't approve of the Ponytail. "Why are you here, Caton? I'm not open yet, or can't you read the sign in the window?"

One corner of my ex-husband's mouth lifted and his brown eyes narrowed. "Don't take that tone of voice with me, Eve. You should remember your place. I had to see if the rumors were true. I can't believe you used your settlement for this place. It's an embarrassment."

His words hurt more than I wanted them to. This man had cheated on me and left me for a younger woman. She represented the witches on the Shadow Council. Lucinda was closer to our daughter, Mina's age than ours. *That* was the embarrassment, not my store.

He never believed running a magic shop was worthwhile. I had always dreamed of opening a place where beings of all kinds could purchase potions and remedies, and magical creatures could buy their supplies.

There was a need for my place in Ravenholde. As it was, witches and warlocks were forced to search high and wide for whatever they needed. The Blue Moon would change that.

And I'd worked hard over the past few months to locate suppliers and develop the necessary relationships to procure items. Not to mention the fact that I had to find someone willing to help me buy the place. Caton had managed to come out of the divorce with the lion's share while I was struggling to survive.

And here he was pissing on my dream, making me feel like a failure before it even began. The days of him ruining my life were over. "Get out of my store. I don't answer to you anymore. Nor do I listen to what you have to say. I'm not open for business. You can come back when I am."

Caton took several steps toward me, making me shrink into myself while backing up. "How dare you talk back to me? You would still be living in that hovel if not for me. I made you who you are today. You owe me everything. Something you'd do well to remember."

That did it. I was done letting him keep me under his thumb. When I did something that he didn't approve of, especially if he thought it made him look bad, he berated me.

He tried to make me feel like I was nothing. He preferred it when I depended on him.

I was worth more than he could ever imagine and I was done allowing him to chip away at my self-esteem. Straightening my shoulders, I rolled my eyes. "You must really enjoy your imaginary world. I thought for sure you'd grow up one day. Let me be clear, I owe you nothing. Nor do I think about you when making any decision in my life."

With that, I turned my back to him and moved behind the glass counter I'd found at a mundane owned antique store a few towns over. I'd been looking for something to display tarot cards and my more expensive crystals.

I was acutely aware of Caton stalking toward me as I lifted a box from the floor. Through the glass front, I saw the black slacks and dress shoes as he moved. "You are nothing without me, Eve. You can stop this charade and give up this endeavor before you fail."

Standing up, I dropped the box on the glass top with too much force. "Did you stop taking your medication when you threw everything away? You might want to reconsider. I hear the Shadow Council can't get a handle on the increase in suspicious deaths, and they are now moving to mundane cities and victims. I'll have some items for sale. If you need scrying water or any potions to help reveal the culprit, come see me." I was opening the next day and didn't have time for this bullshit. I needed to finish setting up my store.

Caton leaned forward, his face turning red with his anger. One lock of his dark blonde hair fell over his forehead. "Watch your mouth. You've got little power and no talent. You were lucky I married you. Nobody else would have."

I snapped my fingers, making the tips ignite with flames. "Someone still prefers living in denial. I can see how you're with Lucinda now. You are the lucky one. I should have seen through your bullshit years ago. Your days of stealing from me are over. Get the hell out of my store. And that invitation for help extends to anyone on the council except you and Lucinda."

I flicked my wrist, activating the wards I'd placed in and around my shop. There was a moment of pure joy when Caton's eyes widened as the spell forced him down the aisle. I barely managed to open the doors with my telekinesis before he crashed into the panel.

I'd have been pissed if his body broke the glass topped panel. Ayesha had helped me finish painting the store name and logo onto the surface the day before. We had the large picture windows to do next.

My heart was in my throat when I followed him down the aisle and slammed the door as he was dumped on his ass. Control of my telekinesis was sketchy at best, and I had no desire to flop in front of him.

After locking the deadbolt, I watched as Caton stood up and brushed himself off. I winced when he glared at me and muttered something under his breath. Given the way he concentrated on me and my shop, I knew it wasn't good.

The sparks that flew when his spell hit my wards made me jump back as a scream escaped from my lips. That turned into a laugh when Caton's suit jacket caught on fire. He'd tried to burn my store down.

In my anger, I had the door open, and I was in Caton's face before reason resurfaced. "You never did learn when to quit. Take your stupidity and stay away from me. My store is protected by more than just wards. They're the strongest protections out there. And will be available to purchase in a few weeks."

Caton lifted his chin and opened his mouth to reply when Ayesha arrived. The Fae leader slammed her car door, breaking the moment. "Fancy meeting you here, Caton. Did you come to support the wife you let get away? I still don't understand how you left her for Lucinda. Then again, we can't all have good taste."

Caton shifted his glare from me to Ayesha. "So, you're behind Eve's latest venture. I was just telling her how pathetic this place is. I will relish its failure even more, knowing it will reflect on you both."

Ayesha's face split into a grin as she walked up the steps and looped her arms through mine. "It will be fun to watch Eve soar without you dragging her down. Your humiliation has already started, Caton. Look around. Countless townspeople have already seen your attempt to attack your ex-wife blow up in your face. Quite literally, it seems."

The tight band around my chest loosened when I realized she was right. Several people were focused on the three of us. The charred holes in Caton's jacket were lingering proof of what he had tried to do.

"You failed to sabotage my new venture, and managed to show the community how much talent I have. I couldn't have asked for better marketing. It's the least you could do after all you put me through." I still hated that I'd given this man the best twenty years of my life.

You're only forty-two years old, not one hundred. The best is yet to come. My life was far from over and I needed to keep reminding myself of that. Ayesha turned, pulling me with her, and walked me back inside my store.

After shutting the door, I locked it and extricated myself from my mentor. Ayesha had been there for me when Caton left me. I was devastated and humiliated that I hadn't seen him for who he really was sooner.

The signs had been there, but I'd chosen to ignore them in favor of keeping Mina's life stable. The desire to leave him had become the only thought in my head too many times over the years. Regret was a bitter pill to swallow.

"Don't," Ayesha told me. "Do not give his words or his

thoughtless actions space in your mind. You need it for all the skills you've honed over the past few months."

I sighed and walked to the back of the store, away from the prying eyes on the street. I didn't want anyone to see me break down. "But what if he's right? I'm doing magic that shouldn't exist. No one has ever combined Fae methods with witchcraft."

Ayesha pulled me to the stairs that lead up to my apartment above the shop. The old Victorian was converted into two separate spaces a couple of decades ago by a fame demon when she opened Ravenholde's first bakery.

My parents used to take me to Callaleh's place for cupcakes as a kid. She made my birthday cake every year until she closed up shop and moved to Wilmington, North Carolina, taking her store with her.

"Just because something hasn't been done before doesn't mean it shouldn't be. You are allowing Caton to get into your head again. It took us months to undo the damage he'd done. You are far more talented than him or Lucinda. You belong on the council, not her." She flicked her hand. "Regardless, you are where you're meant to be. There are big things in store for you." Ayesha's pep talk soothed the hurt that I was yet to banish, making it easier to reclaim my determination to succeed.

I had no desire to make decisions that affected the entire Shrouded Nation. I was happy in my corner of the world, helping where I could. And her belief in me was the reason I'd come to rely on her friendship and guidance. Crossing to the stove, I put the kettle on to boil and grabbed the canister of assorted tea bags I kept on hand.

Ayesha wasn't a witch with the power of premonition, but her last words struck me as foreboding. "Having anything beyond the Blue Moon in the future sounds ominous. Should I be afraid?"

Ayesha shook her head and blinked her eyes several times. "Honestly, I'm not sure. You know I don't get glimpses of the future. It's more of a feeling than an omen. This store was always meant for you and you know it. You'd have opened it years ago if you hadn't allowed Caton to stop you. Did he ever find out that you made potions and tinctures on the side throughout your marriage?"

I shook my head and placed the tea, sugar, and milk on the table along with the mugs, then turned back to the pantry to grab some cookies. "He was clueless about anything that didn't involve him. He saw me as an accessory to pull out when he needed and stuck me on the shelf when he didn't. I doubt the people that came to me talked much about it. The shifters, especially. They would have been looked down upon for going to a witch for help, you know that."

Ayesha frowned as I retrieved the kettle when it whistled like a train. "I've tried to overcome the prejudices separating the species for years. There will come a day when those in charge will realize we have to band together to survive. I've never understood the animosity between some. Particularly the hatred shifters feel toward witches. I get vampires and shifters hating one another. They're natural enemies in many ways, but we can overcome these differences. You opening the Blue Moon is the first step. No witch has ever catered to all the species like you will."

Pouring the hot water into our mugs, I smiled, thinking about the work I'd accomplished lately. It helped to forget everything I'd lost when Caton left me the second Mina went away to college. In some ways, losing my daughter was worse than the divorce. Neither was the house or the status I once had.

Refusing to go down that road and get lost in grief and concern, I focused on Ayesha. The Fae had long white hair that flowed to her waist. She looked younger than me, despite being over seven hundred years old. Until you looked into her eyes. They were the color of Scotland moss in the springtime and had an ancient quality to them.

"I'm only able to open this place because you helped me purchase the house. Speaking of which. I have another payment for you." I grabbed the envelope from my purse and handed it to her.

She narrowed her eyes. "I told you not to worry about payments until you started making money. The support from Caton is supposed to be used for your food."

I lifted one shoulder. "The sooner I can pay you back, the faster I will truly feel like this is mine. Not that I mind being in business with you. You didn't just save my life, you're my only true friend. I want to stand on my own two feet. I need to prove it to myself more than anyone else. I hope you understand."

Ayesha dunked her tea bag in and out of her cup. "It's your time to shine, Eve. Don't let anyone tell you differently. Especially not those witches that act like they care about you. They'll come around to see what you're doing, but their sentiment will be as fake as they are."

I laughed at that. She wasn't wrong about the people I'd grown up with. They never really liked me in high school and only started coming around after Caton married me. They wanted to be close to the head warlock, not me. Only my best friend, Arabelle, was there for me growing up.

She moved to the west coast right after high school. I was missing her dearly when I went to college and met Caton. Belle and I maintained contact through the phone and later on social media, but without having her here I never confided in her about things in my life. It was easier to maintain the façade that I was happy and everything was great.

"I don't know. I thought I'd go to the dark side and become one of Caton's simpering fools. It seems to be all the rage in the witching and warlock worlds," I joked, though the simpering part was one hundred percent accurate.

Ayesha rolled her eyes while laughing. "Har, har my friend. You're a real comedian. What did Caton want anyway?"

That question killed my laughter instantly. "What do you think? He wanted to tell me to close the store and give up because I would fail and was an embarrassment."

Ayesha scowled as she stirred her tea a little too briskly, making it slosh over the sides. "That's because he's worried that you'll show him and his chippie up. If he'd put that much effort into his role on the council, we might get out of this mess before the mundanes discover us."

The shift in topic to the recent string of murders was sobering. "That's what I told him. I might have also taunted him with an offer of potions to help reveal the vampire behind these deaths."

Ayesha's frown lifted a bit at that. "I bet he didn't like that. Using one of your potions will be the perfect way to stick it to him and prove your worth. Although Darick swears none of his vampires are responsible. I believe him. He has too much to lose if he's lying. And if it's a rogue, seeing his or her face won't be all that helpful."

My gut churned as I considered the ramifications of the vamp being rogue. "Whoever is doing this is escalating their attacks and needs to be stopped before they kill enough mundanes to make their police link their cases to ours."

Ravenholde was populated by supernaturals, but we were located close to mundane cities and towns. Years ago, when a nearby Sherriff realized we had no police force, he incorporated our town into his service area. Patrol officers had discovered two of the victims here before the Shadow Council could cover them up.

Ayesha nodded in agreement. "This situation is close to

exploding all over us. The council has been meeting nightly and we each leave with areas to search for cases. There were victims close to Roanoke last night. Once it reaches the city where they have more resources, it'll only be a matter of time until they call in the FBI and Ravenholde is inundated."

I hated being on the sidelines. I felt like I had a voice when I gave Caton ideas to help solve problems that the council faced. Through Ayesha, I discovered that he suggested my ideas more than once to his peers, although he never admitted as much to me.

Now, I had no way to locate the vampire rampaging my town and the surrounding areas. I lifted my lukewarm tea to my lips. "Unless you can get your hands on something personal for me to scry with, it might help map the victims and determine if there is a pattern to who he's choosing. Maybe you can predict where he will go next."

Ayesha clapped my shoulder. "I like the way you think, Eve. Now let's get your store set up for your grand opening tomorrow."

My nerves jumped for very different reasons as I put our cups in the sink and headed downstairs. My lifelong dream was coming true. In a matter of hours, I would open the Blue Moon and I couldn't wait. No more hiding and making potions for people under Caton's nose. I'd prove to him how valuable the community would find my goods and services. *Let's see what tomorrow brings.*

CLICK HERE to continue reading Prime of my Magical Life, book 1 in the exciting new Supernatural Midlife Series.

AUTHORS' NOTE

Reviews are like hugs. Sometimes awkward. Always welcome! It would mean the world to me if you can take five minutes and let others know how much you enjoyed my work.

Don't forget to visit my website: www.brendatrim.com and sign up for my newsletter, which is jam-packed with exciting news and monthly giveaways. Also, be sure to visit and like my Facebook page https://www.facebook.com/AuthorBrendaTrim to see my daily posts.

Never allow waiting to become a habit. Live your dreams and take risks. Life is happening now.

DREAM BIG!

XOXO,

Brenda

CLICK THE SITE BELOW TO STALK BRENDA:
Amazon
BookBub
Facebook
Brenda's Book Warriors FB Group

AUTHORS' NOTE

- [Booksprout](#)
- [Goodreads](#)
- [Instagram](#)
- [Twitter](#)
- [Website](#)

ALSO BY BRENDA TRIM

Midlife Witchery:

Magical New Beginnings Book 1

Mind Over Magical Matters

Magical Twist

My Magical Life to Live

Forged in Magical Fire

Like a Fine Magical Wine

Magical Yule Tidings

Magical Complications

Magical Delivery

Magical Moxie

In the Goddess's Magical Snare

Hunting for Magical Meaning

Meddling in Magical Pursuits

Guardians Of Magical Power

Twisting The Magical Fires

Mystical Midlife in Maine

Magical Makeover

Laugh Lines & Lost Things

Hellmouths & Hot Flashes

Holiday with Hades

Saggy But Witty in Crescent City

Nasty Curses & Big Purses

Fae Forged Axes & Chin Waxes
Demonic Stones & Creaky Bones
Underworld Frights & Sleepless Nights
Pixie Dust & Brain Rust
Magical Hands & Silver Strands
Deadly Quips & Furry Lips

Twisted Sisters' Midlife Maelstrom

Packing Serious Magical Mojo
Cadaver on Canal Street
Seances & Second Line Parades
French Quarter Fae
King's Day Magical Mischief
Etou-Fae the Hard Way
Hurricanes, Heroes, & Hail Marys
Royal Street Romp
Levees, Lost Crowns & Loa

Dame of the Midnight Relics:

Surprised by a Supernatural Start

Supernatural Midlife Mystique Series:

The Prime of my Magical Life
All Good Magic Comes to an End
Sweet Magical Destruction
It Takes a Demon to Know One
The Demon is in the Details
Magic is Only Skin Deep

A Demon is as a Demon Does

Fork in the Magical Quest

The Dark Warrior Alliance

Dream Warrior (Dark Warrior Alliance, Book 1)

Mystik Warrior (Dark Warrior Alliance, Book 2)

Pema's Storm (Dark Warrior Alliance, Book 3)

Isis' Betrayal (Dark Warrior Alliance, Book 4)

Deviant Warrior (Dark Warrior Alliance, Book 5)

Suvi's Revenge (Dark Warrior Alliance, Book 6)

Mistletoe & Mayhem (Dark Warrior Alliance, Novella)

Scarred Warrior (Dark Warrior Alliance, Book 7)

Heat in the Bayou (Dark Warrior Alliance, Novella, Book 7.5)

Hellbound Warrior (Dark Warrior Alliance, Book 8)

Isobel (Dark Warrior Alliance, Book 9)

Rogue Warrior (Dark Warrior Alliance, Book 10)

Shattered Warrior (Dark Warrior Alliance, Book 11)

King of Khoth (Dark Warrior Alliance, Book 12)

Ice Warrior (Dark Warrior Alliance, Book 13)

Fire Warrior (Dark Warrior Alliance, Book 14)

Ramiel (Dark Warrior Alliance, Book 15)

Rivaled Warrior (Dark Warrior Alliance, Book 16)

Dragon Knight of Khoth (Dark Warrior Alliance, Book 17)

Ayil (Dark Warrior Alliance, Book 18)

Guild Master (Dark Alliance Book 19)

Maven Warrior (Dark Alliance Book 20)

Sentinel of Khoth (Dark Alliance Book 21)

Araton (Dark Warrior Alliance Book 22)

Cambion Lord (Dark Warrior Alliance Book 23)
Omega (Dark Warrior Alliance Book 24)
Dragon Lothario of Khoth (Dark Warrior Alliance Book 25)
Cunning Warrior (Dark Warrior Alliance Book 26) Coming September 2023

Dark Warrior Alliance Boxsets:

Dark Warrior Alliance Boxset Books 1-4
Dark Warrior Alliance Boxset Books 5-8
Dark Warrior Alliance Boxset Books 9-12
Dark Warrior Alliance Boxset Books 13-16
Dark Warrior Alliance Boxset Books 17-20

Hollow Rock Shifters:

Captivity, Hollow Rock Shifters Book 1
Safe Haven, Hollow Rock Shifters Book 2
Alpha, Hollow Rock Shifters Book 3
Ravin, Hollow Rock Shifters Book 4
Impeached, Hollow Rock Shifters Book 5
Anarchy, Hollow Rock Shifters Book 6
Allies, Hollow Rock Shifters Book 7
Sovereignty, Hollow Rock Shifters Book 8

Bramble's Edge Academy:

Unearthing the Fae King
Masking the Fae King
Revealing the Fae King

Midnight Doms:

[Her Vampire Bad Boy](#)
[Her Vampire Suspect](#)
All Souls Night

Printed in Great Britain
by Amazon